HIGH RIDER

HIGH RIDER

BILL GALLAHER

TouchWood
Editions

TouchWood Editions
touchwoodeditions.com

LIBRARY AND ARCHIVES CANADA CATALOGUING IN PUBLICATION
Gallaher, Bill, author
High rider / Bill Gallaher.

Issued in print and electronic formats.
ISBN 978-1-77151-114-8

1. Ware, John, 1845?–1905—Fiction. I. Title.

PS8563.A424H54 2015   C813'.6   C2014-908209-6

Editor: Marlyn Horsdal
Copy editor: Cailey Cavallin
Proofreader: Christine Savage
Design: Pete Kohut
Cover images: John Ware, Glenbow Archives NA-263-1 (detail)
Horse and rider, Glenbow Archives NA-4571-11 (detail)
Author photo: Jaye Gallagher

The title of this book was adopted from the song of the same name by Diamond Joe White.
Both the title and the epigraph on page 1 are used with permission from the artist.
The song lyrics on page 80 come from "Bury Me on the Lone Prairie"
(also known as "The Cowboy's Lament"), which is in the public domain.

Canadian Patrimoine
Heritage canadien   Canada Council   Conseil des Arts   BRITISH COLUMBIA
                         for the Arts   du Canada   ARTS COUNCIL

We gratefully acknowledge the financial support for our publishing activities
from the Government of Canada through the Canada Book Fund and the Canada
Council for the Arts, and from the Province of British Columbia through the
British Columbia Arts Council and the Book Publishing Tax Credit.

The interior pages of this book have been printed on 100% post-consumer
recycled paper, processed chlorine free, and printed with vegetable-based inks.

2 3 4 5   19 18 17 16 15

PRINTED IN CANADA

For Philip Teece, who welcomed
me into the circle.

CONTENTS

He was born a high rider, born to make his mark upon the day.
—Diamond Joe White, "High Rider"

PROLOGUE

Far from being the colour of his name, Mustard was a black stallion. Yet the appellation fit, because it described a temperament as hot as the condiment. He was one of a few "green" horses on the roundup—animals that required breaking. This was usually a relatively simple task, but not with Mustard. He would let you stand beside him and stroke his neck, make you think he was easygoing, that he'd be quite happy to go prancing off with you on his back. But throwing a saddle on him brought out his inner beast. He would go crazy, bucking blindly into a brick wall if one was nearby, wanting only to rid himself of the load on his back. The day before, he had tried to destroy the chuckwagon. He broke the fold-out table, scattering cooking utensils and a bag of flour everywhere, and sent the crew scurrying to safety. The cook was so angry he wanted to shoot him, and any member of the crew whom Mustard had embarrassed would have eagerly provided the gun. Some referred to him as "that fucker of a bucker," and there was no one left in the outfit willing to ride him. Except John Ware.

He had watched it all with great amusement, and this morning, when the others avoided their black nemesis, he grabbed a hackamore and reins from the supply wagon, jammed his Boss of the Plains Stetson down to his ears, and strode to the animal's

3

side. John stroked him for a minute or two, talking softly, and slipped on the hackamore, an act that Mustard always tolerated, as if he were trying to fool a man about his real intentions. While the stallion was digesting that small change in his life, John leaped onto his back. Mustard's eyes bulged. He reared, snorted, and flew into his mad gyrations.

Some of the crew whooped and cried, "Ride 'im, John!" while Mustard spun in circles so fast, John almost lost his bearings. But he hung on as the crazed animal crashed into another horse, nearly knocking it to the ground. His back arched and his nostrils flared, moaning like a demon, Mustard bucked in ever-widening circles. Someone yelled, "John, the river!" Another yelled with even more alarm, "Get off, you fool! You'll be killed!"

About fifty yards away was the Oldman River, flowing at a good spring pace below a twenty-foot cutbank that dropped straight into the water. Unaware of the river's proximity, John was as much into the ride as Mustard, and he rowel-raked the animal's flanks, angering him even further. Also oblivious to the precipice, Mustard reached the edge at the beginning of another spin, but this time, when he descended, there was nothing but air beneath his hooves. Until that moment, John had not realized how precarious the ride had become. He saw the water twenty feet below and knew that he was in trouble: if the fall did not injure or kill him, he would probably drown.

Horse and rider seemed suspended in mid-air for a split second, then plunged straight down, frozen in position like a granite statue honouring bronc-busters, and splashed explosively into the river. They sank beneath the surface and John could not see a thing—not because of the muddy water, but because he had his eyes clamped shut. He was still on Mustard though, his legs gripping so tightly he worried he might break the animal's ribs. He could feel the chaos of the ice-cold water around him, feel it surging up his nose, and Mustard thrashing beneath him. He sensed he was still right side up, but in a spate of panic did not know whether they would ever rise to the surface or if he should let go and try to flail his way up and to shore. But then they broke into the air and the horse began swimming, his wild eyes scanning the bank for a place to land. Gasping, John leaned forward, wrapped his arms around Mustard's neck, and hung on for all he was worth. Reaching a low spot farther downstream, the animal clambered out of the water, heaving for air, slipping on the slick, muddy bank, with John still on his back and breathing with some difficulty himself. Once on dry ground, Mustard stopped and hung his head, still panting, all the fight gone out of him.

John heard a rousing cheer and saw the crew at the top of the cutbank, waving their hats at him. He tugged off his dripping Stetson and waved back. He noticed that the spot where Mustard had launched himself into the air was the only part of the bank that dropped straight into the river. In most other places, it sloped. He thanked his lucky stars. Had they hit a slope, horse and man would have tumbled into the water and might not have survived the fall.

He urged Mustard up the grade to the camp, where the crew greeted him with a smattering of applause and congratulations. He dismounted and said, as if he did this sort of thing every morning after breakfast, "Nothin' like a mornin' swim to take the fuss out of a horse." He reached down, pulled his boots off, and dumped the water out of them. "That river can sure get a man wet."

There were laughs at the understatement and John felt pleased, knowing that he had once again proved himself to men who believed that he might not be up to their standards because of the colour of his skin. It was the way of his world, and it had been like that for as long as he could remember.

ONE

No better than a snake!

Abe Lincoln had asked, "Why should there not be a patient confidence in the ultimate justice of the people?" but John Ware was tired of waiting for it. On his way out of Georgetown, he purposely passed the colonnaded stone courthouse, glad he was seeing it for the last time. The justice it dispensed mirrored a South that had not yet turned a blind eye to colour, and that was only one of the reasons he would not miss the town, or South Carolina for that matter. He avoided Front Street, with its stone-built homes and businesses occupied by people who had little time for his kind, and took grid-patterned side streets to the main road leading out of town, whistling softly as he walked. The post-dawn air, which would soon give way to the oppressive heat of the day, was warm and pleasant. The land was level and grew stands of pine, oak, sycamore, maple, and flowering magnolias. Occasionally a driveway reached back from the road, marking the entrance to a rice plantation. A few still operated in limited fashion, while others had gone to seed.

Before long, he neared the plantation on which he had been born and raised. Even from the road, he could see that weeds now surrounded the red brick columns marking the entrance to the estate. He could also see that the main house, a square, white two-storey box with a veranda across the front and a portico

7

supported by four columns, had not been maintained, and that the slaves' quarters had been dismantled. Probably for firewood, he surmised. A rider on horseback was coming down the oak-canopied driveway, and John wondered if it might be his former master. He did not have a single fond memory of the man; the few he had of the plantation existed only because of his family.

———

John, his parents, his seven brothers—four older and three younger than himself—and his two younger sisters lived in a one-room log cabin in which they sweltered in summer and shivered in winter. It was one of six cabins forming the slaves' quarters. The man who owned them like chattel was Sebastian Chambers II, who had inherited the plantation from his father. A widower with no children, he was short and thin, a pinch-faced, miserly man who, like many born into it, believed he was entitled to wealth and that it was part of the natural order. He had few virtues; however, while other plantation owners did not care if they broke up families, Chambers at least kept John's together. This did not rise from any wellspring of altruism, but from an assumption that his bondsmen would be more productive and less prone to rebellion if their families remained united. Even better, these families had children, who would grow up to have children of their own and supply him with an unbroken line of free slave labour.

Chambers usually allowed Saturday afternoons off so that his slaves could tend to their personal chores, such as laundry and cleaning. On Sundays, slaves attended church in the morning and, because there never seemed to be enough food, spent some of the day catching catfish in the creek that meandered through the edge of the plantation. Sometimes they would gather with a fiddle or a banjo outside their quarters and sing and dance to forget the misery that cloaked their daily lives. Christmas was the only time of year when Chambers displayed any generosity, allowing his slaves three consecutive days free of work. He also permitted exchange visits to and from nearby plantations. It was a time of unusual conviviality, enhanced by the strong corn whisky that was supplied by most of the masters, with the exception of Chambers. He did not approve of the custom, though his own drinking habits were excessive.

Beyond those small concessions, Chambers was cruel and drove his slaves without mercy. John's childhood was more about work than play. He and his fellow slaves, about forty altogether, not including children too small to work, laboured from dawn until dusk on any task Chambers had a mind to set for them: working in the rice fields and the plantation's large vegetable garden, digging irrigation ditches, building and mending fences, and cleaning out his horse and mule stalls. There was never a shortage of work to do, because he believed that idle slaves meant less production, and idle hands meant the Devil himself was lurking in the vicinity. It was his further belief that an educated slave was a dangerous one, so there was no schoolhouse on the plantation. There was a small church, however. The slaves were steeped in religion and despite their illiteracy knew many biblical passages by rote. The one most often repeated on the Chambers plantation was, "Slaves, obey your earthly masters with deep respect and fear. Serve them as sincerely as you would serve Christ." Most did.

To entertain himself and his friends on special occasions, Chambers would make all of the teenage boys gather in a roped-off ring and fight until only one remained standing. It was usually John or one of his older brothers, for they towered above the others and were stronger. Still, they didn't like hurting their friends, and they themselves always came away with some part of their anatomy bruised and sore. They dared not pull their punches either, for fear of incurring Chambers's wrath. And no matter how serious the injury, he expected the boys to be in the fields the next day.

A more dangerous form of entertainment was one that John actually enjoyed—riding Chambers's mules bareback. The animals had nasty dispositions and always tried to trample thrown riders. Once he hit the ground, a boy had to be quick to get out of the angry beast's way. The spectacle never failed to delight Chambers and his guests. But as he got older, John's height and long legs allowed him a firmer grip on the animals, and once he rode one to a standstill. The planter never made him ride again.

Chambers demanded deference at all times. His slaves had to stand and bow when he came into their presence. They could not sit down until he left. He carried a whip that seemed attached to his right hand, for John had never seen him without it. Chambers used it at will, as much to reinforce his superiority as to mete out punishment. A sycamore tree grew in front of the slaves' quarters; he would secure transgressors to it and whip their behinds and backs, sometimes until they bled. And no one dared cry for mercy.

Given the ethos with which the slaves grew up, most believed theirs was an inferior race, but John's father was vitriolic in his opinions about their master, and white folks in general. He was, however, wise enough to know that the best way to avoid the cutting sting of the whip was to be submissive and obedient. He hated being that person, but he was a practical man and saw it as little more than a way to survive. Otherwise, he possessed considerable integrity and dignity, and his role as a decent, responsible father, combined with the respect he received from the other slaves, allowed him to maintain those qualities, as well as his manhood. He found solace in a deep and abiding faith that freedom from bondage was inevitable and would come in his lifetime. He repeatedly advised John never to run away, even when stories began circulating about Negro insurrections and the possibility that the northern and southern states would soon be at war with each other. "You'll probably only get yourself shot," his father insisted, "when the only thing worth dyin' for is defendin' your mother or sisters."

As it turned out, that almost happened during John's fifteenth summer. It was a humid Sunday afternoon and he and his father were at the creek, fishing. He had just pulled his third catfish from the murky water when Thaddeus, his youngest brother, came running up, breathing hard.

"Come on, quick!" the youngster cried. "It's Nettie! She in some trouble!"

"What kind of trouble, boy?" his father demanded.

"Master Chambers gone and hurt her bad!"

John thrust the string of fish into Thaddeus's hands and he and his father rushed to their ramshackle cabin at the end of the short row of slaves' quarters. Reaching it first, John burst through the door to find his mother and siblings gathered

11

around twelve-year-old Nettie, trying to console her. Tears smeared her pretty face, her right cheekbone was swelling, and the eye above was red. When she saw her father enter behind John, she blurted between gulps of air, "Master . . . done . . . a thing to me . . . an' hurt me bad! An' . . . he boxed me . . . when I tried to get away!"

Rarely quick to anger, John felt the heat of it rise from his gut and flare across his chest. He was at the cabin door in two strides and then outside, running along the tree-lined path to the main house, heedless of his parents' calls to come back. Through his rage, he saw Chambers stepping down from the veranda stairs onto the pathway. When the planter saw John charging toward him, he uncoiled his whip and let it fly. The tip hit John on his right shoulder and bit into his cheek, but he never felt it. Reaching Chambers, he shook his fist in the man's face and cried, "You ain't no better than a snake!" It was the worst name he could think of; he hated the slithery devils. "You lay your hands on my baby sister again and I'll kill you!"

Chambers snarled, his breath a blast of sour mash whisky. "You insolent nigger! You do not speak to a white man like that, let alone your master!" He brought the whip handle up and struck John in the face. Without thinking, John lashed out with his fist and caught Chambers square in the eye, knocking him to the ground. The planter lay there dazed, as much from shock that a slave had struck him as from the blow itself.

John shook his fist again. "You been warned! She's only a child an' I'll kill you!"

He turned and strode back to the slaves' quarters, trembling from anger and from the horror of what he had said and done.

Slaves didn't strike their masters and get away with it. Chambers might not shoot him, because good workers were hard to replace and John was one of the best, but at the very least, he would be in for a severe whipping.

Back in the cabin, John's kinfolk were frightened, but he detected a glimmer of pride in his father's eyes. "You went too quickly, boy," he said, his voice trembling. "It shoulda bin me gone and put that man down in Hell where he belong!"

"It was right for me to go, Pappy." Their roles temporarily reversed, the son tried to ease the pain of failure the father felt. "You might notta come back. At least I got a chance."

A half hour raced by and Chambers still had not shown himself. The Wares did not know what to make of it. Surely he was not going to let the matter slide by without doing anything about it. That was inconceivable. A few minutes later, James, John's eldest brother, who was stationed at the window, said, his voice quavering with alarm, "Here he come!"

John looked out and saw the reason for the delay. Chambers had taken time to change his clothes and clean up, presumably, John guessed, because he did not want his slaves to see him in a dishevelled state. But he was sporting a blackening eye that he couldn't conceal, and it was obvious he hadn't come to parley: he had a pair of holstered pistols strapped around his hips and he was carrying his whip. He stopped in front of the cabin and spoke in a loud, clear voice so that all of the slaves could hear him, his plantation English accent so distinct and recognizable that even a blind slave who had never heard him before would have known that an owner stood outside.

"John Ware will come out of his cabin and face his punishment!

He has one minute. Every extra minute that he makes me wait will mean one full day without food for every slave on this plantation."

Nettie began to cry, as did her mother and younger sister, Millie. The three huddled together for comfort. John's father and brothers were anxious and fidgety. Together they could have gone out and overwhelmed Chambers; after all, he was a single man against many. But it wasn't only Chambers they'd be up against; it was a powerful, widespread system that would run them to ground and lynch them, if it didn't shoot them or beat them to death first. His mother begged John not to go outside, but he knew he must. He could not make the rest of the slaves pay for his misdeeds, regardless of the punishment. His mother and sisters wailed in torment. Nettie ran to him and grabbed his shirt in an effort to stop him. "Let *me* go!" she cried. "Maybe if he got me, he leave you alone!"

His sister's bravery brought tears to his eyes. He gently removed her hand, knelt, and laid his palm on her cheek. "You ain't goin' nowhere, child. This ain't your affair no more." He took her in his arms and held her as if she were gossamer. "You wait right here for me. I'll be back soon. I promise." The words tumbled out with a bravado he did not feel.

He stood, gave her thin shoulder a squeeze, and walked out into the yard. Once the other slaves saw him, they came out of their quarters too, bowing to Chambers, assembling in family groups without a whisper among them, fear and apprehension etched on their faces.

Chambers transferred his whip to his left hand and drew a pistol with his right. He aimed it at John's chest. "You will remove your clothing and go directly to the whipping tree. I will not repeat myself. I will shoot you instead."

John would never forget that voice, as cold as the creek in winter. To ignore its command would have meant certain death. In a strange way he felt relieved—he was only going to be whipped and not executed. He undressed, frightened and embarrassed at the same time, trying to still his trembling body. But he held his head high in defiance and walked to the sycamore with as much dignity and grace as he could muster. Chambers instructed another slave to tie John's wrists together around the bole. Not until John was securely bound did the planter holster his pistol. Before administering the beating he cracked his whip in the air, and many of the slaves recoiled at the sound, particularly those who had felt its awful bite on their backs. He set to work with a fury they had never seen before. John heard his mother's and sisters' high keening, which tore into his soul as much as the whip tore into his flesh. He kept repeating in his mind, "Oh, Mama and baby sisters, don't you be weepin' for me now! Don't you be weepin'!" and soon he was no longer certain whether the words were contained in his mind or if he was crying them aloud. He fought to stay conscious through the whipping, so that he could walk away from it strong and defiant, but the excruciating pain became more than he could bear and he blacked out.

That had been several years ago. Sometimes it seemed like a bad dream, but the ugly scars across his back and rump testified to its reality. (And often they itched terribly.) The days immediately following the whipping were the hardest John had ever endured, Nettie and his mother comforting him in the evenings after work by rubbing a soothing balm into his wounds. Yet he felt a modest victory, because Chambers had never gone near Nettie again.

Not long after the incident, the rumours of war became reality, and that was accompanied by new rumours of the abolition of slavery. When the war ended and abolition became law, John did not understand how life could still be so difficult. Despite his inability to read or write, he understood the writing on the wall. It spoke to him with glaring clarity: South Carolina was no place for a coloured man. To make matters worse, most of the state, including the area around Georgetown, fell into an economic slump. The rice crops, which supplied most of the country, failed because there were no slaves to work the plantations, and many planters, so accustomed to keeping their tidy profits to themselves, were unwilling to negotiate wages with freedmen. Even if they had, they would have been short of workers because the labour of women and children was no longer available to them. And more than ten thousand black men had gone north with General William Tecumseh Sherman when he and his Union army had marched through South Carolina on their way home from their destructive tramp through Georgia.

On an immediate level, the war and Reconstruction had done what John's former slave master had not—split up the Ware family. Four of his brothers had joined Sherman and stayed in the North after the war, and his three remaining brothers, believing that there was a greater tolerance for coloured folk there, had later joined them. But John wasn't interested and stayed behind with his two sisters and their parents. Nettie and Millie were live-in domestic servants in Georgetown, and John worked as a blacksmith for a thoughtful white Republican named James Ball. Together, the three siblings supported their parents, with whom John lived in a small wood-frame house at the edge of town, where other coloureds had gathered to form a community. But two years had passed since the Confederacy surrendered, and even a fool could see that the Southern Democrats, with their racist policies and white supremacy beliefs, were going to control the region. John's position was that they could control whatever they wanted but it wasn't going to include him.

Hope for a decent future lay in some place other than South Carolina, or anywhere in the Lower South for that matter. Therefore, it was time to go, to leave behind this land of cruel deeds committed by heartless, single-minded people. He would walk west into Texas; he would go as far as it took to put the last plantation behind him, until he found the ranches with horses and cattle that he had heard so much about. The stories excited him, because he had always loved horses. His former master had kept a pair in a small stable, and John had enjoyed cleaning out their stalls and caring for them. He had a natural affinity for the animals, but then most white folks had always considered him and his kind a related species.

His parents did not want him to go west. Instead, they implored him to go north, to find a wife and raise a family among his own kind. It was safer, they insisted. Heading west meant running a gauntlet of the Ku Klux Klan several hundred miles long, and only God knew what he would find in Texas.

"Near as I could learn," said his father sagely, "coloured folk are as scarce as trees out that way. Mostly white folks an' Indians. How're you s'posed to find a wife in that bunch?"

John shrugged, knowing he would never be able to offer any responses that would satisfy his father. "Settlin' down ain't somethin' on my mind just yet. And far as I know, there ain't no ranches up north."

John told James Ball that he was leaving and that he would never forget the kindness shown him. "Ah, it weren't so much kindness as it was respect, John," Ball said. "If a man don't hold respect for all God's creatures, what good is he on this earth? Anyway, I'm truly sorrowed to see you go—you been a mighty fine hire and any man out west would be doin' himself a great favour by takin' you on."

At the end of the day, John collected his pay, a small bonus that Ball called "travelling money," and a note of reference. He visited Crowley's store on Front Street, a place he had avoided because it always reminded him of what he did not have and could not afford to get. He purchased a rain tarp, a blanket, a tin pot to boil water in, a cup, a good clasp knife, and a flint to light fires. At home, he gave half of the remaining money to his parents and then he visited his sisters to say goodbye. Nettie sniffled her way through the parting and hugged John as if she did not ever want him to go. They had formed a special bond after Chambers had raped her and John had risked his life for her. But the incident had turned her world darker, and she had never been the same. In the deeper shadows at the edge of her mind lurked men in the guise of their former master, and it instilled in her an unshakable fear. Unlike Millie, her younger sister, she never spoke of the possibility of marriage. John did not like leaving her and boasted that he would own a ranch one day and would send for her. Perhaps it was a hollow boast, but he could think of nothing better to say and he wanted to leave her with good feelings.

That night sleep eluded him. After breakfast the following morning, he wrapped a single change of clothing in his bedroll, along with a package of biscuits his mother had baked, tied a rope to each end, and slung it behind him with the rope slanting across his chest. He kissed his tearful mother and doubtful father goodbye, stepped out onto the road in the still, post-dawn air, and put his back to the rising sun. He was twenty-two years old. Spread out before him was a world he knew very little about.

John remained on the road in front of the plantation as the clip-clop of horse hooves coming up the oak-edged driveway grew louder. John's heart rate accelerated as Sebastian Chambers, mounted on a grey mare, rode out onto the road and turned toward him, apparently on his way to Georgetown. John had seen his former master around the village a couple of times but had always avoided any encounters, uncertain of what he'd do if their paths crossed. But it is curious how fate sometimes plays its hand in a man's life, how stepping out in new directions can sometimes take him to places he never imagined he'd go. Now, with no one else in sight, John saw an irresistible opportunity.

Chambers appeared to be paying John scant attention as the gap between them closed, but the planter was intentionally directing his horse toward John so that he would have to step out of the way. John kept his head down to hide his eyes from

Chambers, letting the horse get close to him. As it brushed by, he reached up and yanked the planter from the saddle. Startled, the horse whinnied and galloped several yards down the road, while John dragged his sputtering bundle into a grove of pine trees and threw him to the ground. Chambers got to his knees and held up his arms, cowering.

"Don't kill me," he pleaded. "I have no money!"

John sneered. "I don't want your money! Do you remember me?"

Chambers shook his head. He looked awful and it was difficult to believe he was the same man who, without a stitch of compassion, had dictated the terms of John's life for so many years. But along with fear, John could see recognition dawning in his captive's bloodshot eyes. He lifted his shirt, half-turned, and displayed his scars.

"You did this to me when I was a boy. And you hurt my baby sister so bad she ain't never been right. Maybe you disremember but I don't. It's been stuck like a knife in me every day."

Without a gun and a whip to fall back on, Chambers's belligerence and arrogance had vanished. He whined, "I could have you arrested for this!"

"Well, you better make sure they hang me quick 'cause I'll find you and beat you until you're blacker than me. Truth of the matter is, I could do that right now and it'd be no more than a snake like you deserves."

Chambers remained kneeling in the pine straw, his lips quivering, perhaps imagining all sorts of horrid punishments, but said nothing. He looked terrified, a look that John had seen on many a slave's face before Chambers took his whip to them. For the first time in his short life, he understood what real power over another human being felt like. It filled every nook and cranny of his body and he knew that he could do anything he wanted to this man. He could beat him to a pulp or he could kill him and no one would ever be the wiser. Yet he sensed the danger in carrying it too far, of having to live with the consequences. He reached down, grabbed the planter by his coat lapels, and hauled him to his feet. Chambers seemed much shorter than John remembered, and twice as contemptible. His face was flushed red and his breath reeked of whisky. He covered his face with his arms, fearing a punch. John drew him close. "Look at me!" he demanded.

Chambers moved his arms and John glared into his eyes. "You're lookin' into the face of your *master*, boy," he hissed. "You belong to me now and it'll mean your life to forget it! I see anybody on my tail and I'll be back for you, and there'll be no good place for you to hide. You clear on that?"

He held Chambers's eyes. The man nodded that he understood.

"Speak to me, boy! I want to hear you say it loud!"

"I understand, sir," Chambers whimpered, his eyes glistening with tears.

John cast him aside like a corn husk used for privy paper. The planter staggered, smacked into a tree, and tumbled to the ground. He rose up on one elbow, breathing hard, sobbing now. He would not look at his captor. Satisfied, John left him there, returned to the road, and continued on his way. He knew that Nettie, gentle soul that she was, would be proud of how he handled himself. He also knew that while it would be better to forget Chambers and everything connected to him, it probably wouldn't be happening any time soon. Maybe not until John had grown so old that his memory failed him completely.

TWO

I'm just passin' through.

As John made his way through South Carolina, asking for directions when he needed to, he did odd jobs for food, mostly for coloured folk but once for a sympathetic white family. All along the way, he found other black men in transit, most still looking for displaced members of their families—wives and children, brothers and sisters, aunts and uncles—to give true meaning to their freedom. Three weeks later, he reached the Savannah River, the murky waterway separating his home state from Georgia. An amiable freedman who lived off the river's bounty and a vegetable garden rowed him to the far side. John offered to pay him but the man refused, saying, "I got a boat, a roof over my head, I eat when I want and I work when I want, and I got plenty of both. Don't need your money."

Georgia had not yet recovered from the war. The destruction left in the wake of Sherman's march to the sea was still evident as John passed burned-out plantations and desperate coloured folk (who even in their crisis shared with him what little food they had). And of all the white folk he would meet over the course of his journey, it was the Georgians who acted the most defeated, the most bewildered by the Confederacy's loss and the added insult-to-injury presence of Federal soldiers still occupying the large towns. Some were angry, too, and a dark-skinned man had to use great care not to step on any toes. As an old, grey-haired black man put it, "We mighta got emancipated on paper, but we still Jim Crow to them, and that ain't no better than a draft mule. Last week a coloured boy over to Newman town was burnt at a stake. Talk is some white folks carted off bones for souvenirs once the flesh was gone. The people who done the burnin' musta been ghosts 'cause when the Federals got there, nobody'd seen nothin'."

Alabama was as bad if not worse. After John crossed the Chattahoochee River, a freedman warned him to keep alert because the Klan was everywhere. Sometimes they seemed to materialize out of thin air and their favourite tree decoration was Jim Crow; indeed, they had lynched a black man the previous week for looking at a white man's wife the wrong way. "You be okay in the big towns where there's Federals; otherwise you'd best be careful. You see a pack of white men on the road, you prob'ly seein' the makin's of a lynchin' party."

John heeded the man's advice and gave small towns a wide berth; in isolated areas, he hid in copses when he saw two or more whites together, unless they were a family. He felt safer in Montgomery town because of the large contingent of Federal soldiers, but he did not linger. The Alabama leg of his journey was often hunger-filled. He could not find much work and spent a considerable amount of time searching in the woods for food, eating catsear leaves and greenbrier buds, plants he and his fellow slaves had foraged on the plantation. He found blackberries, past their season and desiccated, but made a kind of soup from them. Once, he got lucky and came upon a creek in which the water level had dropped, leaving ponds here and there along the edges. He followed it away from the road for a hundred yards or so, until he came to a pond that still had a small stream running into it and another running out. Two good-sized catfish were visible in the shallow water, so he gathered stones and built dams at each end, making escape impossible. He used his knife to fashion a spear from a willow bush branch and waded into the water. He stood stock-still. When the first fish swam by, he stabbed at it and missed. After several failed attempts, he realized that the fish was not where it appeared to be, that the water was somehow distorting its position, so he made the necessary adjustment. He speared one and then the other, grabbing them behind the gills and flinging them onto the bank. He whetted his knife on a stone, gutted his catch, and made a fire. He boiled water from the pond and picked leaves from a sassafras tree to brew tea. The fish soon sizzled over the fire, and there was plenty left over to take with him.

Sometimes there was nothing better than losing himself in thought as he walked along, as it was a good way to put miles at his back without noticing them too much. However, it could prove to be a dangerous pastime in Alabama, so he kept an alert eye on both the road ahead and the road behind, even though it made the state seem much broader than its two hundred miles. Near the outskirts of Demopolis, an industrial town about thirty miles from the Mississippi border, he passed a log house set well back from the road in a sparse grove of pine trees. The entire front yard was a vegetable garden, split up the middle by a path. Two black women were working in the garden, one bent over pulling at something, perhaps weeds, the other using a hoe. It seemed to him a perfect place to obtain some food for his labour. He walked up the path and when the women saw him coming, they stopped working, their stares following him. Both were tall and thin with grey streaks in their hair, and the one holding the hoe looked older.

"Good afternoon, ladies," he said, doffing his hat. "It's a fine day for gardenin', ain't it? I'm just passin' through, bound for Texas, and since I don't see no menfolk around, wondered if I could trade some hard work for a meal. I'm John Ware, recent from South Carolina."

Both women appraised him. The older one spoke. "Well, John Ware from South Carolina, I can tell by your manners that your mama raised you right, and you surely look like you be capable of handlin' a man's work. I be 'Liz'beth Adams and this be my sister, Emma, but you can call her Em and me Liza. Or ma'am, if that sets better with you. There's a heap of small logs in back in need of sawin' and splittin' and pilin', and if you can see fit to do that for us, why we'll see fit to set one more place at the supper table."

Liza led John around to the rear of the house where there was a small henhouse with some chickens scratching nearby, an empty stable meant for one, perhaps two animals, and a pile of logs cut into six- to eight-foot lengths.

"Mr. Avery, from down the road a piece, sawed these up for us and said he'd be back to buck 'em and split 'em into firewood, but the poor man's been ailin' lately. It's your job now if you be up to it."

"I'm up to it," John said. He removed his shirt so as not to get it sweatier than it already was. Liza looked at his broad chest and powerful physique with approval.

"You be a mighty fine specimen," she said wistfully and returned to the garden.

He went to work. In an hour or so, he had all the logs bucked and some split when Liza instructed him to wash up at the well pump and join the sisters for supper.

He sat on a straight-backed chair at a table cobbled together from an old plank door, while Em served him generous portions of salt pork, black-eyed peas, and mashed potatoes. They did not take much for themselves and he hoped it was because they were light eaters and not because they were low on food supplies. Afterwards, over cups of sweet chamomile tea, Liza told John that her husband and Em's had gone north during the last year of the war to fight for the Union.

"They'scaped from Griffin's plantation over yonder where we was slaves. Borrowed two of the master's horses and rode away into the night. Believed they were obliged to help in the fight to free us, but they never come home. Been three years now, so I guess they ain't never comin'." Liza sighed at the idea of it, a deep sadness in her eyes. "Don't even know where they's buried, or even if they got a decent burial. Our children was sold off before that, taken somewhere in Looziana. I birthed two daughters and Em birthed three. A day don't pass that we don't hope to see 'em comin' up our path." She paused for a minute, as if to shake off the longing. "Anyway, the Federal soldiers come and occupied the town at the war's end and brought some good things with 'em, but also a heap of confusion. This place here belonged to some poor white folks who up and left when the No'therners arrived. A lot of 'em did that. Didn't like the changes that were happenin'. We found this un and moved in. It woulda been a cryin' shame to let it go to waste, and the garden puts food on our plates."

Em interjected. "A few white folks around the area don't care much for us livin' here. Ain't none too happy that we took a white family's house, never mind that we ain't slaves no more."

The sisters asked John about South Carolina and were curious about why he was going to Texas. "You lookin' for kinfolk?" Liza asked.

He shook his head. "They's spread out over half the country, but I'm luckier than most 'cause I know where they live. A lotta the folks I pass on the road are like you—they can't find the ones that mean the most to 'em. You can always tell because they's the sad ones."

He told them his reasons for going to Texas and asked about the lay of the land to the west.

"Don't know much about it," Liza said, "except that Demopolis ain't far down the road, sittin' as pretty as you please on the banks of the Tombigbee River. Heard there's a new railroad bridge that you can use to cross over. Not more'n a few miles from there to Mississip. Can't say what that's like 'cause I ain't never been there, but I wouldn't expect any welcoming committees for a coloured man unless they was holdin' a rope with a noose at the end of it."

John pushed his chair back from the table. "I should finish the job I started and maybe get across the river before sundown."

The sisters looked appalled. Liza scolded him. "Why, you'll do nothin' of the sort, John Ware! It's gettin' too late to be out on the roads 'round here. The stable's empty and clean enough to sleep in, but I'll give it a good sweepin' anyway. We got an extra blanket and pillow if you need it. It'll probably be more comfortable than most places you slept in on your journey. In the mornin', a belly full of grits'll have you steppin' down the road lively as a colt."

John had hoped they would offer accommodations and was tired enough to accept. He split and piled the remainder of the wood before nightfall, then chatted with the sisters over more tea before turning in. They gave him a lantern, but he declined the blanket and pillow they offered and bade them goodnight.

The stable was not any hotel, but it was dry and clear of dust and cobwebs, which would not have mattered much anyway for he had indeed slept in worse places. He spread his tarp, pulled his blanket over him, and blew the lantern out. Exhausted from the day's trek and toil, but content, he was asleep soon after that.

Sometime deep in the night, a racket awakened him. He sat up, trying to collect himself, as the door to the stable flew open. A tall man wearing a hood made from a gunnysack with eyeholes cut in it barged in carrying a lantern in one hand and a gun in the other.

"Get on your feet, nigger!" he snarled.

John's mind was whirling. What was happening? Then he remembered Em's comment about white folks not wanting the sisters around here and made the connection. He thought, You come in the dead of night wearing masks like the cowards you are. But as his father had, he figured that it was best to be subservient. "Yes, sir!" he said obsequiously as he rose to his feet. He looked for a way to disarm his captor, but there was too much room between them, which meant plenty of time for the man to get a shot off. The Klansman moved to one side and motioned John toward the house with the gun. John could hear the sound of things being smashed. He saw in the moonlight that someone had knocked down the woodpile and scattered it. He was frightened of what was awaiting him in the house; he feared for the sisters' lives.

The man jammed the barrel of his gun into John's back and shoved him into the house, where there were three more hooded men, all armed with pistols. The place was a mess, furniture broken, pieces of bowls, crushed pots, and tin cups and plates scattered around the floor. A single lantern flickered, and in its light he saw Liza and Em standing to one side, in nightgowns. Liza's face was bloody and she moaned, "Oh, John, we're so sorry . . ."

The man nearest to her raised his hand as if to hit her. "Shut up, you black bitch! Now you listen and listen good. If you value those scrawny arses of yours, you'd best pack up what you got left and get outta this house fast. This ain't your place and it especially ain't no place for uppity niggers. You'll get clear out of the county if you know what's good for you!"

He turned to John. "Don't know where you're from, boy, but you're in the wrong place. Best you hightail it outta here at first light. We see you around and we'll tear that black hide offa you and feed it and the rest of your ugliness to the pigs."

To reinforce his point he strode over and struck John on the cheek with the butt of his revolver.

John reeled but did not go down. He felt no pain from the blow, only that hot rage flaring in his chest again. Had he been able, he would have ripped *their* hides off with great pleasure. But there was nothing he could do that wouldn't result in his death, and the sisters' too.

With that, the men went outside, mounted horses, and rode

roughshod through the garden before galloping off down the moonlit road. Liza and Em burst into tears and John did his best to console them.

"You poor boy," Liza said, sniffling and laying her hand on John's cheek. "We didn't tell 'em you was here, so they musta been watching."

"We got you into this!" Em cried. "And it ain't even your affair!"

John was still angry. "It's gotta be my affair! Ain't my skin black, too? We can't let 'em get away with what they did to you and your house!"

"But they *will* get away with it," Em said. "That's the sad story of Alabama, and only God can say how it'll end. Probably won't do no good, but we'll go see the soldiers in the mornin' and let 'em know what's happened. Maybe they'll look in on us once in a while. Don't matter though because we ain't leavin'; this is our home now. Besides, we got nowhere else to go. But like I said, this ain't your home, son, so you do as the man said and hightail it out of here at sun-up. Get yourself to Texas and make yourself a future. There ain't nothin' you can do here but get yourself hurt or maybe killed. We'll be all right."

John could see the determination and certitude deep in the sisters' eyes and it should have made him feel better. Instead, it left him with the same feeling of powerlessness that he had felt as a slave, the same deep sense of frustration that stems from always being on the losing side and not having the means to turn it around.

As sleep was no longer possible, he fetched some water from the well so that Liza and Em could clean up while he set about restoring some order to the house, sweeping up the debris and doing his best to straighten the tin cups, plates, and pots. Later, Em made tea that they drank from battered cups. At dawn, while the sisters went to see what they could recover from their garden, he went outside and re-stacked the firewood, paying no mind to their urgings that he should leave immediately. When he finished, Liza served him grits that he devoured with relish, trying to ignore his sore jaw. He gathered up his bedroll from the stable and made to bid the women goodbye. They might look fragile, he told himself, but they're tough old birds, really. They'll be fine.

Outside, Liza hugged him and said, "Thank you, John. You takin' the time to pile that firewood again, when you shoulda lit out of here, has only fixed our purpose more. We can't let cowards tell us what to do so we'll see this through, the good Lord willin'. You go safe as you can now, hear?"

John rarely had a shortage of words ready on his tongue but at that moment they deserted him. He did not know what to say, except to offer his thanks for the food and that he wished matters had been different. He would go safe and he hoped that they would stay safe.

Em also hugged him goodbye and said, "A woman could do worse than to birth a son like you, John Ware. That be the truth straight from the heart."

He walked down the path, through what once had been a beautiful, productive garden, and felt optimistic that it would be again. As he turned onto the road, he looked back and saw the sisters, arms about each other's waists, waving goodbye with their free hands. Liza held a handkerchief in hers. He waved back, and soon lost them behind some trees. He steeled his mind to go forward, because his heart was insisting that he turn back.

⁓⁓⁓

He kept alert as he moved farther westward, and in Mississippi he was surprised to find that conditions were not as bad as Liza thought. He found more than a few blacks working their own farms in the bottomlands and others doing well as sharecroppers. He was pleased for them but not the least bit tempted to settle, although he did stay for a while to help two families build their homes, carpetbaggers from up north come to take advantage of the cheap land prices. After that, he moved on.

At Vicksburg, besides the heavy presence of Union soldiers, John saw signs that a horrific battle had been waged there: shrapnel from burst bombs had been gathered and piled in places like giant iron anthills. He made his way to the docks, where a large crowd had gathered in anticipation of the arrival of a huge riverboat. John could see the vessel beating her way upstream, black smoke billowing from twin stacks. As her whistle sounded an intention to berth, her stern paddles began thrashing the water less vigorously. He asked a dockworker if there was anyone around who would be willing to take him across the river.

"There's a ferry leaving once the riverboat's unloaded," the worker said. "It costs a dollar if there's room. If you don't want to wait or pay that much, you can talk to that fella over there." He pointed to a thin man wearing a grey Confederate kepi and a black patch over his left eye, who was working with some ropes at the side of the dock. "He ain't pretty to look at but he'll probably take you over for a lot less."

John approached the man. An ugly scar that turned his upper lip into a permanent sneer ran up the side of his face and disappeared beneath the patch. He had a wad of chewing tobacco in his mouth. If the fellow were indeed a veteran and had received his injuries in the war, John wondered how willing he would be to row a black man across the river. But he hardly looked at John and said only, "Four bits'll get you there."

John paid and they climbed down a short ladder to a rowboat. When the wash from the riverboat subsided, the man let loose the painter and stabbed the oars into the river, aiming the vessel upstream so the sluggish current would direct it to the dock and road on the far side.

"It's a upside-down world," the man said, "when a white man goes to workin' for a nigra." He dipped his head toward Vicksburg. "But ten thousand Union boys died or give up some of their body parts just so's I'd have the privilege." He spat a gob of tobacco-stained saliva over the gunwale, adding, "I do it but I cain't say I care for it much. The money is all I care about."

John didn't know his numbers but figured that ten thousand had to be at least a city's worth of boys, too many to die in one place. Too many to die, period. He shrugged. "Well, there ain't much I can do about you not likin' it, but I suppose if a man don't change with the times, the past is bound to render him bitter as vinegar. If he ain't already bitter to begin with."

"I ain't bitter, leastways not real bitter. I give up one eye and got turned into a ugly sight by a grenade so's everythin'd stay the same, but like you said, a man's gotta keep up with the times." He fixed his good eye on John. "Even if such times is contrary to what the bible says."

John remembered all too well what the bible said; it had been rammed into his head every Sunday. And while he believed there was a God above, he had little faith in the bible. It was a hammer made of words that owners used to beat their slaves into submission. Still, John had to give the scarred man his due. The change that had come to his world was not sitting well with him, but he did not seem to be the type to hide behind a hood and terrorize innocent folk like Liza and Em. They were silent for a moment, the only sound the big riverboat's engine and the creaking oars. John changed the subject. He mentioned the large piles of shrapnel in the city and since he knew little of what had happened there, he asked the vet about it.

"Lasted nearly two months." The vet lay on the oars for a moment and then let the boat drift. "It was a war between smart rich men, and they got stupid poor men like me to fight it for 'em. You ask me if it was worth it, I'd have to ask you how could it be? Look at me. And all those dead boys just so's I could row you across the Mississip. Don't make no sense at all. No, sir, not one lick."

He began rowing again and continued talking when John said nothing. "Well, that was four years ago but it don't seem that long. The way it pictures in my mind it coulda been last week. Coulda been yesterday for all that matter."

At the far shore, John climbed from the boat and hesitated for a moment. He was tempted to lift his shirt and show the vet the ugly scars across his back, tell him that maybe the Union boys' dying had at least done *some* good. But he didn't think the man was quite right in the head—the grenade seemed to have taken some of his senses along with an eye—and John figured such an exhibition would probably be wasted. He said goodbye and set off on the road through the swampy bottomlands beside the river.

The few words he had shared with the vet had served to arouse memories of Liza and Em. They would be pleasantly surprised if they knew he had reached Louisiana safely, that he was nearly on the doorstep of Texas. As he trudged on, into the rolling woodlands and prairie forming the northern part of the state, he wondered how they were doing.

Beyond Shreveport, numerous stagecoaches passed by on the Texas road, the busiest thoroughfare he had seen so far. He encountered more freedmen, some heading east, some still looking for kin, others bound for the East Texas town of Marshall, which was in the westernmost extension of the cotton belt and on his route.

When he arrived there in November, the weather was unseasonably warm and humid. Marshall overflowed with blacks, many employed on the region's numerous cotton plantations. John felt safer than he had in months. He went to the Freedmen's Bureau, an agency set up to help freed slaves get a start in Reconstruction by finding them jobs and providing food to those passing through. He talked to one of several men working there and showed him the silver dollar–sized holes worn in the soles of his boots, saying he would be grateful if the bureau had anything to replace them. The man went into a back room and returned with a pair that was almost new, donated by a Union soldier. They pinched a bit, but as a big man with feet to match, John would have waited a long time for a pair the right size. He devoured the meal that the bureau provided, but declined the agent's offer of a job picking cotton, even though he would be a "paid worker, not a slave." Instead, he asked, "How far might it be to the nearest ranch?"

"Nearest ranch?" The agent looked surprised. "Don't recollect bein' asked that before. Out around Fort Worth, I suppose, but that's a long way from here. Maybe two hundred miles. Can't tell you if they'd be hirin' freedmen or not. Don't know but that you might even find a peck of trouble out that way. Heard they been murderin' coloured men."

"I'll take my chances," John said, "and I'm grateful for the food and boots."

As he was leaving, he glanced at the bureau's bulletin board, something he hadn't paid attention to on his way in because of his inability to read. Messages and single-page news bulletins containing several items filled it. He did understand some words though and recognized one straight away because he had seen it on several signs: *Demopolis*. His curiosity got the better of him. He removed the bulletin and took it to the agent.

"Can you tell me what this says?" he asked.

The agent took a few moments to peruse the short article and then paraphrased. "It's about a couple of murders near Demopolis, out Alabama way. Two coloured sisters, name of Elizabeth and Emma Adams, got beat to death in their home. No one knows who did it. That's all it says, but it sounds to me like the Klan's been busy."

John mumbled his thanks and left on legs turned as soft as overcooked greens.

Regrets nagged at him. Maybe he shouldn't have strengthened the sisters' resolve to stay by re-stacking the firewood; maybe he shouldn't have let them talk him into leaving. Maybe he should have kept after them until *they* left. Maybe. And maybe it wouldn't have mattered. They were two determined women who knew what they wanted and that they might face even more torment to get it. But his heart felt heavy with the injustice of it all, an injustice that hung over the South like a poisonous swamp gas. That night he thought about Liza and Em deep into the darkness before falling asleep, and they were still on his mind as the sun peeked over the eastern rim of the world the following morning and he set out down the road to Fort Worth. That was all he could do with his life: move forward, walk away from the past and into the future.

THREE

Amos Cole might be looking for a hand.

A week or two past Marshall, the surrounding countryside became more open and the road more exposed to the wind. The days were often dusty and the nights near freezing. But John had finally left the cotton belt and the last plantation behind, and he was glad of that. Dallas offered another Freedmen's Bureau with food and shelter, but he did not stay. Someone said that the Klan had been making their presence known in town.

Thirty miles farther on, Fort Worth sat on a low bluff above a loop in the Trinity River, flying a Union flag. Federal sentries stopped John at the edge of town. They were friendly enough, asking only what brought him this far west. He outlined his quest and asked the soldiers if they knew of anybody looking for a hardworking hand, someone who was not fussy about the colour of a man's skin, or the depth of his experience.

One of the soldiers said, "Well, there's always some outfit wanting a good cowpuncher, but I'm guessing that you don't fill the bill. Could be that Amos Cole might be looking for a hand. He owns the Flint Springs Cattle Company, a small spread a little southeast of here. Can't hurt to talk to him, anyway."

John got directions from the soldier, thanked him for the tip, and headed for Amos Cole's. He munched on the last of his food, a piece of cornbread from a small package given to him the day before outside of Dallas by the last farmer he'd worked for. It took an hour of easy walking to reach the ranch. An overhead sign nailed to two vertical posts straddled the entranceway. He presumed it read FLINT SPRINGS CATTLE COMPANY. A log house with a porch across the front sat a couple of hundred yards back from the road among a stand of scrub oaks. Nearby was a good-sized barn complete with a corral made from mesquite staves, and there were a couple of sheds and a privy. A few pigs and several chickens roamed at will near two large stacks of hay. John opened a squeaky rectangular wooden gate and entered the yard, closing the gate behind him. He'd taken only two or three steps when a man came out of the barn carrying a pitchfork. He slung the implement over his shoulder like a rifle and walked toward John, who figured that the best thing to do was smile. It worked, because the man smiled back and nodded hello. His height matched John's, but he was half the width and nowhere near the same weight. A pure white goatee covered the pointed chin of a weathered triangular face that looked as tough as Texas dirt. The man's eyes were a dark chestnut colour. Not a real old-timer, John thought, but around sixty, anyway. He wore a ten-gallon hat, well beyond its prime, and a grey flannel shirt tucked into faded blue Levi pants, which were crammed into worn and scraped boots. A blue neckerchief with polka dots that may have once been white encircled his neck.

"How do," he said. "Do something for you?"

John kept smiling. "I heard from some Federals up the road that you might be lookin' for a good hand."

The man's eyes scanned John from head to toe. "I suppose that's you, is it?"

John nodded. "Yes, sir, I'd sure like it to be. I'll give you some hard work for a meal and if you like what you see, maybe I can stay for a time."

"You ride?" the man asked.

"Been known to sit an ornery mule or two, but never a horse. But I'm willin' to learn."

The man pulled at his goatee. "Hmm. Well I reckon a mule can be as ornery, if not ornerier, than a horse. Got one in the stable over yonder, in fact. You interested in throwing a leg over her? Could be the ride of your life."

John shrugged. "Don't think I've had that ride yet."

"C'mon with me then."

John walked over to the barn with the man, who then asked him to wait outside. He shed his bedroll and leaned it against the wall. He heard the whimper of a mule, and a couple of minutes later the man came out leading a jittery sorrel jenny by a hackamore. She was as big as any horse John had ever seen.

"This is Connie," the man said. "She's short on manners and pretty much contrary to everything you want her to do, but she'll worm her way into your heart in time if she don't stomp you to death first. You can take her for a ride over that way." Motioning his head toward a gate at the rear of the fenced-off property, he added, "I'll open it for you and away you go."

He passed the reins to John as Connie reached around and tried to nip him. John leaped back. "Whoa, girl," he said. "No cause to be doin' that!"

The man grinned. "She's trying to set the rules. Unless she's hitched to a wagon, she only goes where she wants to and she hates anything on her back. She don't like water much either, unless it's to drink, so I reckon she won't run any farther than the Brazos."

"The Brazos?"

"Yep. The Brazos River."

"How far's that?"

"Oh, maybe thirty, forty miles southwest of here, depending on the route she takes. It's never the same."

John thought he detected something of a jokester in those dark eyes. "Hmm. Never heard of a mule runnin' that far before."

The man lifted his hat and scratched his head. "Well, maybe she don't. But I guess we'll never know because she ain't never come back with the rider."

"Well, sir, not this time," John said.

The man laughed. "I like your grit, but we'll see."

When the gate opened, John grasped Connie's mane and launched himself onto her bare back in one swift motion. The mule let out a whinny, followed by a loud hee-haw, threw her hind end high in the air twice, and took off across the yard and through the gate, presumably in the direction of the Brazos. John flopped around until he was able to get a better grip on the animal's flanks with his long legs, which were as strong as a thousand miles of walking could make them. Connie flew down one side of a shallow arroyo and up the other, through scattered thickets of black, gnarled mesquite trees and intermittent copses of stunted oak and pine, and into more open, bushy country. John hung on, the reins and mane bunched together in both hands. The man had been right: it *was* the ride of a lifetime. Yet he knew that he could stay on Connie, so he let her have her head, let her run as hard as she wanted, so that she would tire herself out, hoping he could handle the fall if she tripped in a prairie dog hole. Once he sensed her tiring, he would start using the reins.

John had no idea how far they had gone and had no sense of the passage of time, but he could not remember when he had enjoyed himself so much. He began to feel Connie weakening; her stride had shortened and she was breathing harder. He hauled back on the reins, but she fought him. Using his considerable strength, he hauled back even harder. Connie pulled up in a partial skid and started to buck. John was surprised at the fight left in her but was determined that there could be only one victor, and it was not going to have four legs. She must have swapped ends a half-dozen times before she slowed and came to a standstill.

She stood there, defeated, head down, heaving for a good breath. John stroked her sweaty neck and talked to her in a soothing voice, telling her what a good girl she was and that what had happened was not such a bad thing. "You been too long without a friend who understands you and now you got one." After letting her catch her breath, he coaxed her into motion and rode her around in broad circles, first left, then right, then he took her through tight circles. He pulled her to a halt and urged her forward a half-dozen times. Satisfied that she knew who was boss, he turned her toward the ranch.

He walked the mule for a while, talking gently to her. He could tell by her flickering ears that she was listening. When he saw the ranch buildings in the distance, he nudged her flanks and rode into the yard at a canter.

The man was at the barn, saddling a horse. His face broke

into a wide grin when he saw John and Connie. John pulled up in a cloud of dust and swung to the ground. He handed the reins to the man and said, "I don't think she'll be wantin' to head for the Brazos no more."

"I'll be damned!" The man removed his hat and ran his fingers through his thinning hair. "I was just saddling up to go look for you." He stuck out his hand. "The name's Amos Cole. Where you from?"

The extended hand reaffirmed John's impression that Amos did not share the same aversion to physical contact with a black man that most whites had. He grasped it. "I'm John Ware, and I'm six months out of South Carolina."

"Don't expect you took a coach."

"No, sir. Got a ride in a wagon here and there, but mostly I walked it."

"You must be tired. Why don't you stick around for a while and we'll see what else you got to offer an old rancher. I can start you off at three squares a day for a couple of days and if you prove your worth, the wage is five dollars a week. You can throw your bedroll up in the barn loft 'cause that's where you'll be sleeping. The privy is a two-holer, and men use the one on the right. The one on the left is for the missus. She ain't never been happy with a man's aim. You'll be chowing down with us in the house. Meanwhile, since we now got ourselves a mule good for something other than pulling a buckboard, you're entitled to one full belly. Come and meet the missus."

John followed Amos to the house and was introduced to Ellen Cole, short, compact, and sturdy, with grey hair and a round, kind face.

"People call me Ellie," she said. "No reason why you oughtn't."

He noticed that her hands were rough and red, the only parts of her that looked as if they might not be aging well. She laughed easily and giggled at things that Amos did not seem to think were funny. John liked that about her, because, regardless of his past, he laughed easily too.

At supper, over a plate of biscuits and beans accompanied by a glass of fresh milk from the Coles' milk cow, John had a chance to look around the house. A big wood-burning stove dominated the centre of a large open space that included a kitchen and living room. At each end was a bedroom with a low loft above it. John could not help but notice the thickness of the front door and the equally thick shutters on the insides of the windows. The shutters each had loopholes in them, and to John, they made the place appear like a small fortress. He asked Amos about them.

"Comanches, first off," Amos said, "but they're not so much of a problem anymore, as a lot of 'em were wiped out by the pox. Even so, there's still outlaws to worry about. Bad hands who think Texas is a playground and that they can get away with murder. They sometimes do. Used to be we had the Texas Rangers looking out for us, but they up and called it quits during the war. The Federals do a fair job now but only in the towns, and they'll be pulling out soon. Anyway, as far as the shutters go, maybe we don't need them, but it's better to be safe than sorry. Besides, when it gets real cold, we close them and it helps keep the heat in."

Ellie made tea after supper, and John learned more about the Coles. It turned out that Amos was actually seventy-two years old and Ellie sixty-eight. They had come to Texas from Franklin, Tennessee, a few years before the war, because they wanted some breathing room, and they wanted a ranch. They got their ranch, but the war came along and took their twin sons, Emmett and Thomas, away.

"Joined the Second Texas US Cavalry," Amos said. "Never did think that one man ought to own another. Don't seem right. Anyway, Thomas was one of the last men to die in that crazy war."

John saw in the Coles' eyes the sorrow that only a parent who has lost a child knows. Amos shook his head. "Weren't supposed to happen that way, him gone and us still here, but there's no accounting for human folly. Been a damned hard road to ride. The war dragged off most of the men capable of working and spending what they earned, and the markets for just about everything dropped faster than rocks down a well. Times are getting better, though. There's still a long row to hoe to real prosperity, but the town's building up again and there's a bit more cash money around to put in a merchant's pocket."

Amos explained that he had one hundred and sixty acres, but only five, around the house and outbuildings, were fenced. Beyond his property, most of the land was unclaimed and therefore considered open range. He kept three hundred head of cattle. There were also a dozen horses running wild there. In fact, Emmett would round them up on his way back from a Cattlemen's Association meeting in Waco. They would have to be broken, but Amos was certain that some of the animals would be good enough to merit training as trotters for harness racing in Fort Worth. Meanwhile, there was plenty to do, with building extra stalls, a corral, and an adjacent holding pen, and installing a snubbing post in the middle of the corral, as well as a host of other jobs. John would earn his keep and more.

And so the following morning they went to work, and Amos liked what John was about so much that he put him on wages at the end of the day. Toiling side by side, each man got to know a little of the stuff from which the other was made. John saw a man who judged him by his work and how he handled himself, rather than by the colour of his skin. Amos learned from John something of what it was like to be a slave, and he understood even better why he had been an abolitionist. He saw in John an intelligent man, unable to read or write, but eager and quick to learn, so he talked of more than just ranch work. He spoke of the stars and the planets and how they all worked together, and about the plant life and wildlife around them, and he began teaching John some rudimentary reading and writing and basic arithmetic.

"You need to know how to sign your name, John. One X looks pretty much like another, and you don't want to be paying for something that ain't your responsibility. It don't hurt to know your numbers in that regard either."

At night, when John wrapped himself up in his bedroll in the barn hayloft, he felt a new kind of power—that which comes with knowledge and contentment. Granted, his friends were few, but he was happy in his mind and was not opposed to spending time there. He reckoned that he had arrived at a special place in his life.

As for the cattle, they were longhorns and pretty much looked after themselves. They took longer to develop than their northeastern cousins and were not sent off to market until they were at least four years old. "We check on the calves in the spring," Amos told him, "brand 'em and remove the fries from the bull calves—you ain't tasted good food until you've had a mess of Ellie's fried bulls' balls—then round up the payers in the fall. The chickens require more tending to than those beeves."

Emmett returned several days later with eleven horses, having lost one to a broken ankle. He drove them into the holding pen. John was in the barn pitching hay down from the loft for the milk cow's manger when father and son entered. He climbed down to meet them. There was no mistaking the younger man's heritage, for he was the spitting image of his father, minus the wrinkles and goatee. In his early forties, he sported a full brown beard and eyes that had seen more in a lifetime than most men care to. He extended his hand to John when Amos introduced them. "Pa tells me you're a good man to have around."

John deflected the compliment. "Well, your pa's a good man to be around."

Emmett threw his head back and laughed in a way that reminded John of Ellie, and clapped his grinning father on the shoulder. "The man could charm a rattler into thinking it should have its fangs removed."

It was from Emmett that John began to learn about horses: how to sit a Western-style saddle and how to use it working with cattle. He told John, "You're gonna need a new pair of boots with higher heels before we begin to break the horses. You slip through those stirrups on a bucking horse that throws you, it'll drag you until you're skinned raw or dead. Maybe both." So he and John hitched up Connie to the buckboard and went into Fort Worth. They ignored the malevolent stares that too often came their way.

"We're going to Van Zandt's dry goods store," Emmett said. "You won't have any trouble there. He's not the kind of man to let skin colour get in the way of a business transaction." Indeed, John found the proprietor respectful and courteous, and came away the proud owner of a new pair of high-heeled leather boots.

Emmett taught him some drover skills, even how to throw a rope, which John practised whenever there was spare time, until he could duplicate or do better than anything his mentor did. Emmett also introduced him to tobacco. He rolled John a smoke and handed it to him. "Try this. It's good for what ails you and helps you relax."

John choked and coughed on the first one but persevered because he was keen to fit in. He was soon rolling his own with one hand, as Emmett did. Seeing John show off his skills one day prompted his friend to say, "You know, John, you always seem to need to prove yourself better than me. Let me tell you that you've more than proven yourself here, and this ain't no contest we're in. You're no less a man than I am and I consider myself a good one."

"Part of me knows that, Emmett, but the other part says that I'll always have to prove myself. The colour of my skin makes that the plain truth for me. Maybe not with you and your folks, but it won't hurt none to practise some here so that I got it right when I need it."

Emmett gathered in the comment and nodded.

Two days before Christmas, John rode the first of the wild horses to a standstill while Amos and Emmett looked on in bemused amazement. John dismounted and, knowing he had impressed both men, suppressed a smile as he asked, "You got any *real* wild ones?"

The Coles laughed and Amos fetched another animal that John rode into submission as well. Amos shook his head and chuckled. "They say that seeing is believing, but what I'm seeing I can scarcely believe."

Emmett said, "Well, I ain't asleep and I ain't dreaming, so it must be real."

The day before Christmas, while John did chores, Amos and Emmett took Connie and the buckboard out and returned a couple of hours later with a rather scrawny pine tree. They set it up in the house, and that evening Ellie decorated it with handmade paper ornaments and bows made from ribbons. It was a custom new to John, and Amos said that it was new to them too, but their German neighbours a couple of miles down the road did it and the Coles had liked the idea. Afterwards, they drank eggnog and sang carols, and before bedtime, Amos read from Charles Dickens's *A Christmas Carol*. John had never had anybody other than a preacher read to him before, and he got lost in the story. It seemed as if Dickens had personally known Sebastian Chambers, although he did not think it likely that his old slave master had found redemption as Scrooge had.

On Christmas Day, the Coles' neighbours stopped by for a visit, as did some acquaintances from town. The Coles introduced John as if he were part of the family, and it felt as strange to him as it probably did to the visitors. They feasted that night on beef, potatoes, and carrots, roasted in the same pot, and had apple cobbler for dessert. Afterwards, they moved to the cane chairs in the living area with hot whiskies.

They chatted for a bit, and Ellie said, "Amos, you'll do the honours, won't you?"

"I surely will." He rose and went to the Christmas tree, where he retrieved five packages wrapped in brown paper and tied with ribbons. He gave two to Ellie, one to Emmett, a large one to John, and kept one for himself.

"Why don't you go first, Ma," Emmett suggested.

"Oh, no," Ellie said. "It isn't fair to make the rest of you wait."

They all tore at their packages, except John, who picked at his, unaccustomed to either receiving or giving gifts. He saw that Ellie had opened her presents to find a new cooking pot from Amos and a fancy apron from Emmett, while Emmett got a new Bowie knife with an eight-inch blade and sheath from his parents. Amos's gift from Ellie and Emmett was a silver-plated timepiece and chain. They had all finished opening their presents and John was still fumbling with his, almost afraid to open it.

"C'mon, John," Amos urged. "Nothing in there that'll bite."

John got the paper off and held the large paperboard box.

"Open it, for pity's sake!" Ellie cried.

John pulled the top of the box off; inside was a black Boss of the Plains Stetson hat. Beneath it, nestled in a pair of home-knitted woollen socks, were a gold eagle worth ten dollars and a double eagle worth twenty dollars. As grateful as he was for their generosity, he wished that he had had the money beforehand so that he could have bought gifts for them. Amos sensed his discomfort.

"John, your gift to us is your presence here. Besides, the double eagle is this month's wages and the eagle is a bonus in hopes that you'll stay on. Now, I ain't a man for making speeches, but I'm telling you this in the spirit of Christmas and all that it means: I've been on this earth a good many years and I've yet to meet a man who works as hard as you do. Never seen a man with as much glue in his pants when it comes to sticking on a sunfishing horse either. So like I said, we've never had such a gift dropped in our laps as you."

"What you do around here to help, John," added Emmett, "is more than a body has a right to expect. You do the work of two men, so you deserve every penny of it. The hat, too. It's the biggest size I could get—I hope it fits."

Ellie spoke up. "And if you'd like a lady's perspective, you're more of a gentleman than most of the so-called 'gentlemen' in town are."

John tried the hat on and the fit was snug, but that meant it would stay where it ought to in a stiff Texas wind. He cleared his throat. "Well, if things don't work both ways, they won't work at all. I can't think of nothin' else I'd rather be doin' than what I'm doin' right here. You've made me feel welcome since the first day I come here and that'd rest easy on any man's heart. My thanks to you."

Amos had a look of childlike anticipation on his face. "We ain't done yet, John. Why don't you have a look in the loft above Emmett's room?"

His curiosity aroused, and more into the spirit of the celebration, John went to the ladder placed against the wall and climbed high enough to be able to peer into the shadowy space. He hadn't the faintest idea what he would find there, and it took a moment for the significance of it to sink in. There was a handmade cot topped by a tick mattress, with a folded blanket at the foot and a pillow at the head. Beside the cot was a wooden box on top of which sat an unlit candle in a brass holder. The realization of what it meant sent a warm sensation flooding through him, and while he had probably shed tears as a child, he had no recollection of it, and had never shed any as an adult. But he now felt them clouding his vision, and a lump in his throat blocked his voice. Behind him, the Coles chorused, "Happy Christmas, John!"

After the brief holiday, Emmett rode south to Waco to attend another meeting, and John broke the remainder of the horses. He and Amos began training two of the best for harness racing. One in particular, a young bay mare, was lightning fast. After John had broken her, he took her out the back gate and let her run. Even carrying his considerable weight, she tore up the furlongs with a speed unmatched by any of the other mounts. Amos commented that she had taken off like a "scalded cat," so Cat became her name.

When Amos hitched Cat to a sulky, John told him, "Seems a shame to hobble that horse to a trot, Amos. She loves to stretch her legs."

"Maybe, but most of the racing in Fort Worth is harness racing and that's where the money is. We gotta try her there first and if she don't work out, well . . ." Amos let the sentence dangle there, incomplete.

On the day of the first race meet, people streamed into town from the surrounding ranches and as far away as Dallas, either as spectators or participants. Emmett, back from Waco, and Ellie joined Amos and John. Unlike the races back east, where horses were bred for trotting, a wide variety of breeds was used here, which made it all the more interesting and entertaining to watch. A festive feeling charged the air and the crowd roared its delight when the races got under way.

Amos and Cat were in the second race, which was exclusively for two-year-olds. Cat got off to a good start, trotting nicely, but lost her rhythm around the first turn and broke into a gallop. The rules stated that Amos had to steer her off to the side, slow down, and let her find her pace again. A couple of other horses had problems, too, which allowed Cat to get back in the race, but in the end, she and Amos crossed the finish line in fourth place, with seven carts on the track.

Amos was disappointed. "Believed she'd do a whole lot better than that," he muttered. "Maybe you're right, John. She always felt to me like she wanted to break away, so maybe trotting ain't in her blood." He lifted his hat and scratched his head, as he often did when there was a decision in the offing. "There's an open race after the harness racing's done and if you wanna ride Cat in it, you have my blessing. You can go saddled or bareback, but bareback may be your best bet because you're heavier than a normal load for a racehorse. Anyway, I hope I didn't tucker her out too much."

The prospect excited John. "I don't think so, Amos. I'd wager she's not even warmed up yet."

Besides the betting that went on, all of the ranchers with a horse in the open race pitched into the prize-money pot, which had built up to one hundred and fifty dollars. It was for first place only.

"You don't come in first," Amos said, "all you'll get is to eat the dust of the leaders, so make her give everything she's got, John."

With the harness racing completed, John mounted Cat and

they joined eleven other horses and their riders at the starting line. Some of the animals were nervous, and it rubbed off on several of the others, which meant a lot of movement and jostling on the line. Cat wanted to run, but John held her head close as she pranced with explosive energy in the small space.

With the horses lined up abreast, the starting gun banged and John felt the strength and power in Cat's stride as she surged forward and flew down the track. The sound of forty-eight horses' hooves pounding on the hard earth was thunderous in his ears, and the danger in being in the thick of it thrilled him. He sensed that Cat could have taken the lead but he held her back, hoping that she would be all the hungrier for it in the home stretch.

The pack rounded the first turn with John in fourth place. He looked for an opening to the inside, against the rail, but there was none, nor was there one to the outside. After the second turn and into the backstretch, he felt that the riders around him might be trying to box him in to prevent him from taking the lead and perhaps winning the race. Around the third turn, the horse directly in front of Cat was tiring, allowing John to slip into third place. Now only two horses remained in front and they were neck and neck. He kept watch for room to make a move inside, desperate to find one, but none appeared. Past the final turn, the lead horses were still jamming the rail; it was outside or nothing. John had a quirt but did not use it; instead, he shook the reins and called to Cat to run. She did not need the encouragement. Like a big cat lunging after its prey, she shot around the outside horse and tore down the home stretch. John felt transported to another world in which human beings rode on the wind. From somewhere far away, he thought he could hear the Coles above the crowd, screaming for more speed. But John's work was done. Cat was in control and she wanted the race even more than he did. Later, Amos would tell John that he had crossed the finish line two lengths in front of the nearest horse, the rest of the field spaced out even farther back. No one at the track had ever seen a horse run that fast.

"You got a good one here, Amos!" John was nearly breathless as he reined up and dismounted in the winner's circle. "Lord, but she knows how to run!"

"That was some race!" Amos's face was lit up like a gas lamp. "Even men I know to be staunch Democrats were cheering." His smile widened. "I reckon more for the horse than for you, though."

On the way back to the ranch, with the cart in the back of the buckboard and Cat in tow, Amos was exultant. "You earned yourself fifty dollars of that prize money, John. And you know what else?" Neither waiting for an answer nor expecting one, he continued, "A man needs a good horse and a horse needs a good man. You and Cat are a pair if ever I seen one. As far as I'm concerned, she's yours. Enough said, now. I'm deaf as a board to arguments."

That's how it was with Amos Cole. Once he made up his mind, it was futile to contest him. John had himself a first-rate horse and more money in his Levi's than he'd ever had before. He thought, A man might feel that the world has done him a bad turn, that he was born in the wrong place at the wrong time. But if he's lucky and he doesn't let it get the best of him, the day will come when such things matter a whole lot less.

For John, that day had come; he felt himself to be a lucky man.

FOUR

No reason for you to stay.

The years folded easily into a decade, as soft butter folds into flour. Amos was now in his eighties and was a little stooped, the rifts in his face a little deeper, but he still had the energy of a man twenty years younger. Ellie hadn't changed much and seemed unaffected by the passage of time, while Emmett's greying beard grew on a face even more burnished by the Texas weather. John's beard, which had been like a mere shadow on his face for so long, had thickened and looked full and respectable. His relationship with Emmett had blossomed from one of employer and hired hand into one of brotherhood. As for Amos and Ellie, they may as well have been his parents.

Emmett said to him one day, "John, you've learned a lot about what it takes to be a good cattleman, but you ought to come to Waco with me for the next meeting of the Cattlemen's Association. You'll see that ranchin' ain't all cattle and horses."

The idea did not appeal to John in the least. "I ain't one for meetins, Emmett. Amos never goes to 'em, so maybe he'd like to go with you. Me and Ellie can look after the ranch while you're gone."

"Pa don't go to those meetings because he don't need to. Besides, he's gettin' too old to go even if he wanted to. But it'd be good for you, John. You'd learn lots."

"Well, if you think I oughta go, Emmett, you'll get no more arguin' from me."

They set out the following morning and were two days on the road, traversing the flat landscape between Fort Worth and Waco. They crossed the Brazos River over a new suspension bridge, paying a small toll, and entered the town during a blustery late afternoon with the dust flying.

"I don't know about you, John," Emmett said, "but my mouth needs a good rinsing out. A friend of mine usually meets me at the Ranch Saloon, and that's where we're headin' first. He always goes to the meetings with me too, and if he's true to form he'll already be there gettin' a head start on us."

The men liveried their horses, walked through the town square to the Ranch Saloon, and pushed through the shutter doors.

"Emmett!"

The voice belonged to a knife blade of a man standing at the bar. Gangly, like a marionette come to life, and redheaded, he sported a huge moustache that tumbled over his upper lip like a waterfall. Coffee had stained the ends brown, and John could see something lodged in it that may have been remnants of his lunch. Emmett introduced John to Seamus Duffield, better known as "Duffy" to anybody who felt they ought to call him something. The two friends exchanged pleasantries and Emmett bought a bottle of whisky. The trio sat down at a table near the rear of the saloon.

They drank the remainder of the afternoon away, with Emmett and Duffy doing most of the talking. Emmett pulled out his pocket watch. "Well, best we get ourselves something to eat before the meeting. They always seem to last a lot longer than everyone intends."

In a restaurant around the corner from the Ranch, they ate

a supper that was disappointingly inferior to one of Ellie's home-cooked meals, and washed it down with coffee. Emmett pulled out his watch again. "Just enough time to get over to Two Street, where the meeting is." Looking at John, he asked, "You ready for this, brother?"

Filled with whisky and food, John felt more like going to bed than to a meeting and admitted it.

Emmett laughed. "I think you'll find it quite spirited. Anyway, we should go. It's a walk over to Two Street and we don't want to keep everyone waiting."

He paid the bill and led the way three blocks to Two Street. The wind had died, the dust had settled, and the evening was pleasant. They came to a two-storey building shaped like a T with the stem at the rear. As they walked through the front door into a large foyer, a curvaceous blond woman who looked to be in her late forties greeted them.

"Mr. Cole! And Mr. Duffy! It's always good to see you! I see you've brought a friend this time, but not to worry, we can accommodate the three of you. Come! I'll see that you get refreshments." She led them into a room furnished with a sofa and wingback chairs. "Make yourselves comfortable, gentlemen. The ladies will be here shortly with your drinks."

She hustled off.

John did not quite know what to make of the place but was impressed. The cattlemen in the district apparently spared no effort to make their meetings as comfortable as possible. A few minutes later, three women entered, dressed in less clothing than was common for the period, each bearing a drink. John was mystified. One of the women walked straight to him and, after handing him a drink, slid onto his lap. She put her arm around his neck, kissed his cheek, and said, "I'm Abby. What shall I call you?"

John swallowed and grew hot. There was a white woman sitting on his lap and kissing him. He looked at Emmett for some kind of sign that this was all right, that it was not going to lead to bloodshed, namely his. Emmett grinned and raised his glass. "Welcome to the Cattlemen's Association meeting. The proceedings are now called to order."

Duffy cackled with laughter.

Later, while lolling in a hot bath, John felt complete and utterly satisfied with life. He had never bedded a woman before; indeed, he had never even held and kissed one. He could not for the life of him even begin to describe how wonderful it felt. She was so soft! And her perfume still lined his nostrils, an exquisite reminder of an evening he would not soon forget. Granted, he would have preferred to lose his virginity to a loving wife instead of a whore, but he had not seen a spousal prospect the entire time he had been with the Coles. And tonight went a long way toward unravelling the mystery he perceived women to be, particularly white women, and that was no small step forward.

In the morning, after they had said goodbye to Duffy and crossed the Brazos on their way home, John asked Emmett, "Do Amos and Ellie know about these 'meetins' of yours? What'll I say if they ask me about it? You know I ain't big on lyin'."

"No one's gonna ask. Besides, Pa knows. That's why he never offers to go. I'm sure Ma knows too. She just pretends that she's not interested in what goes on at a boring meeting with a bunch of men, so that's why she never asks about it. But Ma knows everything, most particularly when it's time to mind her own business."

The ranch was much more prosperous now than it had been when John arrived, but 1873 saw the collapse of an economy that had flourished after the war, and the beginning of a long depression. That year was a hardscrabble one for the Coles, and their coffers dipped at an alarming rate. John refused to accept his wages, and even though Amos did not like it, he accepted the refusal because he had little choice. But when John developed a serious toothache in his lower jaw and asked Amos to pull the tooth out for him, Amos wouldn't hear of it. He would pay a dentist to do it.

Fort Worth did not have a dentist, but Dallas did, so the following morning, John, carrying money from Amos, saddled Cat and loped there, the pain intensified by each thud of her hooves. The oil of cloves Ellie had given him did not help much. Dallas did not appear on the horizon any too soon, nor did the shingle hanging out in Commerce Street that read DR. SINCLAIR, DENTISTRY. And below: PAINLESS EXTRACTIONS.

The dentist was a pasty-complexioned, fair-haired young man of slight build, whose forehead had a noticeably damp sheen. He had a chronic cough, which John did not like because it might be consumptive, but his manner was kind and genteel, his accent that of a Southern aristocrat.

"I can offer chloroform, ether, or nitrous oxide to eliminate the pain," he said.

John shook his head, fearing that he would be rendered senseless and he didn't want that. "Just yank it."

"As you wish, sir. *Fortis an stultus.* But first we must find it. And I would suggest that you grip the arms of the chair with all the strength at your command. Open!"

John spread his jaws and the dentist tapped the teeth in the area John had indicated until he hit the offending one. Despite his grip, John almost shot out of the chair from the intense burst of pain.

"Ah, the third molar is the culprit." The dentist smiled. "Now, open again."

Once John was able to comply, the dentist grasped the tooth with forceps, which looked to John like a smaller version of the pliers he had used as a blacksmith, planted his feet firmly on the floor, and began pulling. An unrelenting pain more intense than a Sebastian Chambers whipping filled John's head and burst into his entire body. The tooth would not budge.

"It is large and stubborn," the dentist announced, "and will require a different plan of attack."

He wrapped his left arm over John's head, grasping him under the chin, and placed his right knee against the arm of the chair. He began pulling again. This time some sideways movement of the tooth was achieved and the dentist wiggled it back and forth, tugging all the while. To John it sounded and felt like miners were working with pickaxes in his mouth, but at last the tooth came free. The dentist held the offending molar up for John to see and said, "*Semper ad meliora.*"

The constant pain that had plagued John for two days had disappeared. His jaw was sore as hell, but the throbbing ache was gone and that was all that mattered. A day or two later he felt fully recovered.

———

The Texas economy began to recover as well, but at a much slower rate. The railroad arrived from Marshall and points east in 1876, and Fort Worth grew and thrived. New businesses popped up and mule-drawn trolleys plied the streets. The Texas Rangers had been reorganized and sent many of the outlaws packing, and the town streets and state roads were much safer. Even so, while the ranch had proved to be a haven for John, the town was the exact opposite. His visits there always met with some form of challenge, from something as simple as white men refusing to step aside on the boardwalks, to threats on his life. Remembering his father's advice, he reasoned that the best response was no response at all.

The shining exception to this hostility was the reception he received at Khleber Van Zandt's dry goods store. Over time, he purchased his own rope and every item of clothing a man needed, from good leather gloves to leather chaps, plus all the required tack.

He sat down with Ellie one day and with her help wrote a letter to his parents, telling them how good life was for him and that he hoped the same for them and Millie, and Nettie in particular. He proudly wrote his signature at the bottom, knowing his family would be impressed. Five months later, he received a reply, not from any of his family but from James Ball, his old boss. Ellie read it to him. Ball began by apologizing for being the bearer of bad news, then explained that Nettie had disappeared. "She went for a walk one day and never returned, John," Ball wrote. "Her employers feared she had taken her own life, because there was such a sense of sadness about her. I think the sadness came from being the last of the Ware family left in Georgetown. Not long after you left, Millie found herself a husband and moved north to be with your brothers. Later, your ma came down with pneumonia and died, and that sent your pa spinning off into a different world. He could not recognize anybody, not even Nettie. He went to bed one night and did not wake up. I believe the burden of those losses was too much for your sister to carry."

Ball concluded by apologizing again for sending such bad news, but John's letter had been brought to him by the Wares' neighbour, and he felt duty bound to answer it. He was pleased but not surprised that John was doing so well for himself.

Ellie handed John the letter, her eyes watery with tears. "I'm so sorry."

John took the letter, folded it, and put it in his shirt pocket. "Thank you, Ellie." He scraped back his chair and went outside to be alone and digest the contents of the letter. He feared also that he might embarrass himself in front of Ellie. Was every man's life so full of "what ifs"?

In 1877 Emmett joined an outfit driving cattle to the stockyards in Abilene, Kansas, mainly to gain the experience to lead his own drive one day. Many ranchers shipped their cattle east from Fort Worth, but the real money lay in trailing them north, where an animal could fetch up to ten times its value in the south. What's more, millions of wild longhorns roamed the Texas plains, there for anybody with the salt to gather up.

When Emmett returned, he and Amos made plans for their own business venture. They had rebuilt a healthy bank account, so Emmett hired some drovers to help him make up a herd from several gathers to trail to Ogallala, Nebraska, in the spring of '78. While the profits were high in terminating a drive at Dodge City, Kansas, some two hundred and fifty miles short of the Nebraska town, the railway through Ogallala served a Pacific coast market, where profits were even higher.

"You'd be more than welcome on these gathers," Emmett told John, "but for the time being, Pa needs your help more than I do."

That was true. The ranch, which had been renamed the Flint Springs Livery and Cattle Company, now depended less on cattle for its income and more on horses that had to be broken and trained, a job Amos had not been able to do for a good many years, but one at which John excelled. Nevertheless, he was keen to go on the drive when it happened, although he didn't say anything to Emmett, or to Amos for that matter. But the northwest had taken on almost mythical overtones for him ever since he had talked to cattlemen who had been as far north as the Montana Territory. Without exception, they spoke of the grandeur of the mountains and the bountiful grass in the foothills, claiming that it was *real* cattle country, and that people were few and far between. It made John think of one day having his own ranch in such a beautiful part of the world.

Emmett and his cowhands, who included Duffy, would go out with a small herd of Flint Springs cattle and use it as a decoy to lure the wild ones along. Over a few months and several gathers they amassed a large herd of longhorns and situated them on good grazing land between the Clear and West forks of the Trinity River, where they could fatten up for the drive. Some would birth calves, and Emmett guessed they would have around two thousand animals to trail north. In the spring the animals would be "road branded" with a light brand that would last for the duration of the trip. Emmett had Duffy and another drover set up camp to watch the herd at all times and a couple of others to spell them off. He rode up to check on them from time to time, especially when thunderstorms were in the vicinity and the cattle might stampede.

John went with him once and the visit only served to whet his appetite to join the drive. One night after supper, when he and the Coles were sipping their last cup of coffee and smoking their last cigarette before turning in, John broached the subject of going north with Emmett. He told them that the north country had been filling his dreams lately, that it might prove to be the perfect place for a man like him to make a new start. He knew that he'd be the greenest hand on the huge drive, but Emmett knew how hard he worked and how quickly he learned. He expected no more pay than the other crew members, plus the same bonuses they made.

"Much as I hate to leave you folks," he told Amos and Ellie, "it's time, I reckon. That's if you'll have me, Emmett."

"I can't think of a reason in the world why I wouldn't," said Emmett enthusiastically. "Except maybe that you'll be sorely missed around here. But that's no reason for you to stay."

Amos grew contemplative. "I guess what surprises us most is that this day took so long to come. We've known for some time that there was much more for you in the world than what we could offer. Didn't say nothing, for selfish reasons I reckon. But when life calls to you, it's best not to turn your back on it, so go with our best wishes, John. We've got plenty of time to find a replacement, and it'll be up to Ellie and me to be fair and not compare him to you. Don't expect it'll be easy."

The winter, though mild, seemed longer than usual to John, even with the work, of which there was never any shortage. In March, Emmett acquired a remuda of forty horses, some of which needed breaking, a task that John gladly looked after. Then he brought Duffy in from the camp to help with training the animals to work with cattle.

Emmett went to town one day and returned with a used buckboard that he and John converted into a chuckwagon. On another trip, upon Emmett's advice, John bought a Colt six-shooter for the drive, along with a hand-tooled leather holster and belt.

"You might need a gun to turn the herd if it stampedes," Emmett said, "but use it only as a last resort. Cattle and gunfire ain't usually a good mix because it can spook 'em even more. You might also need it to shoot an Indian or a rustler, but we'll hope it never comes to that."

Excitement ran high at the supper table the night before Emmett and John were to depart. Eight drovers and the remuda had left that morning, along with a cook and a well-stocked chuckwagon. Emmett was more excited than John had ever seen him, insisting that if their gamble paid off and they got most of the herd to Ogallala safely, the Coles stood to earn anywhere from sixty to eighty thousand dollars after expenses. To John, those figures were almost incomprehensible, but he reckoned his friends deserved every penny of it. He also knew that Emmett would be generous when it came to paying out his men, as long as they pulled their weight.

Early the following morning, the pair saddled their horses and prepared to take their leave from Amos and Ellie. The older couple knew their son would be back, but that it might well be the last time they saw John. Ellie was near tears.

"I was hoping this day would never come, John, even knowing in my heart that it would. You've been like the son we lost, and that's the highest praise I can offer." With that, she reached up and pulled John's head down and kissed his cheek.

A hundred thoughts ran through John's mind, but only one formed into words: a half-baked joke that he could say without his feelings catching in his throat. "I heard that the cook Emmett hired has been known to burn water, so besides missin' you, I expect I'm really gonna miss your cookin'!"

Ellie laughed, the response he had hoped for, but both knew that he would miss much more than home cooking. The Coles had included him in their lives, brought him inside their circle, and made him feel like a fellow human being instead of chattel. Their generosity had allowed him to discover what he supposed he had been looking for all along: the man he had become.

While John was talking to Ellie, Amos had gone into the house. He came back out with a brand new Winchester rifle, model 1876, tucked inside a leather scabbard. He handed it to John.

"A gift to take with you, son, from all of us. It was a good day for the Cole family when you walked through our gate. A sad one now that you're leaving. Maybe this'll help you remember us."

John accepted the rifle. "It was a good day for me too, Amos. When I left South Carolina, I dreamed of workin' on a ranch out this way. Never seen in it me ownin' a horse or havin' a pocketful of money, or learnin' as much as I did. And I surely didn't know I'd meet such fine folks as you. I'm not likely to forget you or forget what you done for me."

True to his habit, Amos lifted his hat, brushed his thinning hair back, and said philosophically, "Well, I guess it's pretty hard to say who done more than the other, ain't it? Maybe that's as it oughta be for folks everywhere."

John grasped Amos's extended hand, the grip still hard and firm. "So long, Amos."

While Emmett said his own goodbyes, John went to Cat's right side, lifted the stirrup leather onto the saddle, and cinched the latigo straps on the scabbard to the metal rings there. If he needed the rifle in a hurry, it would be within easy reach. After one final farewell, he and Emmett mounted their horses and nudged them into motion. Neither of them looked back, but they knew that Amos and Ellie would be watching them until they disappeared from view.

※

When Emmett had gone north on his learning drive, the route taken was the Chisholm Trail, a well-established track that passed through Fort Worth, crossed the Red River into the middle of the Indian Territory, and ended in Abilene, Kansas.

The drive to Ogallala, however, would take a different route that cut through the western edge of the Oklahoma Territory to Dodge City, before continuing on to the Nebraska cattle town and the Union Pacific Railway.

On the short ride to the camp and herd, Emmett told John that he had let the new cowhands hired for the drive know that a coloured man would be joining them. "Most of 'em don't have a problem with it but a couple a diehards named Rufus Pauley and Homer Morgan weren't exactly whistling happy tunes about it. They're good hands, but if they cause you any trouble, let me know and they'll be paid up and sent packing."

"I can take care of myself, Emmett; you know that."

"I do. But for this drive to work, someone's gotta be in charge and that's me. You start taking matters into your own hands and it'll bring nothing but trouble. Meanwhile, the men know your main colour is green and they'll expect you to start as wrangler. It's the low board on the fence post, but few men understand horses better than you do, and I figger when they see how good you are at taking care of 'em and how well you handle 'em, they'll be over to your side without knowing they made the trip."

Emmett also cautioned him about Pépin Gireaux, the camp cook. "Call him Pepper or Cookie, but nothing else. Best not to call him Frenchie, unless you wanna get brained by a cast-iron frying pan. And you'll wanna walk softly around him. Think of the chuckwagon as a country and he's the king, and the rest of us are simply peasants that he feels obliged to feed. He ruled the roost on the drive to Abilene and he puts in long hours, so if he gets a tad crotchety, all you got to do is walk away and don't argue with him. He fries up a mean steak and after you've had one at the end of a hard day's ride, I believe you'll forgive him for most things."

At the camp, when Emmett introduced John to the crew, most nodded cordially and said hello: Nathan Pitt, Albert Jackson, Glenford Pounds, Ben Munger, Reg Haliday, Alex Baily, and "Pepper," the cook. Rufus Pauley and Homer Morgan barely moved their heads. Both seemed like hard cases, particularly Pauley with his thin lips, cold, brooding eyes, and shoulder-length black hair. John was glad to see Duffy's friendly face among the crew and knew that he would be a staunch ally if one were required.

There followed a democratic discussion of assignments: who would ride point, who would ride swing and flank, and who would ride the drags. It all boiled down to experience, and so Ben, Nathan, and Rufus, as the most experienced, got the point, leading the herd; Duffy, Reg, and Alex would ride swing and flank on either side of the herd, keeping it in line and picking up strays. The least experienced, Glenford and Albert, would ride drag, keeping the herd moving forward while eating the dust that it churned up. Emmett was trail boss and scout, and John and Homer were in charge of the remuda. Emmett would have liked a better pairing, but with any luck he would open Homer's eyes to a much broader world. The drag men would spell them off from time to time, as a much needed break from the dust. John liked that arrangement because it would give him some experience working with the herd.

He roped off a corral among some trees and drove the horses grazing nearby into it. In the order of their experience and place on the drive, the men had their choice of mounts from the remuda that would be theirs for the duration. John would ride Cat, who was now thirteen years old but still had a lot of spunk, Emmett had Goldy, a beautiful palomino mare, and Pepper had command of the chuckwagon pulled by two mules.

While the mount selection was under way, Emmett rode amongst the herd and counted them. By his tally, they would be driving a little less than two thousand head of longhorns north. He was a happy man. He cut out an older, dry cow and took her back to camp to slaughter.

That evening, while the men tended to their equipment, John gathered bundles of oak firewood for the canvas sling beneath the chuckwagon, and got the remuda settled down and hobbled for the night. With help from Emmett, Pepper dressed the slaughtered cow and hung it to cool overnight. They would wrap it in a spare canvas in the morning to keep it cool during the day and hang it out again in the evening when they stopped. The men would have steaks and roasts, and when the meat was too old for those luxuries, Pepper would put it to good use in chili and stews.

Pepper ground up some beans and put on a final pot of coffee. Emmett was the first to taste it and he sighed appreciatively. "You could float a saddle in this, Pepper. Damned fine brew."

There were murmurs of approval from the other hands and Duffy added, "Best damned coffee I ever tasted."

Pepper neither smiled nor beamed over the accolades, accepting them not as compliments but as statements of fact.

Most could hardly wait until morning when the drive would get under way; it was what they lived for, and talk around the campfire was wild stories from past drives. When the coffee pot was empty, Emmett yawned. "Well, boys, best we turn in. It's gonna be a long day tomorrow. We'll see if we can get maybe eighteen or twenty miles out of these critters and break 'em into the trail. Get 'em used to heading in the direction we want 'em to, and tire 'em out enough so that they'll wanna rest and not wander off into trouble somewhere. Don't expect there's a cow alive that hasn't tried it more than once in its lifetime."

In anticipation of the coming journey, John didn't feel sleepy; indeed, the whole camp was restless. Men tossed and turned in their bedrolls, and a crescent moon was high in the night sky before he heard some snoring. He lay there thinking about what the coming months would bring. He felt more excited than he had when he left Georgetown so many years before, like an explorer off for the first time to some exotic, unknown land. On a map, it was north that he was heading, but he wondered where the journey would really take him.

FIVE

We got ourselves an outfit here!

John awoke the following morning with dawn a rope of light on the horizon, the sky above still starry. He lay there for a few seconds gathering his senses and focusing on the coming day. He was about to stretch when he became conscious of a weight on his chest. The weight began to move. John froze. Peering over his blanket, he saw an enormous coiled rattlesnake stirring from where it had apparently slid to find warmth in the cool night air. John's bowels felt as if they were shaking themselves loose, and for an instant he did not know what to do. He saw that the snake was lethargic, and without further thought, flung the blanket off. The reptile flew through the air and landed on Duffy, who was just awakening. Duffy yelped and he too threw the snake off, sending it into the cold ashes of the campfire. He had his gun out in a flash, leaped to his feet, and shot the rattler twice, then a third time for good measure. Meanwhile, the other members of the crew were flying from their sleeping rolls and grabbing for their weapons, fearing they were under attack by Indians.

"Goddamned snake, boys!" Duffy explained. "Come at me outta nowhere, flyin' through the air like a goddamned bird! Never seen the likes of it!"

John was tempted to let Duffy think that he had seen his first flying snake, but reasoned it was best to own up to his part. "It was me who did that, Duffy. Woke up with it on my chest and it scared the bejesus outta me. Flung it off without thinkin', and I apologize." He was still shaking, thankful that he had not been bitten and had not fouled himself. He would never have lived it down.

Duffy took some good-natured ribbing from the others and saw the humour in it. He half grinned. "Well, I'da done the same thing. I hate those sonsabitches! Old Saint Patrick drove all the snakes outta Ireland, then sat around on his arse for the rest of his life. Lazy bastard shoulda come to Texas."

Emmett laughed. "Too bad you killed it, Duffy. Don't know how we're ever gonna get you up that fast again."

Emmett let the herd graze for a while, before he, Pepper, along with the chuckwagon, and John and Homer, with the remuda, headed out under a cloudless April sky. Emmett's job would be to find a good bed-ground for the night. Behind them, the herd moved out, an enormous mass of animal flesh surrounded by roiling clouds of dust, led by Nathan and Rufus and contained by the rest of the crew. The object was to keep the herd moving in one homogeneous string, but in those first days it was nearly impossible. What little mind the Texas longhorns had was at least their own, and the swing and flank men were kept busy routing strays out of mesquite and oak thickets.

It was those riders, off in the bushes, who encountered snakes—mostly rattlers, but in the wetter areas around streams and ponds, an occasional cottonmouth or copperhead. Most of the men gave the reptiles a wide berth and left them alone, but not Duffy. His hatred of snakes ran deep and that first day he killed six rattlers before the noon break, sometimes riding out of his way to do it. As a reptile slithered away trying to make its escape, he'd slap it hard with his rope and break its back. "Got another one a them sonsabitches!" he'd cry to anyone within hearing distance. The snakes were all diamondbacks, some four to five feet long.

John could not blame Duffy. The mere sight of a snake, in particular those long, large-fanged devils, made him weak in the knees. On the trail, you always had to check for snakes before you sat down, and stories abounded around the evening campfires of them curling up with a drover at night for warmth. No one had ever heard of anyone dying from a snakebite, but one day a huge rattler bit a grazing calf on the nose. Its face swelled up and it soon collapsed. Emmett put it in the chuckwagon, hoping to save it, and even placed a poultice of kerosene and sliced raw onions on the bite, trying to draw out the poison. It failed and the calf died later in the day. Yet it was not the horror of the incident that bothered most of the men. Losing an animal was like someone picking their pockets.

The days slipped by and the men grew accustomed to handling the herd, while the herd settled into travelling and being kept in line. The days were long, lasting from dawn until dusk, and were made even longer by the two-hour stints on night watch the men took in rotation. Slowly, they got used to each other as well as to Pepper's rants when things were not going well for him, which seemed to happen regularly. But everyone loved his sourdough biscuits—on cool nights he slept with the pot of yeast to keep it warm—as well as his beans, which he soaked overnight to make them tender and tasty. The smell of sizzling steaks would drive the men mad, and best of all, he always had the coffee pot on first thing after stopping, and kept it full.

Over time, Homer came to accept John, perhaps not as an equal, but at least as a fellow human being. Because of their positions on the drive, they had opportunities to talk and that helped. Rufus, on the other hand, was distant and cool, though cordial when necessary, knowing that Emmett would not tolerate any disrespect among a crew living in close quarters for several months. However, around the campfire at night, he would always sit opposite to John, and he was the farthest away when bedding down. With other matters to worry about, Emmett gave no sign of noticing.

Besides Emmett, of all the crew John liked Duffy best. He was gregarious and did not have a discriminatory bone in his body. John knew Duffy and Emmett had fought side by side in the last battle of the war, although they had never talked about it in front of him, not even at Waco. One evening, when they went to a nearby creek to fetch water for Pepper, Duffy told John what had happened.

"The Rebs had run us out of Brownsville, and we was holed up on Brazos Island blockadin' the mouth of the Rio Grande. Our job was to cut off their supply route, but we all knew the war wasn't gonna last much longer. Then Colonel Barrett heard that the Rebs was leavin' Brownsville and got it in his craw that we could retake it. Jesus H. Christ, John, it wasn't real intelligence, it was only rumours! We was more than willin' to fight where we were if we had to, but to go back to Brownsville when we should of waited for official word that the war was over? That was plain crazy! We marched with the 34th Indiana and the 62nd Coloureds—we was the only cavalry unit in the damned war without horses. Turns out only a handful of Rebs left Brownsville and we didn't get any further'n about halfway there before we ran into 'em."

He chuckled mirthlessly. "We only had rifles and a hundred rounds of ammo each, so it weren't exactly a fair fight. Kept us pinned down for about a half hour and then they attacked. That's when Thomas got it. That's also when Barrett sounded a retreat. Emmett hoisted Thomas up on his shoulder—don't know where he got the strength from—and we ran till the Rebs stopped chasin' us. By that time, poor Thomas had bled himself pale as a ghost. Never seen a man more heartbroke than Emmett, standin' there, soaked in his brother's blood. Never seen a man more courageous, either."

"I've known him ten years and he ain't never talked about the war. I can see why," John said.

"He don't even talk about it with me. Never has. Maybe he's holdin' it all inside in case he ever runs into Barrett."

"Maybe. But I'd be surprised. Near as I can tell, Emmett don't live in the past and he ain't vengeful. Don't know that I've met a finer man, 'cept maybe his father."

Duffy shrugged. "You can't tell nothin' about any man. Don't matter how much you know him. We're all carryin' secrets around inside a us."

John reflected on that for a moment, and then, because it had piqued his interest, said, "I didn't know there was coloureds fightin' down that way. Somethin' else he never told me."

"He told you in his own way. With a man like Emmett, honour is everything, and those men of the 62nd were honourable men. He knew they was fightin' for an even greater reason than puttin' an end to slavery. They was fightin' for the honour of coloured folk everywhere. That's the reason you was made so welcome in the Cole household."

Two weeks of dry weather saw them at Doan's Crossing on the Red River. Jonathan Doan and his nephew Corwin, both Quakers, had set up a supply post near a gravel-bottomed ford, much of the rest of the river shore being quicksand. Across the muddy waterway was the Oklahoma Territory, and the next opportunity to resupply was in Dodge City. Emmett took on some more beans, coffee, salt pork, and kerosene, and asked the younger Doan if he had seen any Indians.

"We had a visit two weeks ago," the sapling-thin Doan replied. "I was away hunting and the other men were off getting supplies when a band of Kiowa came close enough to scare our women silly. They never attacked and I can't say why. Other than that, they haven't been much trouble for the big herds going through. Doesn't mean to say that they won't try to steal one of your beeves or demand one as a toll. Maybe even try to stampede them and pick up a few strays. It's best to give them one if they ask. The price of one animal isn't worth the trouble they can cause if they take a disliking to you."

The next day the outfit pushed on, across the Red River. Emmett knew that the two worst obstacles for trailing cattle were water and no water, but unlike their shorthorn counterparts, the longhorns usually had no fear of rivers as long as the sun was not reflecting off the surface and they could see the other side. It also helped if they were thirsty. On drag for a while, John followed the last of the cattle into the river. The cool water rising up the side of his legs filled him with apprehension because he could not swim, but the water never got above Cat's shoulders and she was sure-footed.

Later that day, they encountered thousands of bleached buffalo bones, mottling the landscape for as far as the eye could see. It was as if some great hand had slaughtered an endless river of the beasts all at once and emptied the land of its only living inhabitants. The herd passed through the vast boneyard without incident; the animals seemed to have accepted as their fate to plod on across a country as flat as Pepper's work table and as hot as his chili. It was not until the next evening that they left the last bones behind.

The days repeated themselves, each an exact duplicate of its predecessor—the skies fair, the afternoons hot, the dust never-ending, the landscape unchanged and immense, demanding humility. The bleak emptiness was so awesome that John was glad to be in the company of a dozen men and a herd of cattle. To be out here alone would have been terrifying.

Ten miles south of the Canadian River, they camped for the night, hoping to reach the watercourse the next day. There had been so little water for the herd to drink that the beasts were beginning to get restless. The men sensed this, which in turn put them on edge. Around the campfire that night, they watched the smoke curl toward the ground and felt the temperature rise.

"We're in for a good storm, I think," said Emmett. "Guess only a fool would think that we'd stay dry all the way to Ogallala." He spoke to Homer: "Best you get some horses in here close by so's the boys can saddle 'em up in case we need to get to the herd fast."

The men named their favourites and Homer retrieved them. Once they were hobbled nearby, everyone turned in, hoping they would not need their mounts until they rolled out of bed at the usual time in the morning.

It took John some time to get to sleep, and he awakened in the middle of the night. The fire had gone out and it was pitch black, the air humid and heavy, as still and silent as death. The camp was about three hundred yards from the herd, but he could clearly hear Glenford Pounds, on night watch, singing.

> O bury me not on the lone prairie
> Where coyotes howl and the wind blows free
> In a narrow grave just six by three—
> O bury me not on the lone prairie.

John lay listening to the song for a while. So far, the rain had not come, and that was a good thing. But he wondered why, if he could hear Glen singing, he wasn't hearing any cattle blowing off. His last thought before falling back asleep was that they seemed awfully quiet. Maybe they were expecting something.

In the predawn, a loud crack and rumble of thunder in the west awakened everyone. A streak of lightning flashed across the sky and the herd voiced its apprehension. Emmett leaped up, and without prompting, the rest of the crew did too.

"Breakfast's on hold, boys," he said. "Best we get out to the herd before it's spooked completely! Circle around and keep it contained. Talk nice and sing if you have to. Some of 'em might even listen."

John and the others swiftly gathered up their bedrolls, donned their rain slickers, grabbed their saddles and rifles, and unhobbled their horses from the string nearby. In a few minutes, they were all riding out to the herd, the thunder still rolling and the lightning still flashing, but much closer now. Ben Munger and Albert Jackson were working the tail end of the night shift, and Ben shouted over the noise of the animals, "Glad to see you fellas! These buggers ain't none too happy."

The herd was milling around, fused with great energy, the adults bellowing and the calves bawling.

"We better work some of their energy off, boys!" Like Ben, Emmett had to shout to make his voice heard. "Get 'em movin' toward the river so that if they stampede they'll at least be goin' in the right direction."

More thunder boomed, followed by jagged bolts of lightning stabbing the ground. The brunt of the storm seemed to be upon them but so far it hadn't rained. John could have sworn he saw lightning dancing along the horns of some of the steers, and ropes of fire snaking along their backs. He stayed in the drags where he was supposed to be, talking to the cattle, whacking them on their rumps with his rope to get them moving forward. The herd was strung out over a half mile of flat terrain and he could feel its dangerous power in the electrically charged air. There was a deafening explosion that seemed to engulf him, accompanied by a blinding flash of blue-white light. Cat balked and reared, and John thought someone had set a bomb off under her. His ears were ringing like a soundly struck bell and for a moment, he could hear nothing.

Panic-stricken, the herd bellowed and shot forward, and

John spurred Cat and followed. A smell that permeated the air reminded him of when a branding iron is left too long on cowhide. He saw the cause as he rode past two dead cattle, smoke curling up from their hides, and parts of them burned black. More thunder and lightning came, but it had moved eastward. The rain began, great fat individual drops of water that soon turned into a deluge and churned the slick ground into mud. John rode carefully, knowing that a spill might prove deadly.

Parts of the herd were splintering off and the riders were helpless to do anything but let them go and round them up later. John stayed in position at the rear, waiting for Emmett and the point men to turn the lead beeves back into the rest of the herd in a giant narrow U and halt the stampede. It did not seem long before the animals in front of him began to slow and he saw Emmett and the vanguard coming toward him. They had managed to turn the herd. As the thundering mass approached, John and Homer rode straight at it, shouting and swinging their ropes. Like a wave curling in on itself, the group of lead animals slowed to a walk, melded in with those behind them, and began milling. The stampede was over.

With the herd contained, John reined Cat to the east and began rounding up strays. The rain stopped and the sky cleared, and by late morning, the herd was back together. The trail was greasy with mud but at least it gave the drag men a respite from breathing in dust.

Pepper had coffee with bacon and beans ready for the hungry crew, and the hard and dangerous work made it taste better than usual. Around the fire, the men were jubilant and praise ran high for Emmett, Rufus, and Nathan for getting the herd turned.

"Give yourselves a pat on the back, boys," Emmett said. "It was good work all the way around. We only lost those two beeves to lightning." He grinned. "I believe we got ourselves an outfit here!"

Before they moved on, Pepper and John returned to the dead cattle and took what edible meat they could salvage. Much of it was good only for son-of-a-bitch stew, but even that would taste good at the end of a long day's toil.

The cattle were docile as lambs after their great expenditure of energy and ambled along at a leisurely pace. By late afternoon, the party had reached the breaks of the Canadian River and Emmett called a halt for the day, to let both man and beast rest up after the hectic start to the morning. When Emmett scouted the river, he saw that it was running high and wide, and crossing it would probably be easier on the morrow, provided they did not get any more rain. They camped well back in the breaks, away from the water, where the mosquitoes were not so plentiful.

In an effort to bridge the gap between himself and Rufus, John waited until he caught the point man alone and complimented him on his good work. Rufus pursed his thin lips and glared at John with brooding eyes. He said, "I don't need your praise, nigger boy. You do your job with the horses and the arse end of the herd, and I'll do mine with the front. That's what we get paid for."

John felt a searing heat wash his face, and as Rufus walked off, called after him, "Rufus!"

The cowhand stopped and turned around, his movements slow and deliberate. Their eyes met. Despite the anger that filled him, John kept his voice well-modulated. "There ain't no nigger boys in this outfit. Only drovers. Best you remember that."

John wondered what the future with Rufus Pauley would bring. He was from Alabama and had fought for the Confederates during the war, hence his attitude toward Negroes. Afterwards, he'd drifted into Texas, ending up in Austin, where he had learned to work with cattle. He had cut his teeth with Charles Goodnight and had ridden swing and point on Emmett's learning drive, where Emmett saw and admired Rufus's hard work and dedication to the job. And since you can't be around a man for a couple of months and not get some idea about where he stands on most issues, Emmett knew of Rufus's lack of tolerance for coloureds. Yet he saw a natural intelligence in the man, and felt that given the opportunity, he would outgrow his antebellum attitudes. He also thought that John might provide the stimulus for that growth. So far, Emmett's idea didn't seem to be working.

Emmett waited two days before he decided that crossing the Canadian would be safe, and they did so without incident. The sun had returned and dried out everything that the downpour had soaked. The thirsty ground had sucked up the water and became hard and dusty again.

During the layover, John had stewed over the point man's rudeness and disrespect, and felt angry enough to want to demand an apology. If he wanted a fight, John had a good four inches in height and fifty pounds in weight over Rufus, and even if the man seemed as solid as oak, John felt he could beat him. Yet something about Rufus suggested that he was not a fair fighter, that in a pinch he would resort to that equalizer strapped on his hip called a Colt .45. In the end, John thought of Emmett and the need to maintain good relations in the outfit. He also remembered Sebastian Chambers and decided that revenge was more hurtful to the soul than satisfying. It was best to let it go.

They were stopped for a lunch break and to change horses above the Canadian when the Indians came, but not in the way anyone had expected. Rufus spotted them first, a dust cloud in the distance that materialized into a small band of Kiowa. A couple of hundred yards away, the band rode in a small circle before continuing.

Emmett said, "Looks like they want to parley, boys, so let's not frighten 'em with a show of guns. Better keep awake, though."

But the Indians weren't interested in a fight, despite outnumbering the outfit two to one. They looked emaciated and demanded a toll of one longhorn to cross their territory.

Emmett instructed John to find a dry cow and cut it out for them. "It's a small payment for a trouble-free passage," he told the men, reiterating Corwin Doan's advice. "We ain't had much trouble so far and I aim to keep it that way."

Before they reached the Cimarron River and crossed over into Kansas, small, starving Indian bands stopped them two more times. Emmett paid each of them a dry cow. While some men complained, he still felt he had a bargain. He said to them after the last band had left, "Three beeves ain't nothing, boys. You seen what was left of the buffalo. Nothing but miles and miles of bleached bones. A man has to feed his family the best way he can."

Rufus, who knew what subtraction could do to a man's pocketbook, groused, "Hell, we didn't kill no buffalo, Emmett."

Emmett shrugged. "It don't matter, Rufus. As far as they're concerned, we might as well have."

It was the beginning of June and there had been enough rain th: the grass-covered Kansas prairie was still a vibrant green. The had put the Oklahoma Territory behind them; another wee would see them approaching Dodge City. They had been on th trail for nearly two months and deserved a break, so Emme had promised everyone a pay advance and an evening in tow . From that point on, all conversations around the campfire we concerned with the relative merits of whorehouses, saloons, an gambling halls, and in which of the three it would profit the most to spend their time. After much discussion, they agree that the best establishment would include all three.

Emmett decreed that half of the men would go into tow on the first day, the other half on the second. The outfit woul leave for Ogallala early on the third morning regardless of th severity of any hangovers. Any man who did not show up woul be a man left behind. It was a thinly disguised bluff, of cours because if half the crew failed to show up, the herd wasn't goin anywhere; nevertheless, it needed saying. Emmett found a goo bed-ground with plenty of grass about five miles southwest c Dodge, not far from the Arkansas River, where the men coul bathe if they wished before enjoying the town's amenities. The drew straws to see who would go first, and Emmett gave eac man an advance of whatever he asked for, up to a month's pa

SIX

Eddie Foy's playing over at the Comique.

John, Emmett, Ben, Rufus, Nathan, and Pepper all drew short straws. Even so, Emmett and Pepper took the wagon in on the first day and resupplied it; their fun, however, would be had the next day. John spent the time trimming horse hooves, replacing shoes where needed, and cleaning tack, finding in these small tasks an escape from the apprehension he felt about venturing into town. The first revellers straggled in late the following morning, exhausted and for the most part glad to be back on the open prairie where they could recover, and where temptations of the flesh were temporarily beyond their reach. Even Duffy, who had more energy than most for non-stop revelling, was happy to be in camp.

John and the others saddled up for their turn. Pepper, who had a pot of salt pork and beans simmering by the fire, left explicit instructions as to what the men could or could not do with the chuckwagon. Any man who violated these orders might as well go ahead and shoot himself, and save Pepper the trouble of doing it.

When asked about Dodge City upon his return from his supply visit, Emmett had said little, except that after two months on the trail it seemed a busy place. Other than the occasional herd continuing north, the town was the terminus for most drives out of Texas and was better than most towns at lightening the loads of drovers weighted down by a couple of months' pay and bonuses. Indeed, Emmett had never seen so many drovers gathered in one spot, not to mention an abundance of establishments offering precisely what they craved.

They loped toward town in the mind-dulling late-afternoon heat, passing other herds grazing on the rich Kansas grass to regain some of the weight they had lost on the trail before they were to be sold in Dodge and shipped to points east. When the outline of the town became distinct on the horizon, the concern John had experienced the previous evening reappeared—he had no idea how his presence would be received. Emmett had told him, "No need for worry, John. I think you'll be pleased by what you find." But it was at best a modest reassurance that did little to lessen John's misgivings. On their approach to the city, he and the others paid ten cents each to a nearly fingerless, limping man to use a toll bridge to cross the Arkansas River.

Front Street, Dodge's main thoroughfare, was a broad dirt road split down its length by a railway track that came from the east and ran west as far as Colorado. The men crossed the track to the north side, their destination a gigantic livery stable named the Elephant Barn. As they rode, John's anxiety eased. He noticed several black drovers strolling along the boardwalks and entering and leaving businesses along the street without any apparent problems. He derived no small sense of satisfaction from the fact that it might be a revelation for Rufus, who had not appeared happy about riding into town with a black man, though he had kept his counsel about it.

The men left their horses at the livery stable and, because the owner said that all the hotels were full, paid two bits extra for a space to sleep in the hayloft. As they took to the boardwalk, passing false-fronted buildings, Pepper rubbed his hands together and exclaimed that his first priority would be a frolic with one or more of the town's many "soiled doves."

Emmett laughed and, knowing that the men needed a break not only from the trail but also from each other, said, "Well, boys, it's every man for himself. But don't forget that you've got a job to do and that other people are depending on you to do it. Try to avoid a dose of the clap and for God's sake don't get yourself shot. Maybe I'll see you around town." On that note, the men parted company.

They had passed a barbershop with a sign that read WILLIAM DAVIS, PROP. The door was open and John had seen a black man, presumably Davis, sitting in the barber's chair reading a newspaper, waiting for customers. John decided to start the evening with a beard trim and maybe obtain information about the town before he tramped its streets alone. He retraced his footsteps and went in.

The man got up from the chair so that John could sit in it, and they exchanged pleasantries. Davis, short, thin, and balding, threw an apron around his customer and went to work, asking him where he was from and where he was going. They talked about cattle for a bit and John asked about the town and its coloured population.

"Not many coloured folks actually live here the year round," Davis said, above the sound of the snipping scissors. "Maybe forty or fifty. Most do service work, but that's what this town is built on. You want your hair cut or your laundry done, a coloured will do it, although the Chinks are horning in on the washtub artists. Most of the coloureds you see on the streets are drovers like yourself, passing through. Around here it ain't the colour of a man's skin that counts, it's the colour of his money, and the entire town's set up to empty his pockets before he leaves. Money's the glue that holds Dodge together. Take that away and white folks would soon put us coloureds in our place, which wouldn't be anywhere near them unless it was at their beck and call. In the winter, we go to our respective corners and tolerate each other while we wait for the next herding season. But don't let that concern you. You'll find that you'll get the respect you deserve, whether it's from the white townsfolk or the black, in any establishment. This is not to say that you won't be the butt end of a rude comment or two, but they're more likely to come from white drovers sorrowfully short on good manners. Luckily, the police try to be impartial and if they get wind that someone's causing you trouble because you're coloured, there'll be hell to pay. It's important to them that you want to stick around long enough to spend all your money, not to mention that they get two dollars for every arrest they make."

When he was finished, Davis brushed the cut hair off of John's neck and removed the apron. "That'll be four bits for making you presentable to something other than a cow. And by the way, if you're interested in a good poke, the sporting houses are all across the Deadline, which is what they call the railroad tracks here. It's wilder and rowdier over there than it is on this side. That's where Forrester's Black Beauties are. He has six women in his employ if black's your colour of choice. If white skin gets your poker up, you can try Dodge's Dazzling Dolls, farther down from Forrester's. You can't miss 'em."

John gave a half laugh as he paid Davis, bemused by the

names. "Don't sound like they're on the wrong side of the law here. Wouldn't get away with that back in Fort Worth."

"They wouldn't get away with it here, either, if they didn't pay to keep their doors open. The town fines them on a regular basis to keep up appearances. It's easy, dependable revenue, and besides, it's the town councillors who use them most in the off-season."

Davis walked with John to the door. "What else can I tell you? Oh, Eddie Foy's playing over at the Comique Theater and he puts on a great show twice a night. You'll have to get there early if you want a seat. And you won't find a better place to eat than Aunt Sallie's, a few doors down to your left."

John thanked the barber for the information and the haircut, and left the shop. He felt conspicuous on the boardwalk, until he realized that no one was paying him any attention. He turned into Aunt Sallie's and was lucky to find a seat among a crowded mixture of drovers, both black and white, dance hall girls, and men and women of respectable society. The food—roast pork with potato dumplings and green peas followed by a thick slab of pecan pie, all washed down with a cool beer—was excellent. So good, in fact, that John decided he would be wise not to crow about it front of Pepper.

The heat of the day was dissipating as he left Aunt Sallie's, and Front Street was swarming with throngs of people out to take the cooler evening air. He slipped across the train tracks to the south side of the street where the brothels were located. At Forrester's, he spoke to the pimp himself, describing the kind of woman he wanted.

"Ah, if you want some lovin' with your fornicatin'," Henry Forrester said, "then Annie's the girl for you. She's two bucks extra. It's the time involved, you understand. Meantime, why don't you put your gun on the shelf by the door? It's the law here and it'll still be there when you're done. You're welcome to have a drink in our house saloon while I get things arranged."

John waited for an hour and had three drinks, which he supposed was simply another way of dipping into a man's pocket, then paid the pimp seven dollars, wondering how much of it Annie would see.

However much it was, he thought afterwards that she had earned every penny, as well as the extra three dollars he gave her to tuck away for herself. He was euphoric and reckoned that if he ever found a wife with her warmth and talent, he'd be a fortunate man. Yet on the outer edges of that euphoria lurked a feeling of loneliness. Annie had made him realize what he didn't have and might never find: a wife. The prospects of finding one were disheartening, and he feared that the farther north he travelled, the more dismal his chances would become.

He came to a bathhouse and went in for a hot soak. Then he walked by the livery stable to ensure Cat was being well cared for. Next on his list was a saloon with a card game.

The first he came upon was the Green Front. He pushed through the batwing doors, placed his gun on a rack, and made his way to the bar at the rear, where he ordered a whisky. Cigarette and cigar smoke hung thick in the air above circular, baize-covered tables, each with its full quota of gamblers playing faro or stud poker. A couple of roulette wheels clacked over on one side and a piano player, who might have missed a lesson or two, played a song that might have been "Lorena" on an upright piano that needed tuning. Turning his back to the bar, John watched gamblers so focused on their games that they paid him no mind. He thought he recognized the dealer at one of the faro tables and wracked his brain to put a name to the face. As it turned out, he had forgotten the man's name but felt certain it was the dentist he had visited years ago in Dallas. What was the name on the sign? Simpson? Sinclair? The only differences in his appearance were that his moustache was fuller and he had a small goatee. Rather than a smock, he wore a cream-coloured suit with a light purple shirt and dark blue tie. Otherwise, there was no mistaking that ash blond hair, sallow face, and subdued but unrelenting cough.

John had never played faro but it was similar to the game called skinning that he had learned as a slave. He also knew that the odds of winning were reasonable, as long as the dealer was not cheating. Thirteen cards from ace to king were pasted on a board. The players could put chips on any of the cards, and the dealer then pulled out two cards from a box. He won any chips placed on the first card, while the second card was a winner for the players. All ties went to the dealer, which gave him an advantage, as did the usual carelessness of drinking players (and drinks here were cheap). Chips were available from fifty cents to ten dollars. John watched the dentist closely but could not detect any sleight of hand, which wasn't to say that he hadn't doctored the cards.

When a player rose and left the game, John bought ten one-dollar chips and took his place, having decided that if he lost the ten dollars he would leave. The dentist seemed to take his measure, but if he recognized his new opponent, he did not let on. He smiled that thin smile of his and said, his genteel

Southern drawl recognizable, "You are welcome to the game, sir, and good luck."

It would have been an orderly game if not for the man sitting on John's right, who had brought a bottle of whisky to the table and was being generous to himself with it. He was also becoming more belligerent with each round that he lost. John figured the man was a fool, because large quantities of alcohol did not mix with a game like faro where it was to the player's advantage to keep track of the cards played. On the table there was an abacus-like board called a casekeeper, which allowed players to do exactly that, but it was not easy for a brain fogged by alcohol. The dentist, though, looked happy enough to ignore the man's drunkenness because of his haphazard betting and persistent losing.

John played for an hour and managed to win enough to pay for his frolic with Annie and his meal. He was glad to be winning because he loved the thrill of the bet and found gambling infectious. He might have dipped deeper into his pocketbook had he been losing, just so he could continue playing. The dentist's face had remained passive throughout the game, except that he winced whenever the piano player hit a wrong note and he coughed from time to time. He would then take a sip of whisky, which seemed to subdue it, but John reckoned that the cigarillos he smoked probably did not help matters any. And he still had that sheen of perspiration across his forehead.

A fair-haired, full-figured woman with eyes the colour of robins' eggs, whose large nose detracted from an otherwise pretty face, brought the dentist a drink when he wanted one and sometimes stood behind him watching the play. Now she came up beside him and leaned over far enough that John and the other players could see most of her breasts. She spoke with an accent that John recognized as European, though it was nothing like the German accents he had heard often in Texas. "It'll be showtime soon, John Henry."

"Oh, thank you, darlin'. Why, I might have sat here all evenin' given the charmin' amiability of the company." He looked at the drunk when he spoke, his words icy with sarcasm, adding, "When the deck is finished, gentlemen, so am I."

John broke even on the last few rounds and the drunk lost. The game over, the dentist gathered the cards. "Thank you, gentlemen; it's been a pleasure. A new dealer will join you shortly."

The drunk banged the table with his fist. "You goddamn lunger! Deal another round! You ain't takin' my money just so's you can go runnin' off with some fuckin' whore!"

The dentist smiled. His voice was soft, his eyes hard and cold. "Well, sir, you're no daisy and evidently you would deny a workin' man a much needed respite. Of course, it may be that a cretin like yourself would welcome a wholesale regression into slavery."

The drunk flipped open his unbuttoned waistcoat and reached for a knife concealed there. At the same instant that a derringer emerged in the dentist's hand, John backhanded the drunk so hard it was as if a catapult had flung his chair over backwards. The knife clattered to the floor and John stood and kicked it aside.

The saloon's minder, a giant of a man, came hurrying over. "I'll take care of this." He retrieved the drunk's weapon, hauled him to his feet, and pushed him off through the crowded tables and out the doors.

The dentist arose and said to the two remaining players besides John, "I bid you good night gentlemen and thank you." To John he said, "A night in the sheriff's company ought to improve our friend's sense of propriety. And he would be remiss if he didn't seek you out, sir, and thank you for savin' his life. A split second more and he would have had a bullet in his heart, which would have left me with no end of explainin' to do. I am a friend of the marshal's but I would disdain to use that friendship to my advantage. By the way, I believe that I have had the pleasure of your acquaintance before, but memory fails as to exactly where."

"Dallas. You took out an achesome tooth a few years back. It's Doc Sinclair, ain't it?"

"Ah, my mind summons it now. The man who didn't need an anaesthetic. *Fortis an stultus.*" He offered his hand. "I was merely Dr. Sinclair's assistant. John Henry Holliday's the name. Folks call me John Henry, or Doc."

Another one of those foreign phrases, but one John had heard before in Dallas. This time he asked what it meant.

"A brave man or a fool."

John laughed and rubbed his jaw, remembering. "A fool, I think." He took Holliday's hand and was surprised at the strength of his grip, considering how frail the man looked. "John Ware."

Holliday turned to the woman. "Darlin', please forgive my appalling manners. May I introduce John Ware, an exemplary card player with the fastest backhand on either side of the Mississippi? John, please meet Kate Harony, a confidant and companion."

John removed his hat. "How do you do, ma'am?"

"Charmed, I'm sure," she said, with the air of an aristocrat. But given her provocative attire, especially the revealing gown, and the fact that she hadn't blanched at being called a whore, it was reasonable to assume that the drunk probably wasn't far wrong about her occupation.

"Well, sir," Doc said, "I am in your debt, but I must beg your leave. I promised my sweet Hungarian princess here that we would attend Eddie Foy's performance at the Comique, and a gentleman never reneges on a promise."

"That's where I was thinkin' of goin'," John said. "If I'm not too late to get a seat."

"Then you must join us. As a personal acquaintance of Mr. Foy's, I have no small influence at the theatre, and we would be honoured by your company." He looked at Kate. "Wouldn't we, darlin'."

It sounded to John more like a dare than a question.

"Of course," Kate said coolly, as if it were the only acceptable answer.

John did not much care how Kate felt, but wasn't certain whether he should be pleased with the invitation or not. On the one hand, he liked Holliday's genteel manner, the way he spoke, and his ease with coloured people. His Southern, well-educated upbringing more than likely included a coloured nanny and much playtime with coloured boys. Yet there was another side to him that John found unsettling: he sensed an aura of danger about the man. Being near him was like riding down a bumpy road on a wagon filled with nitroglycerine. And the way his gun seemed to materialize out of nowhere, as if he drew it from the air itself! He would have had to practise a lot to be so good at that. John wavered for a moment, then thought, If nothing else, it could prove to be an interesting evening, something to tell the boys about. He accepted the invitation.

While John collected his gun, Holliday cashed in his chips, gave the house its percentage, and retrieved his slouch hat and a cane that appeared to be more a fashion accessory than a necessity. Kate took Holliday's arm and the trio left the Green Front together.

The air had cooled but was still fairly warm, and the wind that often whipped up dust in Dodge's streets had died in the evening's clutches. The town had come alive now and sounded festive: tinkling pianos, whining fiddles, and raucous laughter emanated from the saloons on both sides of the street. Myriad boots echoed on the wooden boardwalks and a mule-drawn wagon rattled across the railway tracks in the direction of the bridge. Here and there, stoic, saddled horses tied to hitching posts awaited their riders. As they strolled along, Holliday smoked and coughed, and shared his observations of Dodge City.

"Callin' this a 'city' is, of course, an exaggeration of the first order. The word connotes civilization and Dodge is some distance from achieving that status. Perhaps a Babylon, though." He chuckled. "Maybe even a carnival at times."

John thought Holliday seemed proud to be on display with his unusual companions, an apparent prostitute on one side and a towering, coloured drover on the other. Again, it seemed to John that he was daring someone to say something.

Doc and Kate waved at two men across the street. Both wore black suits with white shirts and broad-brimmed black hats, and had similar inverted chevron moustaches. Each wore holstered pistols and carried a shotgun.

"Wyatt and Morgan Earp," said Doc. "On patrol, protecting Dodge's good citizens from the wild and wicked ways of visiting cowherds. Wyatt's cooled the town down some since he took on the job of assistant marshal. He can pistol-whip a villain faster than most men can draw a gun, though some might argue over who the real villain is. Yet even along with several other police officers patrolling the town at night, it isn't uncommon to hear gunshots. These days, though, celebration more than deadly intent is usually their antecedent."

They turned the corner onto Bridge Street, where the Comique was located in a capacious, false-fronted building with large windows on either side of the main door. Holliday said something to the man at the entrance that John could not hear and they entered. Neither tickets nor money changed hands. The interior was hot and smoky and packed with about three hundred patrons, the majority men and several of them drunk. The bar over to one side was enjoying a lucrative pre-show business; Holliday joined the crowd and got drinks for himself and his companions. They took seats near the rear by the door, in moveable hardback chairs that could be pushed aside for dancing. Doc said he needed to be near an exit in case he had a serious coughing spell.

A bevy of dancers opened the show and filled the theatre with a delirious energy. When they finished, the grinning, ginger-haired Eddie Foy came on. He sang, danced, juggled, and told animated risqué jokes that might have had their origin in a Kansas cornfield, yet his delivery was faultless and the crowd showed their approval with thunderous applause and good-natured catcalls. He was reciting a humorous poem about a place in Michigan called Kalamazoo when a thunderclap of bullets crashed through one of the theatre's front windows, shattering it.

99

Women screamed and froze, men gasped and swore, and most ducked behind their chairs. Foy threw himself flat faster than he had during any of the pratfalls he had performed earlier. There was more gunfire, this time outside and farther away, and some members of the audience began rising to their feet. Many simply stood there, uncertain of what to do, while others began swarming toward the doors and through the gaping window. A few rushed to the stage where Foy was sitting up.

Holliday, Kate, and John were among the first outside, where they heard even more firing, but this time well off in the distance. A ring of people had gathered several yards down the street, but John could not see what they were surrounding. A person hidden in the middle shouted, "Move back for God's sake, and give the poor man air!"

Trying to catch his breath, Holliday hurried over and forced his way toward the centre of the ring, people jostling each other aside to let him pass. Some recognized him for the dentist that he was, but he was at least a sort of doctor and would do until the real thing came along. John and Kate followed their companion but stayed on the boardwalk so that they would not get in the way. Four policemen wearing the same dark attire as the Earps appeared and began dispersing the large crowd, as an older, white-haired man carrying a black doctor's bag arrived. Holliday spoke to him but John could not make out the words. He saw the doctor shake his head. Holliday turned and looked at John.

The two doctors were crouched beside the prostrate figure, hiding it from a clear view, but then they rose and John was able to see fully the man dying in the street behind them. It was Emmett Cole.

SEVEN

Rest your mind on that account.

They buried Emmett in Boot Hill Cemetery on the north side of Dodge, beneath a blue sky bleached by a white-hot sun. There was not a breath of wind, and sweat beaded on everyone's brow. Besides most of the trail crew, Doc and Kate and many townsfolk, including the Earps, had come to pay their respects. John scarcely heard the pastor's words and stared dumbfounded at the gaping hole in the ground, the pine coffin containing Emmett's remains sitting beside it, and the headboard with John's words painted above Emmett's date of birth and death: HERE LIES EMMETT COLE—A KIND MAN, A GENTLE SOUL. He had not intended it to rhyme, but it fell pleasantly on the ear and he liked that. The pastor spoke more of God and his mysterious ways than he did of Emmett, about whom his knowledge was understandably scant. John did not know how to tell him about the kind of man his friend had been—the *kind* man that he was. On that long road from Georgetown to Fort Worth, he had encountered a wide variety of people who disliked him because of the colour of his skin, so to find Emmett, not to mention Amos and Ellie, at the end of it was a stroke of the greatest good fortune.

The town council had paid the funeral costs because Emmett died trying to stop a fleeing criminal. He had been walking along the boardwalk toward the Comique when the gunman rode by

101

and fired shots through the theatre's window. Emmett ran into the street as the man raced by and tried to pull him from his horse, which proved to be a fatal mistake. The shooter almost escaped but, in an exchange of bullets, Wyatt Earp shot him as he rode across the bridge leading out of town. Before he died, he confessed that his motive for shooting into the theatre was jealousy. He had had too much to drink and believed that his wife was involved in a tryst with Eddie Foy.

Emmett's dying request had taken Holliday by surprise. He told John, "In so many words, I was instructed to find you and tell you that you are now trail boss and to carry on to Ogallala." Doc had been glad to be able to reply, "I've already found him, sir, so rest your mind on that account." He thought Emmett had heard him but couldn't be sure.

Nathan and Pepper had returned to camp to tell the others the bad news and set up a skeleton crew to mind the herd so that those who wanted to could attend the funeral. The men were stunned. Emmett dead? Inconceivable! "Shit!" and "Dear God!" had been the only words most could get out. Duffy was heartbroken and angry over his friend's death. "You survive a war only to die at the hands of a bloody drunk. Don't make no goddamned sense at all!"

Meanwhile, Emmett's request had hurled John's mind into turmoil. The easy way out would be to sell the herd in Dodge City, but he believed that Emmett had thrown down a challenge. He could not ignore his friend's faith in him and still hold his head up. But would the men stick with him over the month that it would take to reach their destination? Most of them would, he thought, but he was not convinced about Homer and Rufus. Particularly Rufus. If they quit, he might be able to hire replacements because there were plenty of men around Dodge who would leap at the chance to earn good money. But would they hire on with a coloured trail boss? And if he hired black drovers, would that cause even more friction in camp? He considered passing on the job to Rufus, since all Emmett had asked of him was to get the herd to Ogallala—he did not say how. But what Rufus would do with Emmett gone was another matter.

Then there was the issue of money. He could potentially get an extra four or five dollars a head in Ogallala, which represented extra cash for the Coles. And it occurred to him that he could use some of that money to buy the men's loyalty by increasing their bonuses. That seemed a fair solution. While it was the Coles' investment that brought the herd together, it was the outfit that would get it to Ogallala. The Coles took the monetary risk, but the men took physical risks and deserved to be paid well for it. John was certain Amos and Ellie would not object.

He had wired the Coles with the devastating news and prayed it would not destroy them. The ranch would be a lonely place now that Emmett would never return. Maybe they had taken John's replacement under their wings, which might help fill the second gaping hole torn in their lives. In an answering wire, the tears in Amos's words were almost audible, even as the operator read it in a bland voice.

His old friend stated that John was in charge of the herd, if John wanted the job, and that he had no doubts that it would get to Ogallala. It was an affirmation that cleared away much of the burden weighing on his shoulders. What's more, as well as having Doc as a witness, he now had something in writing to show Homer and Rufus, in case they disputed Emmett's dying words.

Both men were in town for the funeral, so John took them aside one at a time, told them of Emmett's appeal, and showed them the telegram. Homer was quick to respond. "Well, I might not of said this a couple a months ago, John, but you proved to me you got gravel. I'll ride with you."

It was not until Homer accepted that John mentioned there would be a five hundred dollar bonus for each man who continued with the drive. That was five times what Emmett had offered, and Homer Morgan departed a happy man, promising not to say a word until John had told all of the men, notably Rufus.

John took the same tack with the point man and did not mention the bonus first. Rufus was as good as they came and John hoped he would stay on, but after reading the telegram, he was silent. He pulled a pouch of tobacco with papers from his shirt pocket and began rolling a cigarette. John sensed his quandary: the man could continue with a "nigger boy" as trail boss and collect the bonus that Emmett had offered, or he could walk away from it. John guessed that both options grated.

John broke the silence. "You don't have to ride for *me*, Rufus. You can ride for the brand. It's Emmett's, not mine. If you can't do that, I'll pay you out right now. You only got to say the word. But what I won't abide is your attitude toward me. The only way we'll get those beeves to Ogallala is if we work together. You'll still be point man, but now you got to take orders from me. Maybe that don't set well with you but that's the way it is. And I can tell you this: I ain't hirin' nobody else just because Emmett's gone. We got that herd bent to our will, so I reckon that the eleven of us can get the job done. That'll mean even more money for everyone at the end of the trail."

John saw the point man's dark eyes flicker with the mention of more money. He took a deep drag on his cigarette and let out the smoke toward John. "I'm in. Emmett was a good man."

John nodded. "Glad to hear it." He held out his hand, which hung in the air as Rufus hesitated. "The black don't rub off, Rufus, so you don't need to worry none about gettin' any on you. And by the way, there's a five hundred dollar bonus if you stay on."

Rufus shook John's hand but there was little in the gesture to say what was really on the man's mind. Nor was there a dramatic rise in his spirit over the increased bonus. "That seems fair to me," he said and left.

John still didn't know where he stood with Rufus, just that if he was to enjoy the point rider's expertise, he was also going to have to deal with the man's dislike of blacks. It would be interesting to see how it all played out. He believed—he hoped—that if worse spiralled down to worst, the rest of the outfit would side with him.

After the funeral, Homer and Rufus returned to camp while John and some of the crew joined Doc, Kate, and the Earp brothers at the Long Branch Saloon for drinks. Having fallen heir to Emmett's money belt, John paid for the round. Toasts went to Emmett, and to Wyatt for catching his killer. Another round followed and the more John drank, the more he wanted to get away from the whisky, the Long Branch, Dodge, and, most of all, the present company. The aura of danger encircling Doc also surrounded Wyatt, and the animosity between Kate and the assistant marshal was palpable.

Doc wanted them to stay longer, maybe play some cards and forget their troubles. John reckoned that the offer more or less summed up John Henry Holliday and Dodge City: no day was so sorrowful that you could not take time to dip into a man's pocket. He left the dregs of his drink. "Thanks for the invite, Doc, but it's time to go. Pepper'll be waitin' supper for us, and it's back on the trail first thing tomorrow."

To a man, the crew stood and joined him, and they walked out together. They rode back to camp at a gallop, racing like lunatics to forget for a while what Dodge City had done for their friend.

———

The weather remained hot, with late-afternoon thunderclouds building on one horizon or the other that never approached them. The spirits of the men were low but they improved daily. John rode ahead ten to fifteen miles each day to find good bed-ground for the cattle. On the fourth day out, Glenford Pounds, who was bringing up the rear with the remuda, said to John, "I don't know if the heat's making me crazy, but I have the sneaking suspicion we're being followed. Every once in a while, I get a glimpse of someone or something over those low ridges to the southwest. Usually it's a dust cloud that comes and goes but it's always in the same direction, so it's not likely elk or anything like that. Maybe Indians."

John was concerned. "I'll get Rufus to scout ahead tomorrow while I go poke around a bit. Maybe I'll see somethin'."

The following morning John rode out alone under a cloudy sky that provided a small measure of relief from the intense July heat. A little bit of rain wouldn't be a bad thing, he thought, although he would rather not have a thunderstorm bring it. The crew had plenty of water, but the land offered few places for the animals to drink and they always suffered the most. He pointed Cat due south, intending to ride that way for a mile or two before cutting west to pick up the trail of whoever or whatever might be following them. The ground was dry, and with the wind ceaseless for the past few days, it was impossible to avoid kicking up dust. On his westerly track, John came upon four sets of hoofprints, three side by side, one behind, of shod horses. Most likely three white men with a packhorse in tow, he figured. Turning north, he found where the riders had stopped for the night. In a deep swale, he saw cigarette and cigarillo butts and the ashes of a small campfire. He followed the tracks to high ground, but all that lay before him was the rolling terrain, the ridges not high, but high enough to hide a horse and rider between them. John followed the trail as it headed north, but after a while, it veered off to the west. He tracked it over a couple of miles, until further pursuit seemed pointless. Either whoever it was had gone or they had seen John coming and decided to deceive him. He turned Cat, nudged her into a canter, and caught up with the herd. He told the others what he had found, but no one quite knew what to make of it.

"Best keep an eye out," John observed.

It rained that night, a heavy drenching downpour that the dry land sucked in, unaccompanied by thunder and lightning, for which the entire crew gave thanks when they bedded down. Around 4:00 in the morning, a low rumbling and the sound of bellowing cattle awakened John. It was a stampede. He arose swiftly, rousing those who had not heard it, and they saddled up in pelting rain and rode for the herd, now a good mile away. By the time they arrived, whatever stampede there had been had turned into milling, bawling cattle, the animals having stopped on their own. The men came upon Duffy, who had been riding the last part of the night shift with Glen Pounds. He was agitated and excited.

"Goddamn rustlers!" he exclaimed. "Caught Glen and me at opposite ends of the herd. They got it all riled up and cut out a bunch from the side. Don't know how many they got and I don't know where Glen is."

While the cattle circled nervously, the crew looked for Glen but could not find him. Even in the darkness, John could make out the churned-up trail of the stolen cattle heading west, but it was impossible to tell if Glen had followed. It would be daylight in an hour and the search for him and the cattle would have to wait until then. He guessed that the rustlers got away with fifty or sixty head.

While the men had coffee and breakfast, Duffy explained what had happened. He and Glen were doing their usual circuits around the herd when Duffy heard several loud pops, like blankets being snapped. The herd reacted to the sudden noise by stampeding. Glen had been at the front of the herd, the direction in which it had moved.

John asked for a volunteer to ride with him after the rustlers. Several men offered, including Duffy, Homer, and even Rufus. John chose Duffy and asked Rufus to take charge of the outfit.

"Have another look around for Glen, boys," he told the others, "and don't let those cattle out of your sight."

At daylight, he and Duffy got some biscuits and jerky from Pepper, filled their canteens with water, and rode out.

Duffy was angry. He had lost several beeves belonging to his friend Emmett on his watch, and that was a scab torn from a sore wound. He would ride to the ends of the earth to get them back and punish those who stole them.

"No place to hang 'em and it's too far to take 'em to either Dodge or Ogallala," he complained. "With any luck at all, we'll end up shootin' 'em."

Neither a hanging nor a shootout sat well with John, and he felt certain that they would not have with Emmett either. But if it turned into a gunfight, so be it.

The two men followed the trampled ground to the west, eyes on the misty distance, searching for signs of their quarry. They spoke little. The rain had slackened, but the clouds were low and visibility was poor. A wind blew out of the west. They loped on for seven or eight miles before John called a halt. In the absence of thudding hooves, the sound of bawling cattle drifted on the wind. They rode at a walk for a while as the sound increased in volume. Reining up on high ground, they scanned the dismal horizon but saw nothing.

"They ain't far," Duffy said. "We need to get around on the other side of 'em. They won't be expecting us to come from the west."

The men turned and moved with caution in a circuitous route, north, west, and south, using the sound of the cattle as a pivot point; it remained stationary, signifying that the herd was not on the move. If the rustlers had a lookout, neither man could spot him. John figured that they had heard in Dodge that the outfit was short a man and would probably cut its losses and carry on to Ogallala.

Once the sound of the herd was east of them, he and Duffy rode toward it, ears tuned to any changes. When the noise level seemed to indicate that the herd was just beyond the next ridge, the men dismounted, ground-tethered their horses, and made their way up the gentle slope toward some scrub brush at the top. They removed their hats and covered the last few feet on their elbows and knees. Hidden behind the brush, John peered out and surveyed the scene below.

Pulling his head back in, he said, "There's three men down there, maybe a hundred yards away, and it looks as if they're gettin' ready to move out. Be easier on us if we don't let 'em get mounted."

"Then let's get 'em now," Duffy said.

Wasting no time, they slid below the ridge crest, jammed their hats back on their heads, and retrieved their horses. Mounted, they drew their revolvers, moved slowly to the top of the incline, and roweled their horses into a gallop. Racing over the crest, John screamed at the top of his lungs and Duffy let out his version of a Rebel yell that sounded like a wolf howling with a scratchy throat. At the same time, they fired warning shots. The men below froze, rooted to the ground in surprise. The startled cattle pushed and shoved each other away from the sudden racket.

"Throw 'em up!" Duffy yelled.

The rustlers' hands shot into the air, mouths agape.

John and Duffy stopped a dozen feet away from the men. John barked, "Get your gun belts off and throw 'em on the ground away from you! I believe you boys've got somethin' that belongs to us."

No one denied the accusation since all the cattle wore the Flint Springs brand, faint but still visible. The holstered guns thumped on the sodden earth.

"Lady Luck's on your side today, fellas," John said. "If there was a hangin' tree within ten miles of here, you'd be swingin' from it. Get your clothes off!"

"Wait a minute, mister—" a tall, bulbous-nosed man protested, but Duffy's gun swung toward his stomach, the hammer cocked.

"Shut up! This ain't no court of law where you get to tell your side of the story."

"You'll get no argument from me, mister," one of the other men said and began stripping. The others followed suit. John sensed their humiliation and it pleased him.

"Take it all off boys, even your underwear," he commanded.

Done, the men stood there with their tanned faces, necks, and hands, the rest of their bodies white as milk. It would have been laughable were it not for the seriousness of the situation. John ordered them to bundle their clothes up and put them in one of the canvas packs on the packhorse. He told Duffy, "Keep your gun on 'em and if anyone moves, shoot him." He dismounted and collected the discarded gun belts, did up the buckles, and slung them over the saddle horn of a rustler's horse. He then cut one of the thieves' ropes into short pieces and used them to bind each man's hands behind his back, pulling the knots tight. With a longer piece, he linked the men together, neck to neck in a rope chain, with about five feet between them. Finished, he pointed to the southeast.

"Dodge City's that way, boys. If I were you, I'd get there before you catch your death."

The rustlers hustled off as quickly as they could, jerking each other with the connecting ropes, stepping gingerly over the muddy ground and small protruding rocks. John and Duffy watched until the trio disappeared over the ridge.

Duffy grinned, clearly happy with the punishment meted out. "Reckon they've got a long walk in front of 'em. Not likely to be much fun in this rain."

John nodded grimly. "Rain's probably better than a scalding sun and mosquitoes. I expect right about now they'll be feelin' lucky that they got away with their lives. At least if they don't, they oughta."

It was early evening when John and Duffy returned with the stolen cattle, all fifty-four of them. The entire outfit might have had a good laugh over the rustlers' punishment were it not for the bad news: they had found Glenford Pounds, trampled to death by the frightened cattle. They guessed that his horse had stumbled and thrown him, before running off to escape the stampeding herd, because it had wandered into camp sometime later. The cattle had been milling over and around him for hours before the men discovered his body, and they buried him right away in a shallow grave, with a pile of rocks for a tombstone.

That was two men gone in less than a week and they were still two hundred miles from Ogallala. The entire outfit was despondent; perhaps even Rufus, who never showed much emotion about anything. As a result, the men were glad to get under way the following morning and pushed the herd hard until late in the day. With Pepper in the chuckwagon and Homer with the remuda, there were now only eight men left to control the herd, including John, and seven when he was off scouting. But just as a man can learn something by repeating it many times, the cattle had learned how to trail and did what was expected of them each day, as long as nothing unforeseen spooked them.

—⁓—

After his return from capturing the rustlers, John noticed a modest change in Rufus's attitude toward him. The point man was by no means friendly, but he was not disposed to friendliness at the best of times. Even so, John felt that the tension between them had lessened. Rufus offered a casual word here and there about small things unrelated to work, and even better, a sleeping spot on the opposite side of the fire no longer seemed to be a priority for him. John had hoped for this sort of progress, yet the thought entered his mind that Rufus might have ulterior motives, and he wondered what they might be. Then he chastised himself for being so suspicious. Better to think good of a man than accuse him of nonexistent crimes. Duffy also noticed Rufus's apparent change of heart but said, "I still wouldn't trust him."

The weather continued foul, with sporadic rain every day for the next week, but their luck held and they encountered no more thunderstorms. North of the Republican River in Nebraska, they passed a couple of drovers travelling in the opposite direction. They said that they were bound for Dodge City because it was more civilized than Ogallala.

"By 'more civilized,'" Duffy commented dryly, "they probably mean there's a better choice of whorehouses."

Two days later John scouted ahead and had to ride only seven miles before he reached the South Platte River, with Ogallala on the far side. He found an adequate bed-ground a few miles to the east and returned to the herd, feeling quite good about himself and life in general.

The following day, he rode into the town, a smaller version of Dodge, and enquired as to whom he should talk to about selling his cattle. He was told the best in town were the Bosler brothers, and he was directed to their office on Railroad Street. The brothers had government contracts to provide cattle to the Red Cloud and Spotted Tail Indian Agencies, as well as contracts out west. They immediately sent a man to inspect the animals and offered John thirty-one dollars a head.

John blanched. "Thirty-one a head? We heard forty down in Texas. We could of got that in Dodge and saved ourselves a lot of sweat and trouble." He wondered if the brothers were trying to gyp him because he was black. He wished that Emmett were here.

"That was down in Texas, son," the eldest brother said. "You're in Nebraska now, and if you can find a better deal around it would be the state's first miracle. The market's getting saturated and if you hold out too long we'll be offering even less."

The deal was not what Emmett had expected, but it still represented a lot of money and there was no need to be greedy. John accepted. The outfit drove the herd to a holding ground north of town and that done, John completed a transaction at the First National Bank of Omaha. He was able to send a fifty-five-thousand-dollar draft to the Coles and pay the crew and himself with the rest. Pepper got the chuckwagon as an extra bonus, and the crew divided the money from the sale of the remuda as well as the extra tack and weaponry, to sell or keep as they pleased.

Later, Duffy asked, "You still headin' north, John?"

"I don't see another direction that draws me. You goin' that way?"

Duffy nodded. "I'll throw in with you, if you like. It'll be a damn sight better than the two of us ridin' alone in the same direction."

They had enough money to make more money, so they agreed that they would go to Montana first to see if there was any gold left in its creeks. They also had money to spoil themselves with Ogallala's whisky and women before they left, and they wasted no time in getting on with it. On their last night in town, they joined some of the crew, including Rufus, for drinks at the Cattleman's Rest, a rowdy watering hole providing nothing even remotely connected to "rest" unless it came in the form of passing out on the sawdust-covered floor dead drunk.

John bought drinks for everyone but wanted to get an early start in the morning, so he and Duffy did not stay late. They made their goodbyes after a couple of rounds, shaking hands with everybody. Compliments on a job well done came from a few, and there were surprised looks when Rufus grasped John's hand.

"I reckon I was wrong about you, Ware," he said.

The words stumbled out but John did not doubt their sincerity. He knew how hard it must have been for someone with Rufus's background to make such an admission.

"I appreciate what you're sayin', Rufus." John smiled. "And I can see it ain't easy for you. But I gotta say that it ain't only me you been wrong about. It's most everyone like me. But I'm glad you took the time to say it."

Rufus nodded but said nothing. The rest of the crew absorbed the exchange in silence, then broke out in good-natured bantering and farewells.

Once outside, Duffy exclaimed, "Well, I'll be goddamned! Just when you think you got a man pigeonholed . . ."

John was happy with the outcome, although he did not know quite what to make of it. But as Duffy had once said, it's hard to know what really goes on in a man's heart.

EIGHT

Let the man see where he's goin'.

In the cool of the early morning, John and Duffy pointed their mounts northwest, leading a packhorse laden with provisions. They rode along the dried-up floodplain of the North Platte River, between the waterway itself and its grassy breaks, which consisted of patternless folded hills and bluffs rising perhaps fifty or sixty feet, cut through here and there with narrow valleys. Rope-like stream beds that saw water only during the spring runoff streaked some of the hillsides, and the dark green, stunted junipers growing on the slopes looked as if somebody had planted them helter-skelter to make the area look less desolate. Some of the draws were thick with them. The land had turned brown in the searing, arid heat, and the shrunken, turbid river, barely distinguishable from the colour of the terrain, looked more like a narrow lake as it flowed sluggishly toward its confluence with the South Platte. Though their surroundings looked unsuitable for supporting life, the pair spotted several mule and white-tailed deer, and felt confident they would not be short of meat during their journey.

The two men made the unlikeliest of companions, as physically different from one another as two humans could be: John tall, wide, and black; Duffy several inches shorter, narrow, and white. Beneath his Stetson, John's hair was short and grew in tight curls against his skull, while Duffy's tumbled onto his shoulders, a red waterfall streaked with white. One face was handsome, with a wiry black beard, the other weather-pounded and trenched, with a thick red one. And while John was in his early thirties, Duffy was old enough to be his father. But they were of like mind and that is the proving ground of kindred spirits.

John had been prepared to make the journey north alone, but he was happy that Duffy wanted to join him. His newfound friend had more than a few stories to tell about the war and Emmett, and it pleased John to hear them. Duffy had been born in Ireland and brought to America as an infant by parents who sought a better life. The only place he knew as a child growing up was the East Texas town of Nacogdoches, about a hundred and seventy miles southeast of Fort Worth. His father had operated an inn and freight service, and Duffy's first job entailed tending to the chamber pots in the rooms and ensuring there was plenty of firewood on hand. He graduated from that to swamping on the freight wagons. While making a delivery to one of the several cotton plantations in the vicinity, Duffy saw first-hand how some of the slaves were mistreated. He had heard horrific screaming coming from the slaves' quarters, and when he looked over, he saw a slave frantically running around with his head on fire. "He had tried to escape and the owner had poured tar on the poor bastard's head and set it on fire. I ain't never heard such a sound come from a man's mouth. The owner didn't want him to die though, so he let the slave use the primer bucket at the well to put it out. That son of a bitch wanted him to live and suffer." Duffy paused in reflection, before adding, "When the war come along, I knew which side I was on. You can't fight to give men the right to do somethin' like that."

After the conflict ended, he drifted north with Emmett, thinking that he might find work in Fort Worth or Dallas, but ended up staying in Waco, where the town was about to build a huge suspension bridge over the Brazos River. The project took four years to complete, and he connected with Emmett whenever his friend came to town for a "Cattlemen's Association" meeting. Those rendezvous were always good times, as John well knew. When work on the bridge ended, Emmett got Duffy a job on a nearby ranch, and later Duffy joined him on the drive to the railhead in Abilene, Kansas. Afterwards, he returned to Waco and continued cowpunching for the same rancher. Emmett had shown up one day and, as usual, they had gone to Two Street for recreation. Later, while they soaked in hot baths, Emmett had said, "I'm thinkin' of puttin' together a herd to trail up Nebraska way. You interested in taggin' along?"

Duffy didn't have to think about it. "I won't say no if you're askin'."

"I'm askin'."

"And I ain't sayin' no."

They had put twenty miles behind them before they stopped for lunch at the edge of the North Platte. Since the river had shrunk considerably, John leaped down a three-foot embankment and crossed the reedy, dried mudflat to scoop out a pot of water. Duffy gathered juniper twigs from the hillside and got a fire going while John strained the water through a cloth brought for the purpose. Finished, he led the horses to the river for a drink while Duffy put coffee on to boil.

The satisfaction of that strong brew in that unfamiliar place, with the responsibility of the drive behind them and a positive future ahead, was immeasurable. Both men were buoyant, a feeling buttressed by money belts stuffed with more cash than they had ever possessed in their lives. The possibility of making themselves even richer as miners was their main topic of conversation, and they decided that Virginia City, Montana, some eight hundred miles distant, would be their destination. They would follow the North Platte to its beginnings in Wyoming and get further directions there. They reckoned it would be comparatively easy on good horses, with no cattle to fret about.

Their coffee and biscuits finished, the men rolled cigarettes and smoked in silence. Finished, John moved to get up when his hat flew from his head—accompanied by the loud crack of a rifle shot from the hillside and the whine of a bullet. There was confusion for a second or two, the friends unsure of what was happening. But they shifted their positions enough that another shot missed them, burying itself in the ground beside John. Under attack, both men responded instinctively. About a dozen feet away was the low bank of the river and they tumbled over it onto hard-baked mud as more shots rang out and small explosions of dirt geysered up behind them.

Out of the line of fire, Duffy exclaimed, "Jesus Christ! What the hell is this all about?"

Pressed tight against the bank on his belly, John shook his head in disbelief. "It's about someone wantin' to kill us. Indians maybe."

"That don't seem very Indian-like to me. Indians woulda

rode down on us, shootin' and yippin'. We'd a been dead as the grass by now."

"Could be it's a hostile, on his own and hungry. Or maybe we've been mistaken for somebody else."

Duffy snorted. "You think there's another pair looks like us anywhere on this good earth?"

John voiced another thought. "Maybe it's someone who knows we had a big payday in Ogallala and wants it without workin' as hard as we did for it."

"Maybe. Meanwhile, we're in a fix and we need to find a way out."

John removed his hat and rose cautiously. Peering through the tufts of dried grass on the bank's edge, he caught a glimpse of a solitary figure on the bluff where the shots came from, moving to another hiding place. John ducked back down.

"It's an Indian," he said.

Duffy took off his hat to have a look, but the soil about two feet from the edge of the bank exploded as the sound of another shot rolled down the hill. They dropped to their bellies again.

"Don't look as if he has plans of leavin'," John said.

"Well, he ain't gonna come down here unless he's got a death wish. Maybe he'll try to wait us out, fool us into thinkin' he's gone. But I think we can get the bastard. We got a good bank for protection, so if I go upriver and you go down, we can maybe get up in those hills and squeeze him from two sides. Make sure you know what you're shootin' at. I don't need two people gunnin' for me."

John didn't need any further prompting. The sooner they got moving, the better chance they would have of getting their assailant. The river curved both ways to their advantage, and John began crawling downriver on his belly over the dry, cracked mud, hugging the bank. He wished that he had his rifle, but it was still in its scabbard on Cat, who, with the other two horses, had galloped off. He had only his sidearm, which would have to do. It meant getting closer to the shooter, but it also meant that he would know what he was shooting at. He kept as close to the bank as his big frame allowed, hoping that the Indian, not seeing any movement, would bide his time and wait for the right opportunity to bag his quarry. Then again, he might also have sneaked around to a gully and be making his way down to the river to get them from the side. John kept that thought handy and glanced behind him every few seconds.

He reached a spot where a dry, narrow stream bed joined the river and calculated that he had gone far enough to be out of the shooter's sight. He peered over the riverbank. He could not see where he figured the shooter was; the slope of a small hill was now between them, but the stream bed ran down a crease between two hills and would provide a route to the top. He watched for two or three minutes, his eyes sweeping as much of the breaks as he could see. When he detected no movement, he drew his pistol, took a deep breath, and rolled onto the bank. Scrambling to his feet, he ran for the crease. It was no more than sixty yards away, yet it seemed twice that distance. Though John had always considered himself fleet of foot for his size, his feet had never seemed as heavy as anvils before. He felt vulnerable every step of the way, but he reached the crease without incident and began picking his way up the rocky incline, one eye on the terrain below his feet and the other on the land above. The heat in the sun-soaked ground radiated up around him and beads of sweat rolled from his temples.

He heard the snake before he saw it, and stopped as if he had run into an invisible wall. Merely looking at the loathsome creature made his knees tremble and he wanted to shoot it. Afraid to risk the noise, he picked up a rock and heaved it at the reptile. Struck a glancing blow on the head, the rattler slithered behind a boulder. John winced at the sound of the rock clattering over the ground. He listened for a while but could hear no other sound. He continued to the top of the crease, giving the wounded reptile a wide berth, not knowing what he feared more, a bullet or an encounter with a snake. The crease ended in a small basin with a scum-coated pool at its centre. He skirted the water and crept on his belly the short distance to the basin's rim.

From his vantage point, he could see the river and the undulating landscape of the breaks. He saw no movement and reckoned that he was about two or three hundred yards from the Indian's position and behind him, if the Indian had stayed put. Below and to his left, a shallow cut studded with junipers ran in the general direction that he needed to go, so John hurried down the slope and slid the last few feet. He moved slowly, careful of where he placed his feet, on the lookout for the gunman and snakes. The excitement he felt tempered his nervousness. He was as much the hunter now as he was the hunted, and that made all the difference.

The crack of a gunshot nearby startled him and he instinctively ducked behind a juniper. Who had fired it? Duffy, he hoped, because it sounded more like a pistol than a rifle. There was no answering fire, but seconds later, he heard a horse whinny off in the distance, followed by the sound of hooves on hardpan. He scrambled to a spot where the cut petered out, about forty feet above a wide draw running at angles to it. Looking down, he saw an Indian fleeing on horseback. He decided not to shoot, because it would have taken a lucky shot to bring him down. More than likely, he would have hit the horse and he did not want to kill or maim an innocent creature. Duffy appeared across the draw, waved, and began descending into it. John scrambled down the grass-covered slope in front of him and met his friend at the bottom.

Duffy's eyes were wild with excitement. "I dunno," he panted, "but I think I mighta hit him. Came out above him as he was about to mount up and got a shot away. You were right, a god-damned renegade Indian!"

Examining the tracks, they saw that the horse was unshod. John also spotted several drops of blood. There was more blood a few yards farther on.

"I think you got him good, Duffy. Wait here and I'll get the horses. We're goin' after him."

John found Cat and Duffy's mount grazing, oblivious now to the affairs of men. He climbed on Cat, grabbed the reins of Duffy's horse, and returned swiftly to his friend.

"I'm seein' lots of blood," Duffy said when John rejoined him. "I don't think we'll have to ride far till we find the son of a bitch."

Duffy holstered his gun, mounted up, and pulled his rifle from its scabbard. John took his rifle out too and they followed the tracks at a trot. The valley widened slightly and, a quarter mile ahead, bent to the right. The men slowed their horses to a walk, scanning the slopes and hilltops. A red-tailed hawk drifted low into the valley ahead of them, swooping down and disappearing around the bend. The hawk was clearly hunting, and they took it as a sign that there was nothing threatening in the immediate vicinity. They cautiously rounded the bend and reined up abruptly when they spotted a riderless horse. The animal had seen them and was warily regarding their approach. Not far away, a motionless figure lay face down on the ground.

They held still for several moments, watching. The only movement was the hawk soaring overhead. The valley was hot and still. They rode toward the downed man, keeping their rifles trained on him, suspecting a trap. They stopped several feet away and John dismounted. He instructed Duffy, "You see even a small tic that I don't, put another slug in him."

He walked over to the prone Indian and prodded him with the muzzle of his rifle. It evoked a small moan. He put his foot against the man's side and pushed him over onto his back. Behind the garish paint on his face and the plaited black hair, John could see that it was no Indian. It was Rufus Pauley.

He was barely alive and his eyes were losing focus. Even so, he recognized the man towering over him. He gasped, "Killed . . . by a fuckin' . . . nigger."

John did not bother correcting him. He reckoned it was a pretty good thought for Rufus to take with him into eternity. The dying man's eyes closed; he took a few shallow breaths and was gone.

"Goddamn!" Duffy exclaimed when he saw who it was, adding a little self-righteously, "I reckon I had him pegged proper. Men like Pauley don't change unless it's to get sneakier than they was as a child."

John was baffled. He had believed that, through the sheer force of his deeds and personality, he had changed Rufus's mind about black people.

Duffy rode back to the packhorse to get a spade and they took turns scooping out a shallow trench. When they were finished, John grabbed Rufus's wrists and dragged him alongside the hole. He placed his boot against his waist and rolled him in, the corpse ending up face down. John considered turning it over but Duffy said, "Leave him be. Let the man see where he's goin'."

They shovelled the dirt back into the grave but did not bother protecting it with rocks. Neither cared much if animals dug Rufus out, nor had they any words to say over the grave. John felt betrayed and had no tears for the man's passing. Indeed, he figured that if the world had any tears at all for Rufus, they would have been better shed at his birth.

They retrieved Rufus's mount, led it back to the river, and linked it to their packhorse. They doused the dregs of their fire, rinsed their cups and coffee pot, returned them to their saddlebags, and continued their journey northwest, still stunned by their discovery. They speculated that Rufus's indirect apology at the Cattleman's Rest was strictly for show, so that it would appear as if he'd had a change of heart concerning blacks in general and John in particular. That way, he would not have been a suspect if his plan had been successful and his victims' bodies were discovered.

He had dressed and painted his face like an Indian, plaited his long hair, and shaved off his moustache in the event someone happened along during the attack, or if John or Duffy got away. He had even removed the shoes from his horse, and had probably hidden his saddle somewhere in the breaks. They believed that as much as Rufus wanted the money, the bonus was murdering John, since the bullets appeared to have first been directed at him. John was lucky to have moved at just the right moment. Otherwise, he and Duffy, along with their horses, might now be in some hidden gully providing a feast for the coyotes and other carrion eaters. Rufus would have ridden off with a small fortune, leaving behind not a single shred of evidence of his misdeeds.

They rode on as the sun sailed the sky in its daily journey between the horizons and the stars eddied against the black void of the night. Long days in the saddle turned into weeks. They holed up in foul weather and pressed on in fair, and one day they reached the crest of a hill and saw that the rim of their world now included the rugged profile of the mountains they had heard so much about.

NINE

Texas ain't in my future.

John and Duffy's arrival in Virginia City went relatively unnoticed. The town sat at the base of a long, ravaged hill called Mount Davidson and was a sprawling, hectic place much like Dodge in its purpose: to relieve a certain type of people of their money, in this case miners rather than drovers. It seemed full of Irish and Welsh, and there were more Chinese than John had ever seen in one place. To his relief, there was also a small community of blacks, many of them entrepreneurs.

At the Boston Saloon, a black-owned establishment, the pair removed the dust from their throats with whisky and filled their bellies with beefsteak and potatoes. Afterwards, they had baths and a frolic at the connected brothel. They spent the following morning checking around town and in the newspaper for the best way to become rich. They were not surprised to find that the rumours they had heard in the small villages on the way to Virginia City were true, that placer mining had run its course and the creeks in the area had given up all the gold they were going to. Miners were still hydraulically stripping the overburden off the hillsides in their quest for wealth, while others were blasting holes and tunnelling, but the ore sought now was silver. The friends could have purchased shares in a producing mine in the Comstock, the area above and behind Virginia City that had produced millions of dollars in gold and silver, or they could have obtained work in those same mines for four times the monthly pay of a drover. Neither option appealed to them. They wanted their own mine.

Through the grapevine, they heard of a man selling a wildcat mine in the hills east of the Comstock, where some predicted the next big strike might happen. He had contracted a cancer, could no longer work, and was letting the claim go cheap. All the necessary equipment was there, including a hand pump to keep the mine from flooding and to wash the diggings. Equally as important in an area with few trees, there was a large pile of timbers for shoring the shaft. The site also included a small cabin. Duffy read the assay reports and found much of the language mystifying. They said that although the mine had not been a great producer, it was considered to have potential. It was also affordable and that was added incentive for John and Duffy to open their money belts. Within forty-eight hours of their arrival in Virginia City, they had become mine owners. They named it the Silver Fleece, based loosely on a story Duffy remembered from his schooldays about Jason and the Argonauts.

They set to work with equal parts enthusiasm and anticipation, and each dawn brought with it the possibility of great wealth. Digging into the hillside with pickaxes and shovels proved to be back-breaking and dangerous work, and they seemed to spend as much time shoring the walls and ceilings of the shaft to prevent cave-ins as they did washing their diggings for silver. Most of what they dug was Montana clay and rock, with barely enough ore to buy food supplies. Their cash dwindled. The first winter slid easily into summer, but the second winter seemed much longer and harder, especially for Duffy, who began to sense the futility of their quest. He grew tired of spending his days underground and unrewarded, and longed to move on. During a trip to Virginia City for supplies, he heard that the ranges in Idaho, near the town of Pocatello, some two hundred miles to the south, had been seeded with cattle and that there was a shortage of drovers to mind them. It was not news he had been looking for, but he received it well. When he got back to the mine, he shared it with John.

"That's where we belong, John, not here. We're cattlemen, not miners. It's time we quit this place and admit that either I read that assay report wrong or it was fake and we was hornswoggled. I figger it's about time we start puttin' money in our pockets instead of takin' it out. It took me some time to know it, but I know it now for certain. We oughta get outta here while we still got somethin' to get outta here with."

John did not share Duffy's pessimism and the words glanced off him with little effect. As much as he loathed parting ways with his friend, he felt driven to keep working the mine. He never entered the shaft without believing that he was only a shovelful away from the bonanza ore, and furthermore, he liked the fact that he worked for no one but John Ware. It was no small feat for an ex-slave and was important to him. He told Duffy that.

"I reckon I understand that better'n most people, but this is plain bloody time-wastin'. I can't abide it no more."

"It don't seem that way to me, Duff. I need to give this everything I got till I got no more to give."

"Well, Lord knows you had enough people tellin' you what do for most of your life, so I ain't gonna add to it. But I'm tellin' you this: I'm leavin', with or without you. It grieves me to do it, but if you stick around here you gotta be the most stubborn man I ever met. Maybe even a damned fool. You ever come to your senses, I'll be down Pocatello way."

John knew it was useless to try to reason with Duffy and, unwilling to part on a bitter note, did not prolong the argument. It was disconcerting and sad, too, to watch Duffy ride off, and for a moment, he wanted to yell at him to hold on while he saddled up Cat to join him. He resisted the temptation, although he wondered if he'd ever see his friend again.

The only way to avoid doubting his decision was to work hard. Duffy's dust had barely settled before John was back in the mine, digging and shoring. The work went much slower without a partner, and while they never talked much as they worked, John missed the small conversations they did have. He wished he had enough money to hire some help, but he did not and that was that. He considered trying to sell Duffy's share but was wary of taking on a partner he did not know, even if someone was willing to buy in. In any event, he missed very few days in the mine, and he hunted in the surrounding hills for game to put food on his table. Cat was his only companion but she was old now, with arthritic joints, and he knew she was in pain when he rode her. So he stopped riding her but always ensured that he made time each day to talk to her. He did not have enough money to buy another horse.

Winter came again, and as it deepened, the thought crossed his mind that maybe Duffy was right, that not only was he stubborn, he was also a fool. When spring finally arrived, he arose one morning and, true to his habit, went out to say hello to Cat, who was usually grazing nearby. It had been a tough winter for her, pawing down through the snow to find grass, and she had weakened considerably. He found her lying on her side, so drained of spirit that she could barely raise her head. She was dying. He had known this day was not far off and was expecting it; nevertheless, he felt heartsick. He sat down with her and lifted her head onto his lap and held her, stroking her neck and talking to her until she passed. His face was wet with tears and he had not felt such emptiness since Emmett died. But as she had served him in life so did she serve him in death: he took the sweetest cuts of meat from her and let nature take care of the rest.

He now felt more alone than he had ever thought possible. Not always aware of it, he began talking to himself. Still he continued to work. Then one night he dreamed of Texas, the Coles, and the ranch that had presented him with such golden opportunities, and when he awoke he declared to himself that his mining days were over. He admitted that he had been chasing after a fantasy and reckoned it had turned him a little mad. It was time to go before he lost his connection with reality entirely. He wanted to return home, because that is what his dream had meant to him, and home was Texas, not South Carolina. He imagined Amos and Ellie as they had been when he had left four years before, active and healthy, and did not think they would have changed much. Despite the fortune John had wired them from the drive, he doubted they would have sold the ranch; it had been their home for too many years.

Many times he lamented the lack of a woman in his life. The prospect of remaining a bachelor until he died, visiting brothels for female company, depressed him as much as anything else. Still, he wanted to be a good prospect for any potential bride and that meant being financially solvent. Now that the mine had proven to be a bust, he would have to find solvency elsewhere, perhaps back in Texas. And it occurred to him that the train ran between Fort Worth and Marshall, where the odds of finding a wife were better than they were here in the North—he had looked but had seen no possibilities among the small black population in Virginia City. It would not have mattered anyway; a man can't go courting when he's broke flatter than the Texas Panhandle.

The truth was he missed Duffy, too. You don't ride out numerous storms with a good man and not feel an attachment to him. You don't let him disappear from your life forever. John decided that the best thing to do was to go to Idaho, find his friend, and persuade him to return to Texas with him.

Since no one was paying money for a worthless hole in the ground, all he could sell were the pump and tools, and he did not get enough for them to buy a horse. He would walk if he had to; he had done a thousand miles once, so he could certainly do two hundred. He bathed in the nearby creek, burned his work clothes, and donned the only clothes he had left, those he wore to town, which were the same as his work clothes, only cleaner and with fewer patches. He gathered up his bedroll, abandoned the mine and cabin as if they had never existed, and walked to the road leading south to Pocatello, reminded of a younger man who had set out from Georgetown long ago with as little to call his own. On the road, he hitched a ride in an ox-drawn wagon brimming with freight, just as he brimmed once more with optimism.

John grabbed his bedroll, leaped down from the wagon, and thanked the teamsters for the ride. He felt dusty and hungry, but his first priority was to find Duffy.

Pocatello was nestled in the last of the hills of the Wasatch Range, where the land flattened into the Snake River Plain. Sandwiched between the Portneuf River and the Utah & Northern Railway, it was like most towns: a collection of wood-frame buildings, the main ones being a hotel with a restaurant and bar, a bank, a general store, a livery stable, and two saloons. The town was quiet, but then it was late afternoon on a Sunday. He enquired at the saloons but nobody knew Duffy. He asked if there was a brothel in town and got directions to the Pocatello Social Club.

He found the club, a few blocks away, on an empty back street. It was a two-storey building with a balcony fronting the second floor, where the club advertised its wares on warm days. The place looked deserted, but when he knocked on the door, an elderly woman with stern features and grey hair answered it immediately. She looked as though she could be somebody's grandmother, and John worried that he might have come to the wrong place. He thought he saw a look of surprise cross her face and wondered if he might be the first black man to knock on her door.

"Welcome," she said with an air of importance. "I am Mrs. Shadbolt." She opened the door wide and stood aside. "Please come in. All are welcome here."

She led John from the foyer through an archway hung with beaded curtains into a room where three other women were lounging in provocative clothing. They saw a prospective customer and sat up, preening themselves like birds. An unattended upright piano sat in one corner (it was played on Saturday nights when the drovers came to town), and a small bar lined one wall. The women looked at him with eyes that longed for business. There was a hardness to their features, the madam's too, but John saw past that to their feminine softness. He had not had a woman for some time and he felt awkward being close to several so available yet so unattainable, but he did not have the funds to acquire their services. He wished he had pockets of cash as Mrs. Shadbolt motioned him to the bar for a drink.

"Thank you," John said, "but I ain't come for socializin'." He explained the purpose of his visit.

Her disappointment obvious, Mrs. Shadbolt was reluctant to divulge information about her clientele. John pressed her, saying that he was Duffy's mining partner and had "good news" for him—a lie only if it was misinterpreted. Besides, how could she believe he might have struck it rich when he was dressed so poorly?

Despite John's clothing, it was clear the madam sensed that the good news might involve money and that imparting information might prove to be a good investment. "I know the man you seek, but the information of his whereabouts is not free. It is worth the price of our services."

John replied, "Yes, ma'am, but I ain't got the money. But I'll come back if I can and pay twice the cost for one of your ladies. That's a promise and the best I can do."

Mrs. Shadbolt only came up to John's shoulder, but she drew herself to a height that seemed much taller and huffed. "This is not a house of credit. For that service, you must visit a bank. I will say good day to you now, sir."

John felt like a scolded schoolboy. "Ma'am, I understand that you're runnin' a business here, but as I said, I'm busted. I'm hopin' that'll change once I find my friend. He might even consider a reward." That was stretching the truth too, but John felt he was close to discovering Duffy's whereabouts.

Mrs. Shadbolt mulled over his words. Then, unwilling to sacrifice the possibility of future rewards for present realities, she said, "He works for the Portneuf Cattle Company, about five miles northwest of here, on the Portneuf River. Follow the road leaving town and take the left fork when you come to it."

John thanked her profusely and left, noticing for the first time the sign on the wall that outlined the club's rules. There were several, most of which were unintelligible to him, but he could read enough now to know that the very first one, in large print, said, "Positively no credit."

On the street, he felt pangs of guilt over his less than honest exchange with the madam, but he believed she was his last resort. His only other option would have been to check all of the ranches in the area, which would have required the one thing he did not have: a horse. And he didn't blame her a bit for wanting money; it was a slow day and she was, after all, a businesswoman. He put the experience behind him and set off on foot for the ranch.

At the fork outside of town, he came upon a buckboard carrying supplies, and the driver offered him a ride. John climbed on board and settled onto the bench seat beside him, a grizzled, bearded man with veined roseate cheeks, bloodshot eyes, and a nose bent to one side, as if a left hook had caught it.

"Don't get many nigras out this way," the driver said in a nasal voice. "Lookin' for work, are ya?"

"Lookin' for an old friend. Seamus Duffield. You know him?"

"Duffy? You bet. Works out to the ranch. You might of come just in time, 'cause I believe he's leavin' soon."

"Leavin'? You know where he's goin'?"

"Far as I know he's headin' north, trailin' cattle up Canada way. I'd go myself if these old bones was up to it."

Canada? It was a vague place in John's mind and he could not even picture its outline. Worse, it looked as if he had arrived too late, even if Duffy had not yet left. His friend was a man of his word and if he had given it to ride north, he would not steer away from that track.

Soon the wagon rattled through the ranch gate and up to the main house, a rambling log structure. Several men were standing about, smoking and talking, and none of them were black. John was disappointed, but that had been his experience ever since he left Virginia City. All eyes were on him now as he got down from the wagon. The driver pointed. "There's Duffy comin' out of the cookhouse." Then John heard Duffy shout his name.

"John!" He hurried over with a grin that now had a tooth missing. "I'll be goddamned if you ain't one of the best sights I've seen in a while! Wondered if that mine had swallowed you up for good." He grabbed John's hand and the two men slapped each other's shoulders with their free hands, their mutual admiration on display for the drovers looking on, curious. "Damned if you don't look a mile or two short of bein' filthy rich. More just plain filthy and like you could use a good meal and a bath. Let's go see if Cookie can rustle you up somethin'."

It was not as easy as Duffy thought. While the ranch never refused transients a meal, a black transient was a different matter altogether, and the cook eyed John suspiciously. But he held Duffy in high esteem and put together a plate of beans for John, with a cup of coffee. Duffy got a cup for himself and the two men sat at one of the long bench tables.

John was ravenous and wolfed the beans down, talking between mouthfuls. He admitted to Duffy that he had been right about the mine being worthless. But the news was no surprise to his friend.

"Well, we named it good because we got fleeced, John. Ain't no use denyin' it. Shoulda took that assay report to a lawyer or someone who knew how to read it proper."

John chuckled. "Most likely would've bought the thing anyway. We was two blind men stumblin' around in places we shoulda never gone. Maybe a bit greedy, too."

They were quiet for a while, and then John told Duffy about his dream and how it seemed to beckon him back to Texas. "I was kinda hopin' I could talk you into ridin' with me."

Duffy gave him a sideways look. "*Ridin'* with you? In case you didn't notice, partner, you ain't got a horse. And I ain't got the sixty bucks it'll take to get you a good one, never mind a saddle. That's two months' wages."

"There must be someone around here that's hirin'."

"You're probably right, John, but for a man of colour it'll be peelin' spuds for pennies at best. Anyway, much as I'd like to join you, Texas ain't in my future. I'm headin' in the opposite direction. I heard good stories about the sweetgrass up Canada way and that there's plenty a room for a man to put down some roots."

John finished the last of his beans. "I bin thinkin' that my roots are in Texas. It's where I stopped thinkin' like a slave."

"I know the truth in that, but you got lucky with the Coles. People like them are as rare as pet diamondbacks. Do you know if they're even still alive? They was gettin' on."

"It's hard to imagine 'em dead. They was so full of life."

The mere thought that they might be gone made John's heart sink. He should have wired the Coles to see if they were still alive. He had wanted to surprise them, the last of their sons returning home, but there was always the possibility that he might be the one in for a surprise.

"Well, they could be alive, I suppose. Don't seem likely though. Either way, Texas ain't no place for a coloured man and probably never will be. Come north with me, John. Far as I know, there ain't never been slavery up there. Tom Lynch, the man gatherin' the herd, still needs a couple more good men and I'll put in a word for you. You'll be earnin' cash again, and he'll even provide a horse and saddle. If you don't like what you see when we get there, turn around and point yourself south. If I don't like what I see, I might even join you for part of the trip, but not to Texas. As I said, it ain't in my future no more."

"Let me think on it."

"I'd never knowingly steer you wrong and you know that. I got a good feelin' about this so don't think on it too long. Tom's got three thousand head waitin' up near the Lost River, and as soon as he's got a full crew together, we're leavin'. Maybe this week sometime. He's still hirin' outta Pocatello House because he won't take just any man that comes along; he wants the best. So I'll borrow you a horse and we can go talk to him right now if you want. All you gotta do is say the word."

A flash flood of thoughts washed through John's mind. It was true that Duffy had never steered him wrong before and John did not think he was now. The drive would last only a month or two, a small slice out of his life, and he'd see some new country. And, as Duffy pointed out, if he didn't like Canada, he could always head back down to Texas. Furthermore, it was a job and he needed one before he could go anywhere.

"Let's go talk to your Mr. Lynch."

⸺⊱✦⊰⸺

Duffy acquired a horse and tack for John and they rode into Pocatello. Duffy was chatty and excited. "Lynch is a good man and he owns a boxcar load of experience. He's from northern Idaho and he's already taken a couple a small herds into Canada for other ranchers, so he knows the trail. He says the ranges up there are among the best he's ever seen and he'll have beeves of his own on them one day, before they're all taken up. Accordin' to him, that won't be long."

They found Lynch eating a late supper in the restaurant at Pocatello House, the town's only hotel. He was a tall, spare man, and looked as hard as ironwood. His thin face was creased and leathery and his bushy brown moustache and close-cropped hair had strands of grey. But it was the man's blue eyes that John noticed most. They locked on his and their message said that here was a man it was best not to fool with. Duffy made introductions and Lynch's response to John was at best cool. He spoke in a forthright manner, what he saw as the truth, and the listener be damned.

"The fact of the matter, Ware, is I've never known a Negro drover and I've never heard of a good one either."

140

Duffy spoke before John could say something he might regret. "You just been introduced to one, Tom. I trailed two thousand head of longhorns with this man from Fort Worth to Ogallala. He started on drag and took over as trail boss after the first one got hisself shot in Dodge City. We had some beeves rustled during a storm and John and me went after 'em. Caught 'em too, and John dealt a hand to those rustlers as good as any I ever seen."

Interested, Lynch said, "I've got the time. Tell me about it."

In detail, Duffy described catching the rustlers and sending them back to Dodge naked and tied together. Lynch laughed but didn't seem overly impressed.

"An entertaining story, Duffy, but every man I've got so far has come recommended by two or more different people. I need good men, *real* good men. I'm particular about who I hire because I can't afford to have any foul-ups on this drive. I'm working for the North West Cattle Company up in Canada. They've paid nearly twenty dollars a head for those beeves and hired me to get them there safely. I take my responsibilities seriously and I don't want to lose a single animal. We've got more than seven hundred miles of rough trail to cover and there'll be rustlers along some of it, which means every man has to hold up his end and more. So I don't know. I only have your word about the quality of this man."

"I wouldn't give my word if I didn't think it could be backed up, Tom. That'll have to do. John here is one of the best there is, so if you don't hire him you'll have to find someone to replace me."

John glanced over at Duffy, surprised yet pleased with his friend's stance. Lynch was staring hard at Duffy, unaccustomed to ultimatums. It seemed a long time before the cattleman spoke.

"Well, I reckon that's as good a recommendation as I could ask for." He turned to John. "If you want the job, you'll switch between helping the cook and taking the night shift. That's all I can offer."

John held Lynch's gaze. "I been in both those places a time or two before, boss. Never lost a man or an animal in either one of 'em." He smiled, leaving unspoken that he was also well accustomed to having to prove himself twice as good as any man with a white skin.

Lynch held out his hand. "Thirty-five a month is what I pay. That's what the other drovers are getting. It's higher than usual, but I want that herd delivered in one piece. You boys be up at the Lost River by Wednesday afternoon at the latest. I want to be stirring up trail dust by Saturday."

Outside, John asked Duffy, "Would you really have quit if Lynch hadn't hired me?"

Duffy laughed. "Hell no! I want on that drive more'n anythin'. For a man who's supposed to spend a lot of his spare time playin' poker, I'm surprised he didn't recognize a bluff when one was starin' him straight in the face."

John grinned. "Well, it was a nice thought. Might as well hang onto it for a while."

Duffy slapped his companion on the back. "Not to worry, my friend, and so's you know my heart's where it's always been, I'll buy you a drink and a bath. The herd's about sixty miles from here and after I square things away at the ranch, we'll have a couple of days to get there, so I reckon there's time for a little celebratin'."

"It'll have to be short, Duffy. I'm a little strapped for cash."

"I ain't. Leastways not for what I have in mind."

As it turned out, Duffy's generosity proved to be greater than a bath and a single drink. It supported several drinks, as well as a trip to the Pocatello Social Club, where business, though far from brisk, had picked up since the afternoon. Duffy happily paid twice as much for John, causing Mrs. Shadbolt's face to alter into what might have been a smile, perhaps from a newly found faith that not everyone was after something for nothing. For her, it had turned out to be not such a bad day for business after all. For the reunited friends, the evening had all the earmarks of heaven.

TEN

Best not to fool with me about snakes.

Tom Lynch had provided John with a good saddle, but a mediocre horse that no self-respecting drover would have been happy with. A week into the drive, John went to Lynch and requested a better mount. Perhaps thinking that he could shut John up, Lynch pointed to a horse in the remuda known to have a mean streak. "You ride that one and it's yours." John rode it to a standstill without any difficulty, amazing everyone, including the trail boss. He always enjoyed the accolades that such feats invariably brought, but it was the acceptance, the subsequent invitation into the white circle, that he cherished most. Later, as they passed by Helena, Montana, one of the point men quit, and Lynch asked John to take his place. It was the end of peeling potatoes and riding night herd, but he knew it would not be the end of having to prove himself. Whenever he was among a new group of white men who did not know him, he had to start all over again.

The outfit crossed the border into Canada and the District of Alberta, where officials counted 3,014 head of cattle and 10 purebred bulls. When they reached the Highwood River, about forty miles southwest of Calgary, John was glad he had allowed Duffy to talk him into joining the drive. It was as pretty a landscape as he'd ever laid eyes on and he doubted he'd be Texas-bound anytime soon.

Back at the Lost River, the name North West Cattle Company, the owner of the herd, had sounded grandiose to John. He had pictured a large ranch house with several outbuildings on a wide prairie, something like the Flint Springs Cattle Company. Instead, it was a solitary log cabin nestled in the foothills of the Rocky Mountains, in the shallow valley cut by Pekisko Creek, a tributary of the Highwood River. Nonetheless, it was a beautiful setting, with the cottonwoods fronting the creek in full fall colour, the drooping willows, and the Rockies, with snow creeping down their flanks, as a western backdrop.

The boss was Fred Stimson, a loud man in his forties with an impressive set of black mutton chop whiskers. He had a deep, abiding love for the sound of his own voice, and it was sometimes hard to fit a word in edgeways once he got started. He hailed from Quebec, where his family owned a farm with cattle, so he had more experience with the vagaries of the creatures than most men. When his father died and left him a quarter interest in the farm, he sold it for twenty-five thousand dollars and decided that the West was a good place to reinvest it. Now he needed ranch hands and asked Lynch if any of his drovers who were not moving on were worth keeping.

"The Negro," Lynch replied. "His name is John Ware and he's got a way with horses and cattle that I've not seen the likes of before. You don't want to let him get away." Lynch had not recommended Duffy, though, saying, "He's a good friend of Ware's with lots of experience, but he might be getting a little long in the tooth to give you the mileage you're looking for."

Lynch and Stimson called John over and Stimson offered him twenty-five dollars a month to stay on.

"Does the same offer go for Duffy?"

"I hadn't considered it," was Stimson's reply.

John looked at Lynch, then at Stimson. "Well, sir, I reckon it needs considerin'. I been his partner for too many years to stay on without him. He goes, and I'll be ridin' alongside him."

John had never heard Lynch laugh as loudly as he did then, no doubt remembering a similar stipulation in Pocatello. He said to Stimson, "I've been down this road before, Fred, and was glad I took it. My guess is that you won't regret taking it either."

And so John and Duffy went to work for Stimson, who was part owner and manager of the North West Cattle Company and the Bar U brand. But the truth was, Duffy *was* getting older and feeling it too, a little sorer from long days in the saddle and a little stiffer from sleeping on the ground. Yet he was not about to admit it to anyone, least of all John, who had the strength and appetite of two men, though he did not move all that fast because of his size. Duffy could at least keep pace with his friend, which suited both of them.

In the spring, Stimson would have the herd burned with the Bar U brand, but for now, their temporary trail brand was wearing thin, and unbranded cattle on open range were up for grabs. So John and Duffy's first job was to prevent the herd from mingling with another large herd that had followed them up from Montana and was passing through to a more northerly range along the Bow River. When the friends saw that herd of four thousand, more than a mile long, amble past their own charges, they knew they were in on the beginning of something big. Adding to that impression was the grass that billowed in every direction beneath a vast, blue sky uncluttered by clouds.

"It sorta takes the longin' for Texas out of a man, don't it?" John asked.

"Texas?" Duffy replied. "The name sounds vaguely familiar. Seems to me I mighta been there once but I don't fully recollect it."

Their job done, they returned to the ranch with the hot fall sun beating down on their shoulders, as it did for the next few days, deluding a man into thinking that he was living in paradise. But they went to bed one night after a warm evening that had seen a glorious sunset of pinks and oranges draped like a lush stole over the shoulders of the Rockies, and awoke to snow on the ground, brought on the back of a furious north wind.

Stimson knew that the cattle would turn their rumps to the wind and drift until it abated. "If it blows long enough and hard enough, those damned beasts could end up back in Montana." He sent the men out to turn the herd, which had already broken up into smaller units as cattle are sometimes prone to do. But the wind was too fierce and the snow too stinging, and the cattle refused to turn. They plodded on, southward. The men had to separate and, afraid of getting lost in the storm, soon gave up. One by one, they fought their way back to the safety and warmth of the cabin.

Unaware of what the others were up to, John continued following a few hundred head, determined not to lose them to the storm. The more he tried to turn them, the more they wanted to disperse into even smaller groups. He figured he might as well let them drift and keep them all together. When the wind abated, he managed to hold them in the relative shelter of a draw where there was still grass poking through the snow. But a savage wind rose again and bit at the herd until they moved on. John felt frozen to the core, and his hands, in summer leather gloves, were so stiff he would not have been surprised if his fingers had broken off into little chips of ice. And to make matters worse, a huge gust of wind blew off his Boss of the Plains hat. He watched it somersault away until it disappeared in the slanting snowfall. He had been in worse winds and could not believe that it was gone. He lamented its loss, and memories of the Coles and Texas flooded his mind. It was as if the wind had severed his last physical connection to them. He wished at that instant to be back in the South, out of this brutal weather. But since that kind of thinking gets a man nowhere, he took his blanket out of his bedroll, wrapped it around his head and shoulders, and focused on the cattle. They were his responsibility now, every one of them.

For two days, the storm roared and kept the herd on the move. John had no idea how far they had gone. He dozed in the saddle and tried to ignore the hunger rumbling in his gut. Parts of his face had gone numb and he thought it might be from frostbite. He pulled the blanket up higher, leaving only a narrow gap to see through. On the morning of the third day, the wind weakened, patches of blue appeared in the sky, and the herd stopped. The drifts were two feet deep but enough grass showed in the sheltered areas that the cattle were able to eat.

John dismounted, so stiff he could barely move. He swung his arms to get some warmth into his body, pumped his legs up and down, and broke into a prolonged jig until he had enough movement in his limbs to gather wood and build a fire. While collecting windfall in a nearby copse, he spotted a deer, a small buck. He returned to his horse, slid his rifle from its scabbard, and, with a lucky shot, brought the animal down. Once he got a good fire blazing, he retrieved the deer, slit open its belly, and stuck his hands inside to warm them. Then he cut out the liver. He was so hungry that he considered eating it raw but instead seared it on the fire, his stomach in knots with the wait. After he had eaten his fill, he was so weary, he could barely keep his eyes open. He built the fire even bigger, got the rest of his bedroll, wrapped himself in it like a mummy, and slept.

He awoke to something prodding him. Pulling back his blanket and tarp, he saw Duffy and Fred Stimson standing over him. His face ached where the frost had penetrated it.

"Figgered you for dead," said Duffy. "You look dead."

"I can't be," John groaned as he moved. "Far as I know there ain't no pain in bein' dead."

"Goddamn it, John!" Stimson exclaimed. "You should have left the herd and headed back to the ranch house like everybody else! You could've got yourself killed!"

"Thought of that many times, boss, but I didn't want those beeves to get lost and maybe end up with someone else's brand on 'em. Figgered you might appreciate it if I stayed close."

Stimson shook his head in disbelief and gratitude. "Appreciate it? Without a doubt. Expect it? Not in the least."

Later he told Duffy, "Damned if Lynch wasn't right. I'm glad I listened to him. That man is one of kind, and I've at least got to buy him a new hat."

Stimson did exactly that on his first trip into Calgary, a Boss of the Plains like the one John had lost.

John stayed around the ranch house until his face healed, then he and Duffy spent the rest of the winter leading an ox-drawn sledge with hay for the herd. After the lovely fall, the sudden onslaught of winter had taken the district by surprise and people had to get used to its ferocious persistence. By the time spring rolled around, many of the Bar U cattle lay dead, and most of the herd up along the Bow River had been wiped out.

"Remember that Texas place you talked about?" Duffy said to John. "The one I said I couldn't recollect too good? Well, it's all comin' back to me now."

Spring found them on a roundup along the Oldman River, some fifty miles south of the ranch, because that was how far the storm had pushed the cattle. Like Duffy, Stimson, and Lynch, the rest of the crew were old cattle hands, although new to John. Some had been wary of him until his plunge over the cutbank into the river on Mustard, the "fucker of a bucker" that no one else could ride, had brought them onside. Or so he thought.

One day, he reached for the horn of his saddle to mount up and his hand landed on a dead snake some prankster had looped around the horn like a lariat. He jumped back in shock and tripped and fell, cursing. It was only a large bull snake, but that did not matter. It was a snake and it had its usual effect on John. He was determined to find out who had committed the prank and confronted every man in the outfit. No one admitted to it. Duffy had no idea who might have done it, but his fear of snakes was almost as deep-seated as John's, so he was not a suspect. John was incensed and let everyone know it.

"I ain't afraid of nothin' except snakes," he told them, his eyes hitting hard on theirs. "I hate 'em, even dead ones. Somebody's had a good laugh on me, but I'm warnin' all of you, I don't find it funny. Neither will the man who did it if I get my hands on him. Best not to fool with me about snakes."

None of the crew was bold enough to scoff at the warning or ridicule what to many of them was an irrational fear.

Practical jokes were common on trail drives and roundups, but that spring they all seemed directed at John. One morning someone hid his saddle, as well as the spares, so he had to ride bareback all day, and one night his bedroll disappeared while he'd gone to relieve himself. A few days before the end of the roundup, he was bedding down next to Stimson's floorless tent, which the manager shared with a cattleman named George Emerson. John preferred to sleep under the stars when the weather was nice, as did a couple of the others. He spread out his bedroll, went to relieve himself, came back, and climbed into bed. He had just managed to get comfortable when he felt movement against his back, like something trying to get out from under him. In his mind it could be only one thing—a snake! He shot out of his bedroll, fumbling for his pistol. At that point, he noticed a rope being pulled out from under his tarp and sliding into Stimson's tent. He jammed his gun back in its holster and in two quick steps was at the front of the canvas shelter. He grabbed it with both hands and yanked it away from its occupants, throwing it to the ground. Stimson and Emerson were sitting up, with silly grins on their faces, and John saw the rope coiled on Emerson's lap.

"I told you . . ." he yelled, lunging for Emerson, who raised his arms to fend off the attack. John had meant to grab the prankster, haul him up, and punch him. Instead, he tripped over Emerson's feet and went sprawling on top of him, banging his mouth on Emerson's head. He felt a tooth pierce his lip, heard Stimson shout, "John!" and felt the cold barrel of a gun against his temple.

"Back off! Back off! Goddamn it, John, don't make me shoot you!" Stimson warned.

There was a tremor in his voice and John did not know whether that meant Stimson would pull the trigger or not, but he obeyed. He was angry, but not so much that he was willing to die over it.

"For God's sake, John, it was a joke! That's all. Just a joke," the manager said.

John got to his feet but Stimson kept the gun trained on him. "I told you, those kinda jokes ain't funny, and I'd punch the next man who pulled one on me." He said to Emerson, "Get on your feet and we'll settle this like men."

Stimson waved his gun. "I'll be the only one settling matters here, John."

Duffy came over and threw his arm around his friend's shoulders. "Come on, John. Leave it be. This won't get you nowhere." He tried to steer John away, but John broke from his grip and faced Stimson.

"I'm done here. You get yourself another nigger boy to play with. I'll be out to the ranch next week to collect my pay."

"No need to be rash about this, John." Stimson was still sitting up in his bedroll, although his gun was no longer pointing at John. "You'll see it better in the morning light. George was just having a little fun."

"Maybe so, but it's always me you're playin' with to have your fun, and I ain't nobody's toy."

Amid Duffy's protestations, John collected his bedroll and tack, and stalked to the remuda. Saddling his horse, he ignored the night wrangler's query about where he was going, and rode off, disappearing like a ghost in the star-filling dusk. He had not gone far before he heard a rider trotting up behind and Duffy joined him. They rode side by side in silence for several minutes in the descending darkness. Duffy was the first to speak.

"Fred's kickin' himself back there. He don't wanna lose you."

"Then I reckon he's smart enough to figger out what to do about it."

"I'd be surprised if he wasn't workin' on that right now."

John considered Duffy's words, trying to subdue his frustrations. "Well, it never shoulda been a job that needed doin' in the first place, Duff. I don't ask for nothin' I ain't worked hard to earn and that includes respect. It don't seem right that I always have to work harder than everyone else to get it."

"It surely don't, brother. And it don't seem right that a lotta folks born with a white skin somehow think it's a better colour than yours. It's a goddamned impossible notion to me. But throwin' a fit and runnin' off ain't worth a pinch of coon shit either. Sounds like you're whinin' and that ain't a bit like you."

Mulling over Duffy's words, John said nothing.

Duffy added, "Could be that they was pickin' on you so's you'd know you belonged."

"That's a funny way of showin' it."

"That it is. But like the Devil, a man's admiration for another man comes in many disguises."

———

John decided that he would not return to the Bar U, at least not right away. When he went to collect his pay, Stimson apologized for allowing the pranks to get out of hand and offered John a five dollar a month raise to return. John was tempted to stay, because he was beginning to believe that maybe Duffy was right, that perhaps flattery and admiration actually did hide behind different masks. But he felt in need of a change, and it wouldn't hurt to stay the course in order to let everybody know that he, like Lynch, was not a man to fool with.

John shook his head. "I took work somewhere else for a while, Fred. Maybe in the fall."

Stimson looked off into the distance. "The offer might not be good in the fall, John."

But John didn't hear much conviction in the manager's voice. He looked at Stimson, holding his eyes. "Well, that may be, but it ain't in me to accept right now."

He was about to mount up and depart when Tom Lynch hailed him. His old trail boss was with George Emerson and the pair came over.

"Glad I caught you, John," said Lynch. "George and I are heading to Montana to bring back another herd and wondered if you'd care to join us."

George nodded in agreement. "First thing, John, I owe you an apology. It was me who coiled that dead snake on your saddle and me who put the rope under your bedroll. It was a damned fool thing to do and I regret it. When it comes to a good horse or a good man, colour doesn't mean a thing. And you're a good man. I know that." He offered his hand to reinforce his sincerity.

"Well, I mighta overreacted some," John admitted, taking

Emerson's hand, "but when it comes to snakes, I ain't never been shy about lettin' my feelin's show. Anyway, if a man takes the time to apologize, I ain't one to deny it. Much obliged." To Lynch, he smiled and said, "I appreciate the offer, but I found the country that's gonna be my home and I ain't leavin' it. Not even for a little while."

He mounted up, touched the brim of his hat, and rode off. He did not know if Lynch and Emerson believed him when he said he was never leaving Alberta, but he had never spoken truer words. He would have his own ranch here one day, of that he was certain. He would have a wife, too, although of that he was less certain. The country was not exactly crowded with black folks—in fact, he had yet to see another one—which made him a bit of an oddity. But maybe Calgary held the solution to that problem, and he decided that it wouldn't hurt to make a trip there one day to see if it harboured any similar oddities of the female kind.

He took work, with a couple of other men, digging a long irrigation ditch near the town arising at the Highwood River crossing. The hours were long and the labour hard, but it at least relieved the stiffness in his large frame, put there by long hours in the saddle. He also discovered that he felt lonesome not being around Duffy, so he rode out to the Bar U from time to time for a visit, and Duffy would come to the crossing. They found a comfort in each other's company that was not available in other men.

Astonished, John watched, with the knowledge that his decision to stay in Alberta was the correct one, as herd after herd poured into the country. By summer's end, there were more than twenty thousand cattle in the district. The word was that many more herds were expected. It seemed he was not the only one bent on making these prairies and foothills home.

He stayed away from the budding town and also from Calgary, saving his pay. He returned to the Bar U in the fall, rejoining Duffy, who was happier than anybody with his return. There were friendly nods from the other ranch hands who knew him, even a "good to see you back" from one man. Fred Stimson showed his pleasure by making good on his promise of a raise.

ELEVEN

Some things are worth holdin' on to in a man's memory.

The Bar U Ranch had fallen into a predictable rhythm of work—buildings rising from the earth, corrals and fences built. In the fall, the crew gathered hay for winter feed and moved the herd to a closer pasture. During the winter, hay had to be taken to it and ice broken in the ponds so that the animals would have water to drink. It could be rough work when it was forty below, and only those with hardier dispositions stayed on. In the spring, the roundup began again, the cycle repeated itself, and another year passed.

During the summer of 1884, John took some time away from the ranch and went with Duffy and a couple of friends to look for gold. There were rumours of a lost mine somewhere in the foothills, and John and the others were no different from prospectors the world over: they set off in search of a lost treasure, believing they could find it. But after a summer of traipsing up and down creeks and rivers, they had to admit defeat. It was not a complete waste of time for John, though. The foothills became lovelier as they rose into mountains, and Alberta impressed itself even deeper on his mind. It became part of him as he had become part of it.

After his return from prospecting, he rode into Calgary to make a homestead claim. While ranchers used thousands of acres of land for grazing their cattle, they leased it from the government and did not own it. The railroad from the east to the west coast was near completion, and the government was encouraging settlers to the North-West Territory by offering homestead rights on rangeland. Most of the ranchers opposed this, but their complaints went unheeded. John paid ten dollars and claimed a homestead west of the Highwood River crossing.

He left the government office not feeling anywhere near as buoyant as he should have. The frigid reception he had received from the clerk disturbed him, as did the cold stares and snide comments made by passersby. The atmosphere made him shiver. He discovered what was going on from a man who stopped and warned him that he would do well to get his "black hide" out of town without delay. It was not welcome in Calgary and could be downright dangerous for the man wearing it.

"Why's that?" asked John. "I ain't been in town long enough to have offended anyone."

"It's not so much you, personally," the tobacco-chewing stranger sneered. "It's your kind."

"My kind? What'd my kind ever do to you?"

"Your kind are heartless, murdering devils. Your kind took a good man from us, slit his throat wide open over at McKelvie's store. We just hung him for it. Our first nigger hanging, and with any luck at all, the last one."

The news and the vitriolic nature of the encounter stunned John. At the crossing and at Fort McLeod, where the spring roundups began, the townsfolk and his fellow cowboys treated him with respect and in some cases showed deference because of his enviable skills. But the only thing Calgarians noticed when he entered their town was his black skin. To them, it was no different from the one they'd strung up for murder, a hanging that must have taken place while he was roaming the foothills, because this was the first he'd heard of it.

Wanting to avoid trouble, he did not linger in town. But he wondered about the killing. Was the black man the real culprit? Because this was not the South, he supposed there must have been witnesses. Perhaps it was a violent reaction by a man fed up with others denying him the right to buy food for his table. Granted, that was no cause to take another human being's life, but if it was the last insult heaped on an ever-growing pile . . . Some men might snap under the onerous weight.

He told Duffy about his experience and his concerns, but his friend was optimistic. "I wouldn't take it too much to heart, John. Word'll eventually spread up there about the kind of man you are and life'll get better. Wait and see."

"The only way it'll get worse is if they lynch me for somethin' I didn't do."

"That ain't gonna happen. There's law and order in this country."

"Well, from what I heard up in Calgary, the law is pretty quick to order a hangin'."

John chose a good building site on his claim, about a half mile back from the river, and he and Duffy cut several poplar trees upstream, trimmed them, lashed them together into a raft, and poled them to where they could be hauled to the site with a horse. They had four tiers of logs up when Fred Stimson sent word that he would appreciate their presence back at the Bar U for the fall roundup and work over the winter. It meant more dollars saved toward his ranching future, so John accepted, as did Duffy.

The roundup and winter passed uneventfully, but spring ambled in bringing trouble. In late March, near the tiny village of Duck Lake, some five hundred miles to the northeast, a skirmish between half-breeds and the police left a dozen men dead. It did not come as a surprise. Word of a possible uprising along the North and South Saskatchewan Rivers had been in the rumour mills for some time. Then Cree Indians, members of Big Bear's band, massacred nine civilians at Frog Lake, which was a bit closer to home, and the entire territory was on alert. Government soldiers were on their way from the east, while a local rancher mustered a force in Calgary.

John considered enlisting but Stimson advised against it. He did not think it prudent for all the able-bodied men in the area to be absent. Several horses had been stolen and cattle killed recently, the meat cut away cleanly with knives rather than torn out as a predatory animal would do, raising concerns that the local Indians could not be trusted. To deal with these problems, Stimson organized John and several others into a militia referred to as Stimson's Rangers. Members received government rifles, and their job, in addition to ranching duties, was to patrol the area and keep it clear of Indians. Meanwhile, all the women in the area sought the safety of the mounted police fort in Calgary.

John patrolled but never ran into any real trouble. Whenever he or the authorities thought Indians were within threatening distance of the cattle, he ordered them to move on, back to their reserves. When one small band refused, John offered encouragement by throwing his lasso over the top of their teepee and pulling it down. He dragged it off a hundred yards in the direction he wanted them to go. Sullen and angry, the band moved on.

The need for such tactics was rare. John's presence usually provided the incentive for the Indians to obey. His size and black skin were mysterious to them, and they believed he might have special powers. Anyone who was not an Indian was by default a white man, so they called him the "bad black white man." John could not have cared less what they called him. He did not think much of the Indians, especially the men, whom he considered lazy, spending most of their time sitting around talking while the women did all the work.

Meanwhile, battles between government soldiers and the half-breeds and Indians flared up along the North and South Saskatchewan Rivers, but by May, the rebellion was over, with government forces victorious. Life in the territory eased back to normal, and John and Duffy rode to Fort McLeod to join the spring roundup.

The first thing John did when they arrived was visit the government office and register the brand "9999" as his own. He liked the number 9, the way it curved in on itself like a contained stampede. It would be his lucky number, four times over, and it would soon be on his own cattle. Most likely because he was the first black man to register a brand, the agent asked, "How many cattle do you have?"

John did not like the agent's tone of voice and detected a hint of suspicion and malice in the question. "None," he replied, "but I aim to fix that directly." He caught the man's eyes. "And I ain't stealin' 'em, either, if that's what you're thinkin'."

The agent looked chagrined and said nothing.

Fort McLeod was spilling over with drovers, most of them down from the several ranches on the southern ranges below Calgary. John reckoned there must have been a hundred riders, fifteen wagons, and five hundred horses that set out on that first day. They would spread out between Pincher Creek in the west and Willow Creek in the east, and head north, like a vast net, gathering in the cattle that had drifted south, separating the brands into herds for the owners to return to their home range. Mavericks were considered property of the group, or "association," and could be sold to help defray expenses.

Such was John's popularity on the drive that the Fort McLeod newspaper ran a story on him, lauding his outstanding skills as a cattleman and rider. Duffy bought a copy and read the full article to him. John was flattered by the accolades and pleased that there was not a single mention of his skin colour. It made him think of the bitter reception he had received in Calgary, and he grew determined to return there in hopes of changing a few minds.

After the roundup, John bought nine young mavericks from the association. He and Duffy branded them and headed for his claim near the Highwood. Even if it was a small herd, it was *his*, with *his* brand, and he was driving it to *his* ranch. He would have been fooling himself to say he did not feel proud.

Duffy, on the other hand, was quieter and less talkative than usual. Up until the morning they struck out on their own, he had shared John's enthusiasm, but now he seemed gathered within himself. John recognized this as a sign that his friend was holding something back.

"Somethin' botherin' you?" he asked.

"Nothin' that's worth talkin' about." But a few moments later, Duffy added, "I still got all the body parts I was born with, but I gotta admit that some of 'em are feeling a little the worse for wear these days. Been thinkin' that maybe I've ridden my last roundup. Not even sure about the work anymore. Maybe Fred'll take me on as a cook or somethin'."

John was concerned. "No need to worry about that, Duff. We'll get the cabin built and you can take it easy there. Put your feet up. You earned it."

"Well, I got a little cash put aside, so I could pay you some."

"Pay me for what? You don't eat more than a bird, and it'll be good to have someone to keep an eye on the property when I'm away. I oughta pay you, and I will when I get the money. And if you wanna turn your hand to cookin', you won't hear me complain. I ate your cookin' before and it ain't killed me."

Duffy was silent for a bit. "Can't say I feel good about eatin' from another man's plate, but I guess I could earn it."

"Since when do partners get bothered about whose plate they're eatin' from? Besides, it ain't nothin' you wouldn't do for me, so it don't make much sense to waste good breath talkin' about it." John spurred his horse to the other side of the small herd so Duffy could not argue. He heard him mutter something but ignored it.

Upon reaching the Highwood crossing, John bought a tarp and supplies, and at the homestead, the friends set up a lean-to as sleeping quarters. They got a fire going and John cooked some bacon and beans. He ended up eating most of it, as Duffy claimed that his appetite was "takin' the evenin' off."

The following day dawned bright and sunny, with mosquitoes already swarming. When John asked, Duffy said that he was feeling better and that a little hard work would do him good. He even ate breakfast, observing, "It musta been somethin' passin' through me, I guess."

The first thing that needed doing was to collect more trees, so they rode upstream about a mile to where there were several stands of large poplars. In order to avoid getting in each other's way, they worked in different stands.

John liked this kind of physical activity, swinging the axe, getting into a smooth rhythm, relishing the thud of the blade slicing into the tree that sent tremors up his arms, seeing the chips fly. Sweat poured off him, which held the mosquitoes at bay but attracted pesky flies and other insects looking for a drink. Still, it was easy to forget the surrounding world at such times, and he failed to notice that Duffy was not making a similar sound. When it finally penetrated his mind, he looked over at the copse where his friend was working and was startled to see him leaning against a tree, doubled over, clutching his stomach.

"You okay, Duff?" he called.

Duffy answered with a series of moans and dropped to his knees.

John flung his axe aside and ran over.

"Goddamned pain in my gut," Duffy gasped. "A real son of a bitch!"

"What can I do?" John asked, more concerned than he let on.

"Let me rest a bit. I'll be right soon enough."

Duffy lay on the ground, still clutching his midriff, trying to suppress his moans. John knelt beside him and laid his hand on his friend's arm, hoping it would provide at least a modicum of comfort. He waited anxiously for what seemed an eternity before Duffy began to breathe more easily. "Seems to have let up," he said grumpily. "Whatever the hell it was."

"Maybe you shouldn't be swingin' that axe for a while's what I'm thinkin'."

"I ain't settin' on my arse while you do all the work, and there's a fact you can chew on."

With some effort, Duffy rose, grabbed his axe, and went back to work. Before long, the pain had him doubled over again. "Get the horses, John," he croaked. "I think I oughta see a doc."

"Nearest doc's in Calgary."

"Too far. There's a vet at the crossing. Maybe he's got somethin' that'll kill this pain before it kills me."

John retrieved the horses and helped Duffy into the saddle. He seemed to teeter for a few seconds before mustering enough strength to catch himself.

"Okay?" John asked.

Duffy nodded. "If we take it slow, I'll be all right. If I die, this saddle's as good a place as any." He managed a half-smile.

"Don't you even think of quittin' on me, partner. I won't abide it. You hang onto the horn and let me take the reins."

"Ain't nobody takin' these reins. Not even you."

John mounted his horse and the pair set off at a walk downriver. Anything faster and Duffy's pain worsened. At this pace, they were a good hour and a quarter from the crossing, and John worried that his friend might not make it. They rode in silence, the only noises Duffy's laboured breathing, the quiet thud of horse hooves on the soft ground, the creaking of leather, the animals snorting at the mosquitoes and flies, and the wind that arose from time to time to blow the insects away. John never took his eyes off Duffy, who seemed to be holding his own. Suddenly, Duffy cried, "Oh, shit! Shit!" He leaned onto his horse's neck and fell from the saddle, hitting the ground with a cry of pain that made John shudder. He leaped down from his horse and rushed to Duffy, who was now curled into a fetal position.

"I can't sit the horse no more, John," he panted. "Pain's way too bad. Better fetch the vet and a wagon."

John hated to leave Duffy alone, fearing what he might find upon his return, but saw no other option. He got Duffy's water canteen and left it by his side, then flew into the saddle and urged his horse to a full gallop. He didn't slow until he reached the crossing and went immediately to the vet's house on the far side of the community, praying the man was at home. John breathed a sigh of relief when the vet himself answered the door. Quick to respond to his visitor's plea, the doctor grabbed his medical bag and some blankets. Hurrying outside, he and John hitched up a wagon, linked John's horse to it, and drove off at a reckless pace.

Duffy had not moved. He was delirious, saying incomprehensible things. Dried tears streaked his face. John could only imagine the pain his friend was suffering, enough to make him cry, a thing that would have to remain unspoken between them. Duffy had also unbuttoned his pants to relieve the pressure on his stomach. His eyes were glassy, but John thought his friend recognized him. He took Duffy's hand—it felt hot and dry. "You

166

go easy, brother, you hear? Doc's brought somethin' to ease the pain. You'll be fit in no time."

The vet placed his hand on Duffy's abdomen and felt around, applying moderate pressure. "He's badly bloated." He felt Duffy's forehead. "He's burning up, too. It could be anything, but my guess is it's typhlitis or maybe his appendix. I've heard of them bursting, causing the level of pain he's experiencing. We'd better get him to Doc Hanson in Calgary. Soak one of those blankets in the river and we'll cool him down a little on the way. I'll give him a dose of laudanum for the pain."

John grabbed a blanket, ran to the river, and brought it back dripping wet. He and the vet made Duffy as comfortable as possible on the dry blankets in the back of the wagon and laid the wet one over him. He tied Duffy's horse to the wagon and they set out on the thirty-mile journey, John driving and the vet administering to Duffy as best he could. The hard-baked ground seemed to be inching by when the vet startled him by tapping his shoulder. "Your friend has slipped into unconsciousness, John, but he's still on fire. You can fly now. He won't feel a thing."

John looked back and his heart lurched to see how pale Duffy's usually ruddy face was. He shook the reins and the horses broke into a fast trot, travelling as fast as the terrain would allow. Once they reached the road to Calgary, John whipped the horses into a gallop, but it was two hours before the town appeared on the horizon. Twenty minutes later, they arrived at the doctor's office, which occupied the front room of his house. John jumped down from the driver's seat, intending to carry Duffy in by himself because it would be quicker. But the look on the vet's face brought him up short.

"I'm sorry," he said, the words laden with sincerity. "Your friend's gone. There was nothing I could do for him."

Most of the crew at the Bar U who did not have duties to keep them away attended Duffy's funeral, including Fred Stimson. Low scudding clouds and rain made the sombre affair even drearier. Stimson said a few words over the grave, as did John.

He stood and held his hat over his heart. He wished he had the skills to write a fine speech that the men here would talk about whenever Duffy's name was mentioned. But all he had were the words on the tip of his tongue. "Some things are worth holdin' on to in a man's memory and Duffy's one of them. I rode with him for eight years and he was straight up all the time, as good a friend and brother as a body could want. We talked some about God and Heaven and Hell, and Duffy didn't believe in any of that. He said he was taught to believe in them, but after seein' what slave owners got away with and his bein' in the war and all, he come to believe all those things were nothin' but 'silly-ass ideas.' So I don't know where Duffy's gone, but I can tell you this much. It's a big hole that's been tore in this world with him gone. In me, too, I gotta say."

That was all that came out, none of it expressing the true depth of the sorrow he felt.

TWELVE

Go home, child.

John lost his motivation to work on the cabin. He missed his friend, which made him think too much of another lost companion—Emmett. For a black man, white friends were hard to come by, and he had had two of the best. Now they were both gone and he was still here, with a dozen acquaintances and no one to call a real friend. On the bright side, ever since the Fort McLeod newspaper had run that glowing article on him and his skills as a horseman, no one referred to him as "Nigger" John Ware anymore, at least not that he was aware of. It was now just plain John Ware, because everyone knew who he was.

Wanting a change of scenery that wouldn't remind him of Duffy, he left his cattle to mingle with the Bar U herds and set off for Calgary to look for work. His spirits were down around his spurs, but at least he had hopes of finding a job: Fred Stimson had put in a good word for him at the I.G. Baker Company.

Along the way, he passed the headquarters of the Quorn Ranch, on the banks of the Sheep River, and stopped in, knowing he'd be fed lunch. Owned by English aristocrats, the Quorn took its name from a town in Leicestershire renowned for its fox hunting. It was being set up as both a cattle ranch and a breeding ranch for thoroughbred studs and native mares, to provide the British cavalry with sturdy mounts. He met the manager, a larger-than-life, pleasant-faced, grey-goateed Irishman named

John J. Barter, called "J.J." by those who knew him. The pair had never met but had heard of each other. Indeed, Barter offered John a job on the spot, but John was keen to pursue work in Calgary. He needed something different for a while.

"Well," said Barter, "when the frantic pace of city life starts wearin' thin, there'll be a job waitin' for ye here if ye're interested. About lunch then. Surely ye wouldn't be declinin' that now, would ye?"

Later that afternoon, John reached Calgary and liveried his horse. He hadn't expected the townsfolk to greet him with open arms, but it seemed that a year had not been long enough to stop the frigid stares and equally frigid treatment. Yet he was determined not to leave unless it proved impossible to find work, and he planned to devote every ounce of his energy to that task. He went straight to I.G. Baker, a mercantile and grocery outfit on the southeast corner of McTavish and Centre. John guessed that Stimson had neglected to mention his skin colour, because the manager was clearly not comfortable with a black man on the premises.

"There's nothing for you in the store," he told John, "but Fred Stimson is a good man and wouldn't steer me wrong, so I can offer you work in the warehouse."

John got the picture. The man might as well have added, "Where our customers can't see you." He felt insulted, but at the same time knew that he probably would not get as good an offer anywhere else. He accepted.

Almost every item that came off the trains and onto the wagons destined for the I.G. Baker warehouse was awkward or heavy, sometimes both. Indeed, John only got the job because the man he replaced had hurt his back. Kegs of nails, bags of flour, wooden containers of sweets, the list went on and on, each piece having its way of raising calluses on top of calluses on a man's hands and moulding his back into the shape of a bent nail. It did not require brains or any of the skill and knowledge necessary to work with horses and cattle, but it was work a man could throw himself into and drown in a river of sweat.

For the rest of the summer, John worked alongside a white man with little to say to a black man; he eventually fell victim to the hard work and left with a strained Achilles tendon. A drunk replaced him, but as winter approached, the new man decided that he would much rather spend it indoors, preferably in a bar. The latest hire was a young man who had stopped off to winter in Calgary before heading to his home in Victoria. He was sandy haired and handsome, with a scar across his right cheek. A strapping lad, he was ideally suited for the heavy work of loading and unloading the wagons, and never shied away from it. John liked that about his new partner and enjoyed working with him. His name was Jack Strong and, among other things, he said he had been at Frog Lake during the massacre and that he had ridden alongside Sam Steele, of the North West Mounted Police, during the hunt for the Cree Chief Big Bear. He said he received the scar on his cheek from a bullet during the Battle of Loon Lake. John had no reason to disbelieve him, for he was not a braggart and his stories rang with authenticity.

As time passed, John noticed that whenever the new employee hired for inside the store was away, management always asked John's partner to replace him, never John himself. He knew why but kept silent about it. Jack was onto it right away, though, and mentioned it one day. John laughed derisively and told him about not getting that job in the first place because of his colour.

Jack shook his head. "What a bunch of fools, but I guess it's their loss, not yours." Later, after thinking about it, he said, "You know, the next time they ask me to work in the store, why don't I tell them I can't and that they ought to ask you?"

"You don't wanna do that, Jack. It'll only get you in a mess of trouble and it ain't worth it, not if you plan on workin' in this town over the winter."

Jack look frustrated. "If I've learned anything in the past year or so, it's that the colour of a man's skin is not where you begin making judgments about him."

"Well, that don't appear to be the case here, Jack. Be nice if it was, but you better let me handle this my own way. It'll be best for both of us."

—⚬—

When John arrived in town, he had taken a small room above the Turf Club, a lofty name for a rather seedy establishment that sat unobtrusively on the west side of McTavish Street, catty-corner from the I.G. Baker store. It had four rental rooms upstairs, two of which had full-time occupants. The club let the two other rooms by the hour over the winter months when business was slow. A set of stairs inside the saloon led to the rooms, as well as stairs outside in the alley behind the club. This was how a man paying to use a room for his carnal pleasures got a prostitute up there without putting himself on display. These men were generally rough-hewn and whisky-sodden, and the women were Indian prostitutes who worked the streets. Such a place had no reservations about accepting steady income from a black man.

As it turned out, Jack Strong knew the other full-time tenant at the Turf Club: Tom Fisk, a tall, lanky man whose movements seemed uncoordinated, as if he were about trip over himself, a trait that had earned him the nickname "Jumbo." He was an easy man to like when he was sober. Good-natured and humorous, he would remain that way through his first few drinks. After that, he often became maudlin and was prone to complaining, and could go from that to mean-minded in the tossing back of a single drink. He had grown up in central Canada, where he trained as a blacksmith, but when he first came west in 1882, he was involved in the illegal whisky trade that plagued Alberta. He used his illicit gains to buy and train racehorses. This was inspired in part by a love for the animals but mostly by a passion for gambling. He made enough money to build the Turf Club but drank and gambled it away, so now he was a patron and tenant.

He had volunteered for Steele's Scouts during the rebellion for two reasons: he hoped it would get him off the booze and that it would provide him with an opportunity to kill an Indian. Instead, he became even more of a drunkard and an Indian had almost killed him. His left little finger had been shot off on the trail to Loon Lake and he did not have full movement in his left elbow, where the same bullet had shattered the bone. Jack had ridden with Fisk that day and remembered how angry he had been when Steele sent him home with his goal unfulfilled.

The result was that Jumbo had no sympathy for "redskins," as he called them. His brush with death had both scared him witless and angered him. He claimed to have recurring nightmares over it, and that was why he drank. Yet despite his professed loathing for Indians, from time to time John saw him bring an Indian prostitute up the back stairs to his room.

———

December passed and along with it Christmas, which went unobserved by John. He walked through the city often, trying to knit it into his bones, thinking that people would get used to seeing him and realize he meant no one any harm. He kept to the boardwalks where they existed, but otherwise followed the trampled-down tracks of horse-drawn sleighs plying the snowbound streets. He found the excursions pleasant, despite the occasional racist comment. He would usually smile and continue on his way.

One evening as he was nearing the train station, he saw three Indian women wrapped in blankets and scarves to protect them from the weather. They were just standing on the corner and would not have been there braving the cold if they were not prostitutes. John planned to ignore them, as the town authorities did, and walk on by, but he could not fail to notice that one was a young girl about fifteen or sixteen. Her beautiful brown eyes caught John's and she stepped forward.

"You want to spend some time with me?" she asked, coyly.

John's heart caught in his throat. She was very pretty, on the verge of womanhood, and there was a desperate shortage of women in his life. It was one thing to be on a ranch surrounded by men and quite another to be in a city where a multitude of women served as a daily reminder that he had none in his life. Part of him wanted to take this girl back to his room to satisfy the lust that arose in him at times, but he felt sorry for her. She was nothing like the prostitutes he had met in Dodge City or Virginia City, most of whom worked the trade because they chose to and were wise to the ways of the world. He suspected that this young girl was selling herself because she had to help feed her family. He shook his head and continued on his way. Several paces past them, he stopped and turned back. He gave the girl two dollars.

"Go home, child," he said.

She didn't, of course, and whenever John encountered her, he gave her a dollar or two. She always took the money and thanked him, sometimes followed by a diffident, "I go with you?" But she never looked him in the eye again. Life on the street seemed to be sucking out whatever pride she owned. John wondered if he was doing more harm than good by giving her money and considered stopping when he began to smell liquor on her breath. But he figured that drinking might be the only way she could deal with the course her life had taken.

Returning to his room one evening after a walk, he saw Jumbo Fisk leading the young Indian girl up the back stairs. He entertained thoughts of rescuing her but did nothing. It did not seem to be within his power, and he had to consider the possibility that the girl did not want rescuing.

John stewed in his room for about an hour. At one point, he swore he heard a commotion coming from Jumbo's room. Then he heard the door open and close, followed by footsteps along the hall to the stairs leading to the bar. It had to be Fisk; the girl would have left using the stairs to the alley. A few minutes later, footsteps came up the stairs, accompanied by the voices of two men, one distinctly Jumbo's, the other unrecognizable.

He heard the door to Fisk's room open, more voices, and the door closed. The voice he could not identify said, "Let's go get something to eat." The footsteps retreated down the stairs to the bar.

What was going on? John reckoned that perhaps the girl had passed out from too much liquor and Fisk would come back after he had filled his belly and take her again. John decided he would not let that happen. He would get the girl, and if she was awake, give her some money and try to talk her into leaving. If she was unconscious, he would bring her back to his room and when she was sober enough, he would give her money and she could go home. He fretted over the decision for a long time before making up his mind. He cracked open his door and peered down the lamp-lit hall.

Fisk's room was on the side opposite to John's, two doors down. He went quickly along the hall and knocked on the door. There was no answer. He put his ear to one of the panels but heard nothing. He tried the knob. The door was unlocked, which was not surprising, as few people in town ever locked their doors; indeed, most doors were not equipped with locks. He pushed it open and a shaft of yellow light from the hallway made a path into the room. He stood in the entrance, letting his eyes grow accustomed to the gloom. He could make out a figure on a bed to his left, its feet pointing toward the headboard. He was certain it was the girl; her torso appeared to be naked. The idea that he should mind his own business nagged at him, but he cast caution aside. To hell with it, he thought. Fisk would never guess that John had taken her. He would think she had got up on her own and left. He took a few tentative steps into the room.

The fire had gone out in the stove and the room was cool. The air reeked of alcohol and something else. That was when he saw the black blotches all over the girl's face, chest, and stomach, and on the bed. He could even see some on the wall. He knew it was blood. His heart raced. He hurried to her side and recoiled in horror. Some of her insides had been ripped out and her once-pretty face was grossly disfigured, possibly by somebody's fists. John wanted to vomit. His mind was a whirlpool of thoughts, mostly about the stark truth that he was a black man in a room with a dead girl. If someone came up the stairs and found him, he was certain to be the next black man hanged in Calgary. He had to resist an almost overwhelming desire to run, shut the door behind him, pretend he'd never seen anything, and let Jumbo deal with it. He pulled some matches from his pocket and struck one. Water in the basin on the washstand against the opposite wall was dark with blood and a knife lay next to it. On the wall, in between the bed and the washstand, as if a drunken man had lost his balance, was a perfect handprint formed in blood. It did not take any great detective to see that it was missing a little finger.

John left, stopping in his room only long enough to pull on a coat, and ran to get the police before they came to get him. He fretted the entire distance that he would be the chief suspect, no matter what he said. The police had come to the warehouse several times to question him about a theft or some other unsolved crime, and since they never spoke to Jack, he saw these visits as harassment, more than any belief on the part of the police that he was guilty of the crimes. Despite the prejudice he knew he would face, he was compelled to report the crime.

But when he reached the police station, Fisk had just turned himself in, accompanied by a lawyer. The fear squeezing John's chest loosened and breathing became easier. An officer took his story, told him not to leave town as he would be summoned as a witness, and allowed him to go.

He did not want to return to the Turf Club, so he checked the two hotels that were affordable. It seemed neither had vacancies, but John wondered if it were true. With no other option, he went back to the Turf Club.

During the three weeks it took to bring the case to trial, John felt unsettled. He wanted to leave Calgary and never return. Living mere steps down the hall from a grisly murder scene didn't help. He felt badly for the girl, too. The night before the trial, he did not sleep a wink. He feared that Fisk was going to walk away from the crime unpunished. A surprising number of people in town supported the man and, according to Jack, who read the accounts to John, the Calgary *Tribune* reported that Fisk was "a good-natured citizen who wouldn't hurt a feather." On the other hand, the Indian girl, whose name was Rosalie New Grass, was "a dissolute young squaw." What chance, John wondered, did an immoral Indian have against a harmless, upstanding white citizen? About the same, he supposed, as a coloured person.

Half the town wanted to attend the trial, and since the courthouse was too small to accommodate everyone, there was talk of relocating to a larger hall a couple of blocks away. But the presiding judge, Charles Rouleau, decided against it, stating that he didn't need that many people in his courtroom.

The proceedings got under way promptly at 11:00 AM on a

Thursday. As expected, the courtroom was packed. Once the jury was polled, Jumbo came in, escorted by a police constable. There was an attitude about him that bordered on arrogance, as if the court were wasting his time. While the clerk read the charges against him, he turned his head away, seemingly unconcerned. He pleaded not guilty.

The first person to take the witness stand was the doctor who had examined Rosalie's body. After going over the cause of death and the state of the body, the district counsel asked, "In your opinion, Doctor, did this young girl suffer before she found relief in death?"

"She must have suffered greatly," the doctor replied. "In fact, I would say that she suffered excruciating pain, enough to make her bite completely through her lower lip."

There was a gasp from the crowd.

"Have you, in your experience, ever seen the likes of such a heinous crime?"

"No, sir. The amount of fiendish brutality evident in the mutilation of the victim makes Jack the Ripper seem mild by comparison."

Neither the *Tribune* nor the *Herald*, Calgary's other newspaper, had reported Rosalie's mutilation, and the information set the crowd buzzing. Rouleau quelled it with his gavel.

John took the stand next and told of hearing what he believed was a commotion coming from Fisk's room, Fisk's departure, and subsequent return with another man, the one who had said, "Let's go get something to eat." He explained his reasons for going to Fisk's room, describing his discovery of the girl's body and the handprint. As he spoke, the only sound in the stale air of the courtroom was the frantic scratching of reporters' pencils on paper.

"And was there anything unique about that handprint?" counsel asked.

"Yes, sir. It was a left hand and it was missin' the little finger."

Rouleau directed Jumbo to hold up his left hand. The missing finger drew murmurs from the crowd that the judge silenced with a stern look.

After a short lunch break, the clerk swore in the investigating officer, John Ingram. He gave a detailed account of the crime scene, including the bloody handprint on the wall. Then the owner of the restaurant that Jumbo had gone to after the murder testified that he had served him a full course meal and that Jumbo had left nothing on his plate.

The following morning, the defence counsel did everything in his power to paint his client in a different light. A doctor testified that the murder was an act of insanity: Fisk, by dint of too much alcohol, was temporarily insane when he committed the crime and therefore he was not guilty. Two other witnesses testified as to his good character, as did the man who had accompanied Jumbo to the restaurant. When asked why he did not go to the police, he replied, "Because I knew that Jumbo would."

Taking the stand, Jumbo said that alcohol had fogged his brain and he did not remember much about that night. Nevertheless, he did recall that Rosalie had attacked him with a knife when he refused to pay after she demanded too much money. As he was trying to disarm her, he had lost his head. He had no recollection of harming anybody. Given the tone of his voice, he might as well have added, "And if I did, so what? She was only a redskin."

At the first opportunity, district counsel stood and asked Jumbo if he had received any knife wounds.

"No, sir."

"The deceased measured five feet two inches in height and weighed around one hundred pounds. What is your height and weight, sir?"

"I stand six feet four inches and weigh about two hundred and twenty pounds."

Another rap of the magistrate's gavel ended more rumbling from the crowd.

Counsel continued. "Now, Mr. Fisk, after you beat this young girl, after you disembowelled her, after you committed these vicious, bloody acts, you washed up and went out with a friend for something to eat. Do you remember that part?"

Jumbo bristled. "Yes, sir."

"So let me see if I have the sequence of events straight. Liquor causes you to lose your sense of reality, the loss of reality brings on violence, and the violence makes you hungry, which in turn revives your sense of reality. Is that how it works?"

"No, sir!" Jumbo looked ready to jump from the witness chair and throttle the lawyer.

"No further questioning." The prosecutor sat down.

During the afternoon session, both counsels summed up their cases for the members of the jury, after which a court official escorted the nine men to the magistrate's chambers and locked them in. Nobody left the courtroom, expecting that it would not be a long wait for a verdict. However, the remainder of the afternoon passed, as did the supper hour, and nothing came. Rouleau sent everybody home.

Early the following morning, John received a message that the jury had reached a decision and court would reconvene at 10:00 AM. He was at the courtroom well before ten, as were many others anxious to hear the outcome. John listened to those around him and the prevailing assumption was that a guilty verdict was a foregone conclusion. They wondered why it had taken so long to reach the verdict, and there was speculation that perhaps some jurors had bought the insanity defence and the others had needed time to convince them of Jumbo's guilt. The proceedings got under way precisely on time, and everyone rose as Rouleau took his seat on the bench. Jumbo was brought in, followed by the jury.

The Clerk of the Court stood and addressed the jury in a sonorous voice. "Gentlemen of the jury, are you agreed on your verdict?"

The foreman, a man John had seen regularly about town and one who had always turned a cold shoulder to him, arose and said, "We are."

The clerk's voice boomed across the room. "How say you? Is the prisoner guilty or not guilty?"

"Not guilty."

A tidal bore of voices rose to fill the courtroom, interspersed with cries of protest and a few shouts of jubilation, until Rouleau beat the room into silence with his gavel. Jumbo was smiling, but the magistrate looked shocked. John's heart sank.

"Gentlemen," the judge said to the jury, unable to contain his anger, "you have failed in your duty to this court. As such, this court cannot and will not accept your verdict. I direct you back to my chambers to reconsider the evidence presented to you by counsel."

He rapped his gavel and the jury filed once more from the courtroom. One hour later, they returned. The judge addressed the foreman. "You have had time to reconsider the evidence. I will ask you now if you all still agree with the not guilty verdict."

The foreman looked sheepish. "No, Your Honour. Some disagree."

Rouleau was furious. "The constable will return the prisoner to his cell and this court will call for a new trial." He gave the jury a disdainful look. "You are dismissed!"

John waited for a new trial to testify again. He hoped this time for an outcome more favourable to the court's point of view, and he wasn't alone in his thinking. Now that the details of the murder were out, there was open talk around town of a lynching, and Jumbo was under constant guard. The verdict even angered the *Tribune*'s editor, who wrote, "The idea which seems to possess the minds of some people that because a crime is committed against an Indian, therefore the crime is lessened, is inhumane in the extreme."

The second trial for Jumbo began three weeks later. Charles Rouleau presided again, and counsel had not changed, but a new jury of nine men was sworn in. The proceedings were a mirror image of what had gone before. This time, after the summations, Rouleau instructed the jury members that if they found the prisoner guilty, they must also decide whether it was murder or manslaughter. John reckoned it was a way of providing an option for those jury members who did not want to see Jumbo hanged. They left to deliberate and were back two hours later with a verdict of manslaughter.

John was not at all happy. Jumbo was still getting away with murder as far as he was concerned. The man had always wanted to kill an Indian and he had found an easy victim: a defenceless, intoxicated girl. John sensed that Rouleau was not happy either and had no doubt accepted the verdict because it was the best he could hope for. However, one thing within his power was to impose on Fisk the maximum sentence: fourteen years of hard labour in Stony Mountain Penitentiary, which, according to Jack, was the prison that held Big Bear and other rebellious Indians. That Fisk would have to spend those years within the walls that also confined a race of people he despised offered no small degree of solace.

John was at the train station unloading goods on the day Fisk left for the prison in Manitoba. It was raining and a cold wind gusted out of the north as a democrat wagon carrying Jumbo and his escort splashed up the muddy street. Both sat in the back beneath an awning, Jumbo securely trussed for the journey. A short chain with fetters bound his ankles and a thick leather strap extended up to join manacles on his wrists. The escort, a burly constable, had to help him down from the wagon and he shuffled onto the platform and onto the train. It was one of the few welcome scenes John would remember from his stay in Calgary, thanks to a colour-blind judge who did not let a bigoted jury compromise his sense of justice.

Newspaper stories of the trial had raised John's profile in town—in a positive light, he hoped. He had believed that it would put an end to visits by the police every time they had an unsolved crime, but they came once more, this time about the theft of a horse. He could only shake his head. He ached to be sarcastic and say, "Yes, of course, I stole the horse. It's in my room at the Turf Club. I left the door open for you 'cause I knew you'd be askin'." But such humour was futile and so was arguing, so he answered their questions with a politeness he did not feel. To add another blow, the reception he received during his walks around town had not improved much, although he sometimes elicited a smile and a nod of hello among the baleful stares and the heads turned away. He would have been pleased if the store manager had invited him inside to work, but that never happened. Spring arrived and it was time to say goodbye to Jack and the I.G. Baker Company, and to Calgary. He wondered when he would be able to walk its streets without feeling the strong undercurrent of intolerance for any person whose skin colour was not white. Probably not any time soon.

THIRTEEN

Never heard tell of any servants around here.

Early on a May morning, John was back in a saddle again and well into the rolling hills south of Calgary. Spring had come to the foothills as it does to no other place in the world. The smell of earth free from snow cloaked the breeze spilling out of the west, and colourful wildflowers daubed the slopes. The grass was the very definition of green, and adding to the spectacle was the backdrop of snowcapped peaks. He had decided not to return to the Bar U and to go instead to the Quorn Ranch. In his mind, he had laid Duffy to rest, along with Emmett, and could get on with his life. The Quorn would provide a fresh start.

When he arrived at the ranch, there was not an idle hand as everyone prepared for the roundup, readying wagons and horses and mending harnesses and tack. Many of the buildings were still under construction, predominantly barns, of which Barter had said there would ultimately be five.

"I've plenty of work for ye," the manager said, stroking his grey goatee. "I could use ye on the roundup, but I've got a far better job to offer if ye're interested. Why don't ye stow your bedroll in the bunkhouse and we'll talk about it after supper. Ye won't be disappointed. The bunkhouse is over there." Barter pointed to a long, low building across from the barns. "Grab yerself any free bunk. The washhouse is in behind. Ye'll hear the bell when supper's ready, then follow the stampeding men."

The details that Barter laid out after supper excited John. Five hundred broncos would be arriving soon from the south, all mares. Coming from the east by train to Calgary were a dozen thoroughbred stallions to service them. John's responsibilities were to ensure the stallions had their way with the mares, break those of both genders needed for riding or working, and tend to the animals' needs. In two days, he would return to Calgary to pick up the stallions, along with five hunting dogs that were to be shipped with them. On the same train, straight out from England, would be three relatives of the Quorn's owners, who were coming to experience ranch life in the Canadian west. Barter made a face at the idea of it.

"As if there isn't enough to do around here without catering to a bunch of English noblemen. Probably prigs—arrogant arses if ye catch me drift. I can think of better ways to spend our money, too." He sighed in resignation. "Well, in the meantime, ye can make yerself useful and lend a hand building the barns. Forty a month for ye, John. All I want is yer word that ye'll stick around for a while and not be gone in the mornin' like some Limerick gypsy."

"I ain't goin' nowhere. Leastways, not just yet."

They sealed the agreement with a handshake.

Two days later, as the roosters crowed in the dawn, John was trundling in a buckboard into Calgary to pick up the Quorn's guests, the horses, and the dogs. He was curious about the noblemen but the horses and dogs thrilled him most. As the train pulled into the station, he was not pleased that he had to greet the Englishmen first.

Barter had been right in his sight-unseen assessment of his

187

guests. They were standoffish, their noses as high in the air as a fine stallion's but with less of a reason to be there, John thought. All three wore derby hats above pallid faces, their clothes cut from fine cloth. They looked out of place, but their attitude seemed to indicate it was the place's problem and not theirs. One, a short, stocky man with a square jaw, languid eyes, red-veined cheekbones, and an officious attitude introduced himself as *Mister* Leechman.

"May I present *Lord* and *Earl* Wootton," he said.

It was not a question and he emphasized the titles. Both men were as thin as hitching posts, of medium height, with fair hair and aquiline facial features. John presumed they were brothers, in their early twenties, and saw nothing noble about them. They might have been born into privilege but that did not mean they were men of substance. That was true of plantation owners and he suspected that it was also true of British noblemen. Neither of them offered to shake hands with him, but he stuck his out anyway.

"John Ware." He smiled. "Which of you is Lloyd and which is Earl?"

Leechman blanched. "That's *Lord* Wootton and *Earl* Wootton. *Lord* and *Earl*. They are peerage titles, you must understand, not names."

John's smile widened. "It might be better all the way around to forget those fancy titles here. At least with me, 'cause I ain't ever gonna use 'em anyway. Not likely anyone else will either, so best you tell me your names."

The men looked at John's outstretched hand as if it carried some deadly disease. He could see their discomfort and figured no one had ever spoken to them like that before, particularly a coloured man in wrinkled, dusty clothes, dirty boots, and a Stetson hat. They seemed both aghast and flustered. Leechman puffed himself up.

"You are a servant?"

It sounded more like an accusation than a question.

John shook his head. "Never heard tell of any servants around here, and there sure ain't none where you're goin'. Might as well get used to it."

It might have been John's size that intimidated them, and that he didn't cast his eyes downward; he had not done that for any man since he had been a slave. Or perhaps it was the gun he carried on his belt. Whatever the case, Leechman said nothing further and the brothers remained silent. John wondered if Barter had purposely sent him to greet them as a way of reducing their expectations before they even got to the ranch.

Since their first names were not forthcoming, John let it go. He had horses and dogs to think about. He and Leechman put the luggage in the buckboard, everyone climbed on, and they drove to the unloading ramps for stock.

The stallions were magnificent beasts, seventeen hands if they were an inch, and all as black as anthracite. They were blue bloods who strutted with their heads high and their tails off their rumps, equine royalty who seemed to view the rest of the animal kingdom as mere filler. John had never felt so good about life as he did at that instant. He knew fine horseflesh when he saw it, and these were the very best. To be responsible for them was no less than a privilege. He said to them, as he tied them in two strings behind the wagon, "Ah, the ladies are goin' to love you boys!"

The dogs were fine animals, too, large hounds that whimpered and barked and wagged their tails, and recognized a pack leader when they saw one. The men and the small menagerie set out for the ranch, John and Leechman on the front seat, the Woottons behind on an extra bench seat that had been installed for the occasion. The dogs had stretched out on top of the luggage and the horses trailed behind.

Back at the ranch, John told Barter that the Englishmen had not spoken a word to him on the way down from Calgary, other than to ask where all the buffalo were. "If I was them, I woulda asked a heap more questions, bein' in a new country and all."

Barter laughed. "They didn't know what to make of ye, John. They thought ye were lyin' about not bein' a servant and insisted that I dismiss ye for yer impertinence. I told them I'd do that when those mountains over yonder crumble into dust. They didn't like it, but I think they'll come around. They really don't have much choice. If they don't come to terms with it, their stay'll seem a lot longer than planned."

He put John in charge of selecting horses for the guests. "Gentle is the watchword. Inasmuch as it could be good fun, we don't want to send our guests home with any fractured bones. We'll never hear the end of it."

John culled three mares for the guests, sweet-tempered animals that were unlikely to embarrass their riders. At Barter's request, he saddled and bridled the animals. He also tended to the horses when the men returned from their ride, which was bewildering to John. A rider's responsibility was more than just sitting in the saddle; he ought to look after the horse himself. If he did not know how, he should have someone teach him.

John was prepared to be that teacher, but the visitors were not interested in learning. Even more perplexing were the English flat saddles that they insisted on using. John called these "sweat pads" and considered them an insult to any horse worth riding.

The hounds had been brought to the ranch so that the English visitors, as well as a few neighbours of English stock, could partake in something akin to a traditional fox hunt. The obvious lack of foxes in the area was no deterrent, for there were plenty of coyotes. That their host considered them prey surprised the Englishmen, who held a rather romantic view of the animal sitting on a hilltop howling at the moon. But to ranchers, coyotes were vermin and fair game for any man with a gun. Hunting them down with dogs, if not efficient, might at least prove to be fun.

Barter arranged a hunt for the forthcoming Sunday and invited John along, in case anything went wrong. A dozen men and the five hounds, with Fred Stimson taking the lead, rode out in the morning, heading west into the foothills. The sun radiated intense heat and there was not a breath of wind. Stopping even for a few seconds was enough to bring swarms of mosquitoes down upon the group. The Woottons, whose first names John had learned were Harold and Alfred, seemed bothered the most by them and were not shy about complaining. The rest of the group offered no sympathy.

The visitors sat their horses well enough, when they were not pumping up and down, which struck John as a strange way to ride. The small bit of arrogance that he had knocked out of them the day they arrived had crept back, and they kept trying to take the lead. Stimson told them clearly to stay behind, that he was the leader. The order did not sit well with either of the Woottons, but they grudgingly complied.

Then Stimson spotted a coyote along a creek bank about the same time as the animal heard the group's approach. The dogs saw it and let loose a cacophony of baying and barking. They tore off in pursuit, with the riders on their tails. Harold, ignoring Stimson's order, quirted his horse in an effort to gain the lead. John, with less enthusiasm for this kind of sport, was bringing up the rear. The coyote veered to the left and the dogs and horses followed, as if they were on a line connected to it. The hunting party traversed a rough patch of ground and Harold's horse stumbled. One second he was in the saddle and the next he was tumbling to the ground. Focused on the hunt, the rest of the group did not bother stopping, but John rode over to Harold, who had risen to his feet, and, reaching down, scooped up the Englishman under one arm, like a sack of flour at the I.G. Baker warehouse. John spurred his horse forward, with Harold lying crossways on his lap yelling, "*I say!*"

John grabbed Harold's mount, which had stopped fifty yards ahead, and rode on to rejoin the group. The dogs had brought the coyote down. There were shouts of, "Good sport, good sport!" Harold, whom John deposited on the ground, was happy to be there for the kill, even considering his ignominious arrival. Stimson, who had witnessed the rescue, grinned. "That was the neatest trick I've ever seen, boys. You two ought to be working for Buffalo Bill's Wild West show. Old Bill'd be turning customers away at the gate!"

Everyone laughed, including Harold, although he reddened and looked embarrassed.

The incident turned out to be the best thing that could have happened. Harold's attitude changed the instant John lifted him off the ground. Barter would later say, with his tongue stuck only partially in his cheek, that it was because Harold had a bit of the damsel in him and any damsel in distress appreciated being rescued by a big, strong man. No matter the reason, it transformed the British lord's stuffiness into respect and freed him to start asking questions of John. He even sought John's advice in matters concerning horses, and asked about the long drives from Texas and Idaho. John showed the brothers how to sit a western saddle and even gave them lessons in roping. With Barter's permission, he took them on a tour of the area and showed them an Indian encampment. By the time the brothers had to return to England, they and John had become companions.

On the eve of their departure, Barter held a small soiree in his visitors' honour. People came from the surrounding ranches to join the fun on one of those perfect prairie nights that made people forget the man-eating insects and harsh winters. John even polished his boots with some soot from the bunkhouse stove. Only the noblemen dressed in near-formal attire. Harold wore a Prince Albert coat, a long, well-tailored, doubled-breasted garment that John couldn't tear his eyes from, deeming it the finest article of clothing he had ever seen. He told Harold so.

Harold said, "If I thought for one moment this coat would fit, John, I would give it to you this very instant. But you have my word that upon my arrival in England I shall have my tailor do one up for you." He eyed John up and down. "The largest size, I expect. God knows what use you'll find for it in this amazing country, but you can wear it hunting coyotes if you wish. Whatever the case, you shall own one!"

The gesture caught John off guard and he did not quite know how to respond. When he had gathered his wits, he protested Harold's generosity.

"Not at all," demurred Harold. "If the coat helps atone in some small way for my reprehensible behaviour upon my arrival here, it will make me very happy."

The summer passed and John continued working with the horses. In the fall, more Englishmen arrived for a visit, much to Barter's consternation, and, given their amicable response to John, he reckoned that they had received some coaching from the Woottons. And Harold was as good as his word, for the visitors brought a package. John opened it to find the Prince Albert coat he had been promised. Accompanying it was a note that read, "With appreciation and best wishes, from Harold."

FOURTEEN

Mostly, you just felt powerless.

Despite job offers from other ranchers, as well as from Fred Stimson at the Bar U, John stayed on at the Quorn. He now had more than two dozen of his own cattle, growing fat with the Bar U herds, which would be the genesis of his own ranch one day, but he did not want to leave what he considered to be the best job in the world. Besides, the horses were like family to him.

As the winter of 1886 approached, there were more than a hundred thousand head of cattle on the ranges south of Calgary. The summer had been hot and dry, with less rain as usual, and grass wasn't plentiful. Some of the ranges were suffering from overgrazing, and many ranchers were unable to stock up on feed for the winter. Any hay for sale was going for the outrageous sum of twenty dollars a load. Winter came on, relentless as a tsunami, and shut the door on any chance of a chinook arriving to warm things up. The price of hay rose precipitously to thirty dollars a wagonload. By the time spring rolled around, many thousands of cattle had died, as well as hundreds of deer, antelope, and rabbits, and the animals that survived were starving. The coyotes, wolves, and Indians had a bountiful season, the frozen prairie a larder full of meat for them.

The Quorn's losses were staggering, particularly among its calves, and John lost more than half of his cattle. Most of the ranchers were beginning to have second thoughts about maintaining large herds and were considering diversifying. A man could also make money with horses, which handled the winters much better, as they had the sense to paw down through the snow to find food. Cattle, on the other hand, would stand there and starve to death.

To compound matters, more and more settlers were moving into the area and fencing off good rangeland for their own use. Ranchers were having to drive their cattle around these properties during roundup and were not happy about it. And it didn't help that thousands of sheep had been brought into the area as well, occupying good cattle-grazing land. The air in the district crackled with tension.

Despite the catastrophic winter and tumultuous changes, John was still determined to have a cattle ranch, but now he reasoned that he should supplement it with horses. He also knew that there was not enough grass for hay on his homestead and that he would have to find another place, possibly farther up the Sheep River.

The good news was that he had done his job uniting the thoroughbred stallions with the mares, and in the spring of 1887, the Quorn was fat with foals. Ironically, it sold many of its horses to settlers, the very people encroaching on its grazing land. Barter brought in a hundred good-quality mares from Ireland and a few English thoroughbred stallions to breed them, and the work kept John busy.

That summer Barter asked John if he would help the Bar U out by taking a few hundred of their four-year-old cattle to Calgary for shipment. Barter had several dry cows that he wanted to include, and he and Fred Stimson felt John was the best man to take charge of the drive. John was not keen to return to the town that had pulled its welcome mat out from under him twice, but there was a nice bonus in it for him, which meant an opportunity to increase his stock. Besides, his father had said that a man might try something twice and fail, but the third time was always lucky.

He held the drive to a leisurely pace so that the cattle could eat and not lose weight; even so, the time passed faster than he would have liked because he was not looking forward to the destination. But Stimson had given him a fine crew of five likable young men with good cattle sense and no fear of hard work, and he was pleased with how smoothly the drive went. They arrived on the outskirts of Calgary around noon on the fourth day and set up camp. The next day, they got half of the herd on the train and penned the other half for shipment the following day. Once the work was complete, John asked the crew, "What'll it be, boys, food first or beer?"

Jimmy Vernam, a tough, sinewy youth who had ridden on point with John, spoke for the group. "Food's plenty enough at the ranch. Beer isn't."

They liveried their horses, and the town lay before the young cowboys like a beckoning oasis. For John, it was akin to entering a corral with an unknown bronco. He did not know how it would react, but he was determined to ride it anyway.

Downtown Calgary had changed since his last visit, as several sandstone buildings now stood in places once occupied by wooden structures. These included the Royal Hotel, which had a bar and was the first one they came to.

"This seems as good a place as any to wash out the trail dust," John said, and they went in.

He bought the first two rounds; it was the least he could do for their good work since they were not getting the extra pay that he was. Then he told them, "You're spending your own money now, boys. This well's run dry."

He did not bother trying to keep up with them. He was at least twenty years their senior and knew well how too much beer can make a man feel in the morning when there was still work to do. What's more, like most young men, they talked about and among themselves, and did not include John much in the conversation. He refused to think it had anything to do with his colour, more the difference in their ages. It was fine by him, as he found much of what they were saying nonsensical chatter anyway. He sipped his beer and drifted off into pleasant daydreams of his own cattle ranch, a lovely wife, and several beautiful, energetic children running around the place.

Loud voices interrupted his reverie. At first, he thought they came from his imagined sons, but it was only his crew getting noisy from too many drinks and trying to talk over the general din of the bar. He sensed trouble and suggested that they take a break to eat, and since the Bar U was paying for it, there was a chorus of agreement. The boys downed their beers and went off unsteadily to the piss troughs in a backroom. John waited at the table and when he saw them coming out, joined them at the main door. Sitting nearby, a drunk with an American Southern accent said in a loud, abrasive voice, "Next time you boys oughta leave your nigger servant at home! He don't belong here!"

Jimmy Vernam sneered. "He isn't our servant, mac. He's our boss."

"The boss of what? Didn't know we had a Nigger Town here."

"You mean-mouthed son of a bitch!" Jimmy was about to go for the man when John grabbed him by the arm.

"Whoa, Jimmy, we don't need none of that. Let's go."

John's ire was up too, but he kept it out of his voice, knowing that trouble here would only lead to more trouble later. He motioned with his head for the rest of the crew to follow and steered Jimmy out the door before a melee erupted. He heard the drunk call, "Go back where you come from, nigger boy!"

"Jesus, John," Jimmy said on the street. "You don't have to take that shit. You shoulda let me at him. I'd've taught the bastard a lesson he wouldn't soon forget."

"You let me fight my own battles, Jimmy. The man's too drunk or stupid to learn anythin' and you'd only end up in jail. Come on. Let's get somethin' to eat and head back to camp. We still got work to do come mornin'."

"Goddamned Yankee," burped Jimmy. "*He's* the one who oughta go back where he came from!"

He broke into a chorus of "The Maple Leaf Forever." The rest joined in, except John, who did not know the words and knew he was already making a spectacle of himself simply by being with a bunch of inebriated white cowboys. They walked up McTavish Street toward the café, their boots clattering noisily on the wooden boardwalk in front of the I.G. Baker store, the boys singing lustily. People crossed to the other side of the street to avoid them. Suddenly, a policeman clutching a truncheon burst from the alley that ran along the north end of the store. Moments later, another policeman came running from across the street to join him.

"Okay, boys," one of them said, "you want to sing, we've got the perfect stage for you, and you won't be disturbing the peace like you are now. You're all under arrest."

"What? You gotta be jokin' us." Jimmy was ready to argue with the constable, but John interrupted.

"Hold on a minute, sir," he said diplomatically. "We're just gettin' somethin' to eat, then we're headin' out of town. I'll see that the boys go quietly. There ain't no need to arrest anybody."

"Nobody's going anywhere, except with us. You're drunk and disorderly and disturbing the peace. Now let's move!"

"I ain't drunk," John said, indignant now. "And I wasn't singin'. I don't even know the words to the damn song!"

"You can tell that to the magistrate. Meanwhile you'll haul your black ass along with us and not give us any grief." Glaring at John, he slapped his truncheon onto the palm of his hand to emphasize his words.

John was outraged. It was one thing to be insulted by an ignorant drunk, yet another when it was a sober policeman. He felt like banging the two constables' heads together to knock some sense into them. But he knew it would be all over the front page of tomorrow's newspaper if he did.

"Lead the way," he said. "We won't give you any trouble." To his crew, he added, "C'mon, boys. We'll get this sorted out at the police station."

But there was nothing to sort out as far as the constables were concerned. They ushered their charges without ceremony straight into a large cell in the basement of the station. Metal benches lined the walls, and the boys, after some complaining and giggling, stretched out on them and went to sleep. John spent a long, sleepless night, gripped once again by the frustration of powerlessness. He wondered why he bothered wasting his time in Calgary. His mind was in turmoil, but Jimmy and the others slept a deep, beer-soaked sleep and awoke before dawn feeling hungover and sheepish.

The first words out of their mouths were apologies to John for landing him in jail, but he did not blame them. In fact, they might very well have been there because of him, but he did not mention that. After a breakfast of weak tea and gruel, they were loaded into a wagon and taken over to the courthouse with a couple of other cowhands who had been jailed on similar charges. Their guard led them through a back door into a holding area in the basement and a bailiff took them upstairs to the courtroom, one at time. John was last.

Magistrate Sidney Pritchard was about John's age and had a face perfect for playing poker or sitting in judgment of others; it was impossible to read. In the gallery with a dozen other spectators were Jimmy and the rest of the crew. Beside them sat Fred Stimson, and John felt a surge of hope that he would have someone to vouch for him if necessary. He reasoned that Jimmy and the others had been fined and released, otherwise they would have been taken back to the lock-up.

Standing before the magistrate, John felt more angry and persecuted than nervous. Pritchard looked down on him from the bench.

"The charge against you, Mr. Ware, is drunk and disorderly. I presume you have a story. Would you be so kind as to share it with the court?"

John struggled to keep his voice at an even pitch. "I wasn't drunk, sir. I only had a little more than two beers, and it takes a lot more than that to get this body drunk. I'd of taken those boys out of town quietly, too, if your constables had let me. That's the full truth of it, because I ain't much for lyin'. That's Mr. Fred Stimson sittin' back there," he said, looking over his shoulder at Stimson, "manager of the Bar U, and I'm sure he'd say a word in my favour if you asked."

"I know Mr. Stimson." Pritchard looked toward the gallery. "Do you know this man, Mr. Stimson?"

The manager stood up and spoke. "I do, sir. He worked for me and he definitely does not have a reputation for drinking or telling lies. He now works at the Quorn for J.J. Barter, who, I'm certain, would vouch for him too. He also has a homestead along the Highwood with a small cattle herd, and there isn't a rancher between here and the Milk River who wouldn't hire him as top hand. And I'd wager that the horse isn't born yet that could throw him." Stimson sat down.

The magistrate looked at John. "Why do you think you were arrested, Mr. Ware?"

John pulled up his sleeves as far as they would go and held his arms out. "Don't know what else it could be but this old black skin."

Pritchard's face remained passive, but John saw something flicker in his eyes. The magistrate banged his gavel and said to the courtroom, "This case is dismissed." To John he added, "I'd like to see you in chambers, Mr. Ware. Would you join me, please?"

Surprised at the request, John went through a door a few paces to the side of the bench, which the magistrate held open for him and shut after he passed through.

Pritchard sat behind a desk and gestured to the chair in front of it. He smiled. "Have a seat." He stroked the neatly trimmed, grey-flecked black beard that framed his angular face, and leaned forward with his elbows on the desk. Light from a side window reflected from his Macassar-oiled hair. "What are your origins, Mr. Ware? Where are you from?"

"South Carolina."

"You were a slave, I take it."

John nodded. "Yes, sir."

"You escaped on the underground railway?"

"No, sir. I left a freedman after the war. Abe Lincoln might of looked kindly on coloured folk, but most of South Carolina didn't care what he thought. None too pleased with it either."

"What brought you to this part of the world?"

John shrugged. "Mostly luck, I reckon."

"You weren't so lucky last night, although I should add that you did the right thing by co-operating. Any other course would have been disastrous for you and quite possibly every other person of colour in town. In any case, you seem certain that it was the colour of your skin that brought you before me."

"Well, as I said, I wasn't drunk and I wasn't disturbin' the peace. I had as much right to be on the street as anybody. And when a man refers to my rear end as a 'black ass,' I figger he don't like my kind too much and would rather haul me off to jail than listen to reason. So I don't know what else it could be." John had to force himself to be polite. "Maybe you got an idea, sir."

Pritchard interlaced his fingers and poked his thumbs into his chin. He puffed his cheeks and blew out some air. "It's patently clear that a white skin has many advantages over a black one here. That's a shameful thing to admit in a place that is so far from what you most likely believed you'd left behind, but there you have it."

John pulled at his nose to ease the dryness in it from the close air in the room. He felt more than a little odd about where he was and who he was talking to, but he refused to speak anything less than his mind. "It's funny. When I first come here, people referred to me as Nigger John Ware. I didn't like it because it made me feel different and less than the white men around me. I knew the only way to change that wasn't by complainin'—it was by hard work. Now all you need to say is John Ware and folks know who you're talkin' about, from the Highwood to Fort McLeod. I don't feel my colour nowhere else except here in Calgary."

Pritchard looked at John as if he were measuring him for a new Prince Albert coat. "You know, I've been doing this job for a few years and I've grown to be a pretty good judge of character. Not only do I recall seeing you unloading supplies at the Baker warehouse, which must be one of the hardest jobs in town, but I know of you from the Fisk trial. My sense is that you are a responsible, hard-working man who started life in the worst possible circumstances but made every effort to rise above them and did. I find that admirable, Mr. Ware. And by the way, you may rest assured that I will speak to the chief of police about the disgraceful behaviour of his officers.

"So for whatever it's worth, please accept my apologies on behalf of the townsfolk. Most particularly for their inability to see past the colour of your skin, when all it indicates is that you had parents of colour, and not what kind of people they were. Nor, for that matter, the kind of son they raised."

"I can't say that I ain't known that all my life," John reflected. "It's somethin' every coloured man knows. Life don't care how he plays his hand. It usually finds a way of stackin' the cards against him and he ain't got the power to do anythin' about it."

Pritchard nodded thoughtfully. "I understand. But you have my word that what happens in the town at large will never happen in any proceeding over which I preside. Insofar as the town is concerned, I believe men of your calibre will bring the necessary change and I will do my utmost to enhance it." He paused. "Now, to move on. I must confess that besides a need to clear the air, I had other motives for inviting you in here. I believe Fred Stimson is also a good judge of character and he seemed convinced that you're among the best horsemen in the district. What makes you so special?"

John gave the question due consideration. "I guess I don't make the mistake that a lot of people make, thinkin' that horses think like men. They don't. They think like horses, and if they can't be boss, they want to know who is. I just let 'em know who's boss, that's all, without bein' mean about it. They respect that."

Pritchard smiled. "Have you ever sat any real ornery ones?"

"Yes, sir. I like the real ornery ones best."

"Tell you what. Perhaps your arrest last night was fortuitous. I've got a real mean one, a gelding with good breeding that could be a moneymaker at the track if I could only get a saddle on him. A few men have tried but all have failed, and breaking horses isn't one of my strengths. There's twenty dollars in it for you if you can let him know his place in the grand scheme of things. Are you interested? What do you say?"

John grinned, pleased with how the meeting had gone and the

sudden turn it had taken. "I say I think you better have twenty dollars ready, sir. But I got some cattle to get on a train first."

Pritchard reached across the desk with his hand outstretched.

"We have a deal then." He gave John directions to his home southeast of the city, across the Elbow River, adding, "Come along when you've finished. It's a short ride and not too far out of your way back to the Quorn. We'll even feed you. Mrs. Pritchard sets a fine table."

Dragon, the gelding, lived up to his name, for he had fire in his eyes and his breath was as hot as a smithy's forge. Even so, he gave John little trouble. Later, Pritchard rode him, and afterwards the two men talked about horses in general before Pritchard said, "You must be hungry."

John waited while Pritchard tended to Dragon, and the two men went into the house, a large, whitewashed, gable-fronted structure with dormers and a bay window looking out onto a wraparound porch. Margaret, the magistrate's wife, was tall and thin with fair hair. To John, her face looked like a feminine version of her husband's. The angles were softened somewhat but the resemblance was quite remarkable. She seemed a serious woman, not very friendly, but keen enough to have company for supper and intrigued that it was a black man. She set the table with beefsteaks and gravy, potatoes mixed with carrots, homemade biscuits, and a pot of coffee. She bade John help himself.

"Don't be shy. You look like a man who can eat more than most."

It had been years since John had sat at a supper table in the presence of a white woman. He had found it an easy thing to do with Ellie Cole, but Mrs. Pritchard was a different matter. She was much more formal and proper, and during the meal she peppered John with many questions about his background, mostly about slavery. He answered the questions as politely as he could, hoping she would soon grow tired of the topic. All it did was dredge up memories that he had long ago deemed unworthy of bringing to the surface, thoughts better forgotten, or at least kept tucked away in a part of his mind where they weren't readily accessible. He had made a good life for himself in Alberta; so far it was lacking only a good woman. It went without saying that he knew how the past moulded and shaped a man, but that did not mean he had to dwell on it.

Pritchard sensed John's discomfort. "Give the poor fellow a rest from the interrogation, Margaret, or he'll never come within ten miles of our place again!"

"Oh, I am so sorry," Margaret apologized. She added earnestly, "But I find the subject of bondage quite fascinating. May I be so bold as to impose on you one last question?" Without waiting for an answer, she asked, "What did it *feel* like being a slave?"

No one had ever asked John that before and he had never given it much thought. He knew he could say much about it if pressed, but he wanted an end to the discussion and gave the shortest answer he could think of. "Some days it didn't feel like nothin' more than a heavy weight on your shoulders, and other days it felt like someone was chokin' the life outta you and didn't have the decency to let you die. Mostly, you just felt powerless."

Margaret glanced at her husband, then at John, and nodded slightly. "Thank you, Mr. Ware."

She served an apple cobbler for dessert while John and the magistrate chatted.

"Do you have any children?" John asked. He wondered why he had not seen any, when the house was clearly large enough for a family.

Pritchard replied, "We have two boys, twelve and fourteen, at school in Toronto. They'll be home for their holidays next week."

John said reflectively, "A man needs a wife and children in his life." He added with a wry grin, "Who knows, maybe a pretty coloured girl'll come my way sometime soon."

No sooner had the words left his tongue than he regretted them. They were heartfelt, but he wondered if the Pritchards might deem them silly and maudlin. However, the magistrate responded with encouragement. "Calgary's growing so rapidly that there's recently been a large influx of stonemasons and carpenters, a few of them coloured and with families. It seems logical that at least one of them would have a nubile daughter." He smiled. "Maybe you ought to think about taking some time to find out, and then go introduce yourself."

A good idea, John reckoned, but he needed to figure out how to go about doing it in a town he had little use for, and which did not seem to have much use for him. He could only hope that the situation would improve because of men like Pritchard.

John declined the Pritchards' invitation to stay the night, saying he had to get back to the Quorn. He would be making some of the journey in the dark anyway, so he thanked them and promised not to be a stranger. Margaret filled his canteen with fresh water and gave him biscuits for the trip. Pritchard shook his hand. "You spoke earlier about a coloured man's lack of power.

That may be true in some cases but I don't believe it to be true in yours. The power you have comes from just being yourself. I believe thinking people will eventually open their eyes and see what lies beneath the skin. As for those whose minds have never been blessed with rational thought—well, you'll always have to deal with them, but with any luck they'll be a small minority."

John shrugged noncommittally. "I reckon time's got to tell that story."

He thanked the Pritchards again for their hospitality, mounted his horse, and loped off, thinking about the magistrate's comments. Being "himself" wasn't as easy as it sounded. When he was living in Calgary and working at the I.G. Baker warehouse, his "self" had wanted very much to visit a brothel or perhaps take one of the Indian prostitutes back to his room. He had carnal needs like every man. But he hadn't, because he deemed it contrary to the kind of image he felt obliged to project, which was not that of a whoring black man. Was that his real self? Or was it the other one? Both, he decided, but the one that really mattered was the one other people saw.

He skirted Calgary, and the idea crossed his mind like a bad joke that he ought to thank the two constables who had arrested him. They had unwittingly put an extra twenty dollars in his pocket, half a month's pay for less than an hour's work. Then again, he did not think it likely that they would find much humour in it.

FIFTEEN

We got us a visitor.

John's herd grew, and by the spring of 1890, he owned seventy-five head, including several calves. It could only continue to grow, which meant he needed better grazing land than he had along the Highwood, so he went in search of a new property higher up the Sheep River, west of the Quorn and closer to the mountains. He remembered the land from his brief foray looking for gold, and knew it to be rich with grass in some areas. All he needed was a good building site, which he found in short order—two flat acres in a hollow, well above the meandering stream and surrounded by lovely, low-lying hills that rose in the west into the Rockies. There would be plenty of sun for a garden, and there were meadows above and below the site, and another one, suitable for hay, across the river. He returned to Calgary and made a claim but did not dally there. He moved his cattle to the new property and sold the other claim to an eager settler.

Meanwhile, the High River Horse Ranch, with more than nine hundred horses, offered John a better-paying job as foreman, which he accepted. J.J. Barter let him have his choice of horses as a parting gift, and he chose Molly, a two-year-old chestnut filly with a white blaze that he had trained himself. Barter also let him have Bismarck, a young boarhound that had attached itself to John.

The new job had come along at the right time. John had been

wanting a change for a while, as well as more money to invest in his future; it seemed to fit in with the change the district was experiencing. There were more settlers and more fences, and railroads were under construction south to Fort McLeod and north to Edmonton. Even the Indians seemed to have settled into their own niche and no longer posed a threat to the livelihoods of ranchers and farmers. About the only thing that had not changed was the shortage of women in the district and the total absence of them in John's life. Since it took a strong woman to handle the hardships of ranch and farm life, most of the men outside the cities and towns were bachelors. But that too was about to change.

The Canadian Pacific Railroad was offering inexpensive trips to Ontario where matchmaking organizations had been set up. A few men took advantage of the arrangement and returned with wives. John considered it, because some of the cowboys from the east had mentioned the sizable black populations there, many of whom had arrived via the Underground Railroad. But in the end, he didn't go. He believed that it would be an exercise in frustration, if not a waste of time and money. He had pretty well resigned himself to the dreary prospect of bachelorhood for at least the foreseeable future, and perhaps the rest of his life.

Whenever the opportunity arose, he loaded tools onto one of the ranch's wagons and drove up to his property to work on the new house he had begun. Sometimes one or two of the ranch hands would join him to help, but usually he toiled alone. He was careful and meticulous, because this would be his home on the ranch that he had dreamed of for so long and he wanted it to be something a man could be proud of. Unlike the rough log structure beside the Highwood River, this would be a home he could bring a wife into without embarrassment. He figured that by the end of the following summer he would have it finished, and a stable and corral built as well.

One of John's tasks as foreman was to drive to the I.G. Baker store once a month for supplies. He customarily did his business as quickly as possible and left, although he found it interesting how the attitudes of the clerks had changed. They now treated him with the same businesslike respect they treated most of their other customers. This was partly due to his regular appearance in the store; however, before he left the Quorn, the Calgary *Herald* had published an article about him and his riding prowess, and that, more than anything, had served to change many minds, inside the store and on the street as well. He was no longer a strange black man in town and he was grateful for the progress.

On a Saturday near the end of May, with a cool breeze tumbling out of the mountains, he hitched up the buckboard to a pair of horses he had trained for the task and headed for town with a long shopping list. Calgary was busy and there was no place in front of the store to leave the wagon, so he turned around and left it across the street.

A bell tinkled as he entered the store, and the smell of spices—cloves seemed to predominate—and floor wax mixed with leather and tobacco smoke flooded his senses. He was awaiting his turn when the doorbell tinkled again and another customer walked in. To John's surprise, he was black. The man saw John waiting and joined him. Wearing workman's clothes, he appeared to be in his mid-forties and was of medium height with a round face and a pleasant smile that stayed in his eyes even after it left his mouth. He nodded to John. "Busy place."

"Always is this time of year." After they exchanged a few pleasantries, John put out his hand. "John Ware."

"Dan Lewis. Pleased to know you."

Lewis was a cabinetmaker from Ontario who had brought his family west two years ago for the same reason nearly everyone else had come—to have a better life. He lived in Shepard, a tiny community about ten miles southeast of Calgary, where he had a business building high-quality furniture. The two men chatted until a clerk became available for John, and Lewis did what John hoped he would: invited him to supper.

"A week this coming Sunday. Come around three o'clock. We'll eat around five or five-thirty."

John wished it could have been sooner than Sunday; even so, the invitation felt akin to winning a valuable prize. "I'll be there. You can count on it."

On the way back to the ranch, he thought of the questions he should have asked Lewis. How large was his family? Did he have any daughters? Given his age, it was possible Lewis had daughters old enough for marriage. But Lewis might have been suspicious about any such probing, thinking that John had other motives for accepting the invitation besides a good supper and a visit with a fellow black. Whatever the case, Lewis seemed like a decent, interesting man with whom to spend an evening, and if he happened to have daughters, so much the better. John would have to dig out his Prince Albert coat from the box under his bunk and polish his boots. He had attended several social events during his time in the district, but he had never looked forward to any of them as much as this one.

He was clattering along the road, lost in his rambling thoughts, when he encountered J.J. Barter on his way to Calgary. It had been a while since they had seen each other, so they stopped their wagons side by side to trade news.

"Good to see you, J.J. How's things at the Quorn?"

"Well, I'm glad I ran into ye, John. One of the boys at the High River Ranch was out this marnin' and came across that damned wolf tearin' up one of yer foals. He took a shot at it but missed. The beast ran off into the woods quick as a cat. But it sounds as if it could be the same animal that killed a couple of our foals over the last year or so."

Every rancher and settler on the southern range knew of the wolf and called it "the King." Those who had caught a glimpse of it said it was the biggest grey they had ever seen, big enough to take down a man. It hunted by itself, its prey the easy food supply of foals and calves.

Barter continued, "Anyway, the lad tracked it for a while but lost it up along the Sheep River. If I were ye, I'd get up to that claim of yers as soon as ye can and check out yer herd. That foal may not be its only victim today. Seems to have a likin' for calves, too. There's a fifty dollar reward for the man who gets him."

By the time the two men went their separate ways, John had forgotten all about his supper date with the Lewis family. He had been lucky so far, his herd untouched, but now all kinds of horrible images stormed through his mind. He knew he had best do as Barter suggested and get to his claim without a moment's delay. But first, he had to deliver the wagonload of goods to the ranch. He slapped the reins down hard on the team's rumps and rattled and shook with speed along the bumpy road.

John ate a hurried supper and packed a bedroll and some food, knowing he would be gone overnight. He climbed on Molly and left for his claim, with Bismarck trailing behind. Clouds obscured the upper slopes of the peaks in the west but the sky above was clear and the air warm. He rode quickly, without being reckless, along the Highwood and onto the trail up the Sheep that he had practically worn himself. His mind was on the King, and the closer he got to his property, the more worried he became.

Nearing the homestead, he saw a raven fly into the air and begin circling. The sight made his gut heave. The trail rose and from his new vantage point he could see past the house to the broad meadow above it. A dozen ravens were tearing at a bloody carcass, while beyond, his small herd of cattle, bunched together, looked on. He nudged Molly and galloped down into the hollow, past the house, and up the far side. As soon as he appeared on the meadow, the ravens flew off to nearby trees, their raucous croaks protesting the interruption of their feast.

The carcass was one of John's calves, and he cursed his luck. Its neck and belly were ripped apart so severely that it had to have been done by a wolf, and recently, too. Probably this morning, as near as John could determine. He could see that it had eaten most of the animal's organs except the stomach, and it looked as if the ravens had been taking their fill of that. John dismounted, pulled his rifle from its scabbard, and called

215

Bismarck, who was sniffing around the carcass. He looked for tracks but the ground was rough and churned up by the cattle. He walked the perimeter of the open space, peering into the woods, but saw nothing. He thought he might be wasting his time, because the wolf could have crossed the river and disappeared into the wilderness beyond the hay meadow. But as he was about to return to Molly, Bismarck shot ahead to a puddle, a remnant of the last rainfall, and began whining. He stood at the edge of the forest, staring in, his tail high and wagging. John glanced down and noticed paw prints beside the water, where it appeared the wolf had stopped to drink. The prints were huge, big enough that John had no doubt that they belonged to the King. They indicated that the wolf had entered the forest, and Bismarck's stance reinforced it.

It was too close to nightfall to go traipsing through the woods after a savage beast, and Bismarck would still be able to pick up the scent in the morning. John did not think the wolf would return for the uneaten carrion, because it had not in other cases, seeming to prefer a fresh kill. He had an idea as to how he could take advantage of that, but first he had to get rid of the carcass. He dragged it by its hind legs out of the meadow and a couple of hundred yards up the river, with Bismarck following. Then he took out his knife and skinned the animal, thinking that the hide would make a nice carpet for his new home. He left the remains, certain that the ravens and other scavengers would have them gobbled up in no time.

John and Bismarck returned to the meadow and retrieved Molly, and the three walked down to the house, where John had a firepit and some stacked firewood. He got a blaze going, fetched water from the river, and put coffee on to boil. While waiting, he tended to Molly, removing the saddle and bridle and letting her graze. He took a couple of biscuits out of his saddlebags and once the coffee boiled, he poured a cup and dipped the hard biscuits into it to soften them and add flavour. When he had finished, he freshened his coffee and rolled a smoke. Sipping the hot brew and pulling the smoke into his lungs, he contemplated his surroundings.

Some of the walls were up on the house, built with lumber delivered from Calgary. In his mind's eye, he saw the finished result. It would have a steeply pitched shingled roof to shed the snow, and a porch, with a fancy cast-iron railing along the front. The door would be in the centre with windows on either side, and there would be windows in each end. He would leave the rear of the house plain so that he could easily knock out the wall in case he needed to add more rooms—no reason why a man could not remain optimistic. He had already begun to gather stones from the river for the chimney; he would start it once the walls were up and before the roof went on. Then, to make it really stand out in this wilderness, he would whitewash it.

It was a very satisfying thing to think about, this house, this land, and his small herd. And despite the death of the calf, and no prospects of a bride, he felt quite content with life and with himself. He had come such a long way from South Carolina and the Chambers plantation that he rarely recalled those places anymore. The itches on his back from the whipping scars now needed only scratching, and not reflection. He rolled another cigarette to accompany a second cup of coffee and listened to the crackle of the flames and the rushing of the river. When he finished, he doused the fire, grabbed his bedroll, rifle, and rope, and said, "Come on, Bismarck. We're sleepin' on high ground tonight in case that old King comes to pay us another call."

In the dusk, the pair walked up to the meadow, where the cattle were beginning to bed down for the night. John roped a protesting calf and tied it to a stump near the river side of the meadow. On the opposite side was a rocky bluff, about thirty feet high, which offered a commanding view of his property, and that was where he and Bismarck settled in for the night.

He lay for a long time reading the night sky that he understood so well because of Amos and Emmett, and fell asleep thinking of the Coles, that he should have had someone help him compose a letter to let them know how well he was doing. They would have been proud. But good intentions were thwarted by a busy life and now it was probably too late.

He awakened before dawn and waited for the sky to lighten. If the wolf was going to come for another feast, this would be the time. Bismarck, ever alert to John's movements, awoke with him, and he scratched the dog's neck for a while. The starry sky turned slowly to grey as the earth turned toward the sun. Suddenly, Bismarck tensed and let out the beginning of a whine. John clamped the dog's mouth shut with his right hand and reached for the rifle lying beside him with his left.

"We got us a visitor here," he whispered under his breath.

Bismarck seemed to understand, for he remained quiet, watching for some kind of signal that John needed his services.

A few moments later, the cattle began to rumble and rise to their feet. The tethered calf bawled. Scanning the meadow, John saw the wolf slinking out of the forest, large and menacing. Talk of its size had not been exaggerated. It paused, lifted its great head, and looked around, sniffing the air. Sensing no threat, it focused on its target and broke into a lope, heading straight for the calf, which was now frantic, choking itself trying to escape, its eyes bulging with terror. Its mother, standing nearby, began bellowing her alarm. John raised his rifle to his shoulder and fired as the wolf lunged. The bullet ploughed into the side of its chest. The thud was audible as the beast hit the ground, air exploding from its lungs. Its legs twitched for a moment, and then it lay still. John hurried down the slope and across the meadow, Bismarck racing before him. He levered another shell into the rifle's chamber in case he needed it, but the wolf was dead.

John was elated. He freed the calf, which ran, still bawling, to its mother's side. He heaved the corpse over his shoulder, thinking that he'd done the same with many a hundred-pound sack of flour when he worked for the I.G. Baker Company, and this animal had to weigh half again as much. He carried it down to the house, where he could cover it with a tarp and keep the ravens away from it. Bismarck, leaping, whining, and sniffing, followed.

After breakfast, John spent the remainder of the morning adding boards to the walls of the house and making the first cuts for the windows, whistling and humming as he worked. He finished up around noon and whistled for Molly.

Most horses would want no part of a wolf on their back, not even a dead one, but Molly seemed to trust John implicitly. Even so, as he prepared her for the trip back to the ranch, she showed her dislike by shivering when he threw the carcass across her rump and secured it behind the cantle. He mounted and pointed Molly down the trail toward home, Bismarck needing no encouragement to tag along. He would stop at the Quorn first, keen to see Barter's face when he showed him his prize. One happy man was about to make another man equally happy.

—◇◇◇—

Word of the wolf's death spread, and ranchers along the foothills went to bed with less worry. Barter collected the reward money and brought it to John a couple of days later. He also brought the pelt, which measured eight feet from the tip of its nose to the end of its tail.

"Somethin' to hang on the wall of yer new house, with my and everyone else's gratitude," said a beaming Barter. "Yer the talk of the southern range, John, and I heard the *Herald*'s runnin' another story on ye." He chuckled. "Keep that up and they'll be askin' ye to run for mayor!"

John reckoned that such publicity could only be a good thing; he would find out the next time he went to town if he was right. He wondered if the Lewises read the *Herald*. If they did, and if they had marriageable daughters, it might stand him in good stead. In the meantime, he had a wolf skin for a rug and fifty dollars to buy windows and doors for the house.

The rest of the week dragged by, even though the mares were still foaling and John had plenty to do. He dug out his Prince Albert coat the day before his visit and hung it outside to freshen and to get rid of the wrinkles. When Sunday morning finally arrived, he arose early and polished his boots. There was an unpleasant odour about them, so he cadged some baking soda from the cook and sprinkled it inside. Satisfied, he pulled them on. After breakfast, he combed and brushed Molly, saddled her, and told Bismarck to stay put, that he would be back late in the evening.

⁓

Shepard was not much as far as communities went, consisting of a small cluster of houses on the bald prairie. Among them, he found the Lewis residence, a smaller version of the Pritchard home. He dismounted at the front porch just as his host came out through the door.

"Hello, John! So glad you could make it. You had a pleasant journey, I trust." Lewis stepped off the porch and shook John's hand. "There's water for your horse around back."

The two men traded generalities as Lewis led John and Molly to the rear of the house, where there was a watering trough and a small stable. As John removed the saddle and bridle, Lewis said, "She'll find the hay in the stable once she's had a drink. Come in and meet the family. They've been excited to meet you, especially after reading all about you in the newspaper. You're famous in our household!" He motioned back the way they had come. "We'll go around to the front door. Esther would be mortified if I brought you in through the kitchen."

John placed the tack on a nearby hitching rail and followed Lewis around to the front again. They entered the house and John could scarcely believe his eyes. Standing there were a boy and three women. The oldest was undoubtedly Esther and flanking her were two girls, one of them the most beautiful he had ever seen.

SIXTEEN

A girl wouldn't be so indelicate.

John had never read a book in his life, but he thought that if a book existed about angels, it would contain long passages about Mildred. She wore a white dress that showed off a perfect figure, and her black hair, tied back with a white ribbon, framed a lovely face. Her brown skin was lighter than John's and looked as soft and as smooth as a child's. A sparkle in her eyes reflected a reverence and passion for life. She was nineteen years old, as fresh as a breeze spilling down from the mountains, and appeared so delicate that for the first time in a long while John became conscious of his size and felt too big for the room. His tongue forsook him, at least for anything sensible to say, but he managed a "Hello."

The supper and evening passed far too quickly for his liking. It took every ounce of his will to tear his eyes from Mildred, and he figured the Lewises must surely think him rude. When it came time to leave, he managed to blurt out a request to come calling on her the following Sunday. When both the Lewises and Mildred agreed—with some enthusiasm, John noticed—he felt as if he'd been living in winter all his life and a chinook had suddenly washed over him.

He stewed the entire week, wondering how to conduct himself around Mildred. He even sought advice from J.J. Barter, who told him he had to make sure not to overstay his welcome on that first visit. Fifteen minutes of being alone with her would suffice. Any longer and his intentions might be considered less than honourable.

John decided that parlours were not a comfortable setting for him, so he approached his boss and borrowed a democrat wagon and a team of horses for the weekend, intending to take Mildred for a ride. That was something he understood, and he could show her how to handle the reins and direct the team if she wanted to. He set out for the Lewises' on the Saturday, knowing that the journey would take much longer in the wagon. He slept beneath it on the side of the road that night and reached Shepard with plenty of time for a short jaunt before supper.

He was not surprised when Dan and Esther Lewis said they would love to go along too—as chaperones, John knew, although they did not say that. At least they sat in the back and allowed Mildred to sit beside him on the front seat. She was so close that their arms touched with every bump and turn of the wagon, which was far better than sitting at opposite ends of a settee in a stuffy parlour. And with the Lewises along, the fifteen-minute rule, if indeed there was such a thing, was no longer a consideration.

Thunderclouds had been building for much of the afternoon, and they had gone only a short distance when an electrical storm fell upon them. Soon a torrential downpour pelted the awning of the democrat, flowing over the sides like a waterfall. John decided to turn back. He had just reversed direction when a bolt of lightning exploded around them. A strong smell of burning flesh brought back memories of the cattle drive from Texas. The bolt had struck the horses and both lay dead and smoking on the ground. Dan Lewis was stunned into silence and Esther and Mildred were terrified. Instinctively, John put his arm around Mildred to comfort her. He told her not to worry, that he would get her home safely. He leaped down from the seat and with some difficulty freed the tongue of the wagon from the dead animals. He threw the tack that was worth keeping into the democrat beside Mildred, as the Lewises watched, dumbfounded. Then he picked up the tongue of the wagon and began pulling the Lewis family down the muddy road to the safety of their home. He was soaked to the skin and exhausted by the time they arrived, but the Lewises stayed reasonably dry beneath the awning.

It was an unusual start to their courtship but it did not matter; his image in the Lewis family took on heroic proportions. And the courtship was smoothed because he wasn't the only one doing the courting. More adept at it than he, Mildred steered the course of events along quite nicely. Even so, when it came time to make a proposal of marriage, John once more sought Barter's advice.

"Flowers and poems," Barter said. "Ye can't go wrong. Women are crazy for them."

But it was the dead of winter and there were no flowers, and John did not know any poems. Barter found him one by some love-stricken anonymous writer. The Irishman read it to him a few times until John had it memorized. He had a purse made from the calfskin he had saved when the big wolf had slaughtered its owner, and he gave it to Mildred as a Christmas present. Later in the day, he knelt before her and took her hand in his. He had never felt as awkward in his life as he recited the poem:

Oh, when first I saw your lovely face,
Laugh at me if you will,
My heart jumped clean out of its place,
I could not keep it still.

He thought she might laugh, but her eyes misted over, and when he asked her to be his wife, she cried her acceptance. They were married two months later, on February 29, 1892. Mildred had just turned twenty and John would soon be forty-seven. Sidney Pritchard performed the ceremony, and his face, unreadable in the courtroom, never stopped smiling.

They could not consummate their marriage that night because they stayed with the Lewises and feared being overheard. The next morning, they loaded a newly bought wagon with provisions and began the long, cold trek through the snow to their home on the Sheep River, stopping overnight at the Quorn as J.J. Barter's guests, where again they had little privacy. They reached home late the following afternoon and John carried Mildred over the threshold. He could barely contain himself as he got a fire going and she made the bed. They did not bother to eat supper.

In the bedroom, he took her in his arms and could feel her small frame trembling. He cupped her face tenderly in his hands. "You're shakin', Mildred. Are you scared?"

"My dear John," she breathed in his ear, "I am trembling with anticipation."

He fumbled his way through removing her layers of underclothing and could not have done it without her help, because it all seemed so complicated. When the petticoats had at last fallen to the floor, he removed his own clothes, bold in the weak lamplight, and they climbed into bed. When finally they slept and awoke in the morning, they felt something neither had felt before: completely and utterly together.

Neighbours from adjacent ranches showed up that afternoon to welcome the newlyweds, with buckets of food and a party. They were all white, but like John, all were ranchers, and he felt a kinship with them. They had accepted him into their midst, and in fact admired him enough to seek his advice from time to time. They celebrated long into the night with drinks, songs, and fiddle music. After everyone left, Mildred told John, "I can't say that I've ever heard of white folk throwing a party for black folk before. But I never knew John Ware before." She put her arms around his neck and kissed his cheek.

He pulled her close and held her tightly. She had brought such unimaginable beauty into his life that it was never easy to let her go.

That fall, after a visit with the doctor, Mildred announced that she was pregnant. John had suspected as much because he had sensed something different about her, from the glow in her cheeks to a new maturity. She began to look more beautiful than he had ever thought possible. One night in bed, she took his hand and placed it on her swollen belly.

"Feel the baby, John. It's kicking!" She giggled. "It must be a boy. A girl wouldn't be so indelicate."

He hoped it would be a boy. He wanted a son to raise and he would make him feel proud of his father. If it was a girl, he and Mildred already knew what her name would be. He placed his ear to her belly and heard the baby's heartbeat, marvelling at how one person could have two hearts beating inside.

―――

It was not all good news that year. J.J. Barter died. He was healthy at John's wedding but a short time later typhoid struck him down. It saddened John to lose someone he had known for so long and respected so much, but at least Barter no longer had to contend with the Quorn's ongoing problems as the owners made one bad deal after another. Every year they sent relatives or friends over to holiday and learn about ranching, but all it did was drain the company's reserves. It had nearly driven Barter mad, because few of them ever bothered to learn anything anyway. It was fortunate that the ranch had not collapsed completely under the weight of these poor decisions.

Tom Lynch died too, another significant loss because had it not been for Tom taking a chance down in Pocatello, John might have returned to Texas. He knew that he would not have been able to create the life there that he had forged here.

―――

In March of the following year, the Wares' first child was born, not a son but a daughter. They named her Amanda Janet Ware but called her Nettie, in honour of John's sister. This Nettie would never have to face the terrible ordeal her aunt had faced. A year and a half later, the son John had wanted was born and they named him Robert after his paternal grandfather.

Family life was good for the Wares, but John wished he could say the same for the ranch. The year Robert was born was another exceptionally dry year. A deep frost in June killed much of the wheat in the region and the grass was shorter than usual. John was able to dig irrigation ditches to a lower meadow on his ranch and did not suffer as much as others did. Even so, wolves, seemingly on a vendetta for John's killing of the King, slaughtered twenty-four of his cattle. He managed occasionally to shoot one but could have sworn that it only served to increase their numbers.

In the meantime, he rode as captain for the Bar U and the Quorn on the great spring roundups, and no one objected to a black man holding this exalted position. Everyone knew he was the right man for the job. One of his main rules was no practical jokes against the new, young riders. He remembered how such pranks had affected him and he would have none of that while he was in charge.

His reputation was such that he no longer needed to prove himself to other people, but proving himself to himself would always remain part of his character. Despite having been on the planet for nearly a half century, he still performed work generally done by younger men. He broke horses for the North West Mounted Police and several ranches, and bought horses for himself as well, most of them too unruly for other ranchers to keep. Mildred's heart was in her throat the first time she watched him break a mean one. She told him later that it worried her. "Don't you go breaking that neck of yours. I'd hate to lose something I only recently found, and your children need a father."

How had he ever managed without her? As slight as she was, she did not shirk the hard work required to stay on top of the distaff side of ranching. She usually started each day by picking the bedbugs from the mattresses, and in the summertime, she washed the sheets daily. She fought a losing battle, but it was a battle everyone fought and lost. She kept the house and the children clean and tidy, and everyone's clothes in good repair. She even found time to churn butter, which she sold to their neighbours. In the evenings, after Nettie and Robert were asleep, she read the newspaper to John and, when necessary, did the accounts. Ironically, despite the years she'd been at the ranch, she still did not care much for horses and cattle, and would have preferred city life. She had always attended church regularly, too, and missed the important part it had once played in her life. But John had no love for either the city or the church, and Mildred learned to live with that.

It was the fall of 1896. John had finished repairing a stall in the barn and was nailing eight coyote paws above the entrance to form the number 4 (he had numbered all of the stalls with coyote paws) when the dogs began yapping and he heard Mildred call to them. He looked out and saw Adam Newby riding up on a roan mare. He seemed in a hurry. Newby, a nervous young man and confirmed bachelor, owned the next ranch down the river and had been among those who'd organized the welcoming party for John and Mildred. A drooping moustache and dark pockets beneath his eyes added years to a youthful face. He was one of several Englishmen in Alberta who were trying to turn themselves into successful cattlemen.

After exchanging greetings, John asked, "What brings you up this way, Adam?"

"Bad news, I'm afraid, John. There's been a murder on the Blood reserve and the farming instructor's been severely wounded."

The Bloods were part of the Blackfoot Confederacy, which also included the Peigans. Their reserve was to the south, between the St. Mary and Belly Rivers.

"What?" John was surprised. "Who was killed? Anybody I know?"

"I doubt it," Newby answered. "It was a Blood named Medicine Pipe Stem. Another Blood by the name of Charcoal did it. No one knows why, but they say he's gone crazy and is thirsting for more blood. He doesn't care if it's Indian or white." He paused for a moment before realizing he had not included everybody in the killer's purview. "Or black. There's a chance he could be heading this way, so it might be best to lock your doors at night and keep a gun handy."

John thanked Newby, who turned his mount and rode off. Being on the run, Charcoal would probably be riding hard and would have to change horses often, and a Blood was better at stealing horses than most Indians. He might also decide to slaughter a heifer if he was hungry. John figured the first thing to do was try to determine if Charcoal was actually in the vicinity, and a good start would be to check on his stock. As for the doors, he did not have locks on them, but Bismarck and the other dogs would let him know if anyone came around. And he had a gun. As he walked up to the house to let Mildred know what he was up to, his breath steamed out as fog in the cold air.

He passed through the gate in the fence he had built to keep Nettie from wandering off and drowning in the river. Inside the house, she was playing on the floor; she arose and ran to him, crying, "Poppa!" He scooped her up in his arms, kissed her forehead, and put her down.

Mildred was fixing lunch. "What did Adam want?"

John explained. "I'll have somethin' to eat, then I'd best ride out and check the stock."

Mildred shook her head. "If it isn't one thing it's another. You be careful out there."

John found nothing to lead him to believe that Charcoal had been anywhere in the vicinity. However, the grass looked sparser than ever, and with fences sprouting up everywhere, he wondered how long he could hold out here. He might have to move to some place where the animals could graze properly.

⁓⁓⁓

In November, Charcoal killed a North West Mounted Police officer who was pursuing him. His own people turned him in, and in March, the authorities hanged him. The ranchers on the southern range, John included, were relieved of one worry, but the winter was long and bitter.

When spring finally arrived and brought the annual thaw, it also brought torrential rainstorms. The Sheep River rose higher than John had ever seen it and he worried about his house. He prepared to evacuate Mildred and the children, but after flooding his lower meadow and seeping into his barn and other outbuildings, all on slightly lower ground than the house, the river finally crested.

John wondered about Adam Newby, fearing that his neighbour would not have fared as well. Newby had built on lowland right next to the river, and John would have bet his last penny that his place had flooded. He saddled Molly and rode down to see if his neighbour needed help. When he arrived, Newby was on horseback at the edge of the water. The young Englishman was disconsolate, yet glad and surprised to see John.

"Surely you have your own property to worry about, John."

"My property's doin' fine. Bit of water in the barn but nothin' worse than that. Don't look so good here, though."

Not only had Newby's land flooded, but the river had taken away his house and outbuildings, which were now in pieces somewhere downstream. His horses had gone to high ground and so had the few cattle he owned, but unfortunately they had chosen a small rise of land that was now surrounded by the flood, the water streaming at a good pace around it. They were bellowing in distress.

"Don't know what I'm going to do about them," Newby moaned. "I've been trying to decide whether I should go get them off, but it looks bloody dangerous. The water's moving too fast and it gets deep a short distance out. I don't know how to swim either, if something goes wrong."

"Well, they're gonna lose a lot a weight if they stay there too long," John observed. "Let me see what I can do."

Without waiting for a response, he urged Molly into the water. It was only knee deep at first, but then it rose over his boots, cold and murky, and soon Molly was swimming. He felt the current pulling at them and slid off her back, hanging on to the saddle horn, wondering why he was doing this, because he still did not know how to swim himself. And the water was as frigid as the high reaches it came from. But he reached shallower water safely and reined Molly around behind the herd. Grabbing his rope, he urged her up the slope, yelling and slapping any rump he could reach. The animals soon got the message. They plunged into the river and swam to where they could walk to safety, far away from the water.

"Good grief, John!" Newby exclaimed. "I hadn't expected you to do that!"

John shivered from the cold and shrugged. "I didn't expect it myself. It just sorta happened. Maybe we could get a fire goin' so's I can heat up these old bones."

John returned every now and then to help Newby re-establish his claim on higher ground, and it made him realize how lucky he was that he had not suffered the same fate. He could not imagine everything he owned floating off down the river, not after the hard work and money that had gone into it. But Mildred was right. It seemed to be one damned thing after another.

She became pregnant again and gave birth to another boy in the fall. They named him William and called him Billy. They passed another winter and while there were early concerns about flooding in the spring, the Sheep River behaved itself. But the wolves were back and had already killed two more calves, and the grass was short and sparse again. John figured he'd played out all the rope he had, and one night, after the children had gone to bed and he and Mildred were enjoying a final cup of tea by the fire before retiring, he broached the subject of moving.

"I heard there's still lots of good grass over by the Red Deer River. I think it's about time I went and took a look at it. If I find somethin', maybe you and the children could stay with your parents while I get the stock moved and build us a house."

She admonished him. "Don't think for a single moment, John Ware, that you'll be leaving the children and me behind with my parents. I'll not hear of it. You'll need all the help you can get and that includes me. Now, with that settled, if you think moving is what we have to do, we'll do it. There isn't any sense in beating our heads against the wall here if we can live peacefully somewhere else. But I don't see you getting any younger, so I think you'd best find a place where our roots aren't going to be torn up again soon."

The next day, John rode into Calgary to see what land was available by the Red Deer and to put the ranch up for sale.

SEVENTEEN

Where does that leave us?

The Wares stayed on the ranch for another two years, hoping for a buyer, before reaching the conclusion that, buyer or not, they had to move. The land here was no longer suitable for their herd of three hundred, but there was plenty of it along the Red Deer River valley and John had already scouted it out. The horizon in every direction was as flat as a playing card, the valley with its hoodoos and coulees invisible until you were almost upon it. The land was not anywhere near as pretty as the foothills, but it would keep his business going and that was vital, not only for the sake of his pocketbook but for his soul as well.

After the roundup in the spring of 1900, the Wares were preparing for the move when a buyer finally came along. The sale removed some of the financial pressure and they headed east with lighter hearts. Adam Newby, still appreciative of John's help during the flood, offered his services for the drive. The Wares loaded their belongings onto a wagon that Mildred drove, the three children in the seat beside her and a fourth growing in her belly. With the wheels creaking and moaning, the cattle bellowing and bawling, and several dogs following, they set out on the hundred-and-fifty-mile journey to a new life. Just as when he had left Georgetown and the Flint Springs ranch, John didn't look back. He saw no advantage in it and preferred to fix his eyes on the road that stretched into the future.

He felt the old excitement of a trail drive during the first day or two, but it soon wore off. They had to take a long route, up through Calgary where there were bridges spanning the Bow River, in order to get the wagon across. Ignoring the warnings from the police that the bridges were designed for people and wagons, not for cattle, he sneaked his herd across in the early hours of the morning. Their journey took two weeks through almost every kind of weather imaginable, so that by the time they reached their homestead, they were glad to be there.

Mildred was not impressed. "You could strain your eyes blind trying to find something to look at out here."

John laughed. "Maybe so, but if you were a cow you'd find the grass real fetchin'."

Mildred observed that the Red Deer ran muddy, unlike the Sheep River, which was clear. John would have to dig a well. She also did not like the hoodoos that had formed here and there along the river, saying they reminded her of something she had once seen in a nightmare.

Truth to tell, John did not care for them either. He knew that rattlesnakes made their home among them as well as in the coulees that cut their way a hundred feet to the valley bottom.

With Adam's help, he set to work finding trees along the river suitable for a house and falling them. When they had gathered enough, the Englishman took his leave. He said that once he got his affairs squared away, he planned to join the war in South Africa. John had seen the call for volunteers when they passed through Calgary and would have gone himself if he didn't have a family. He wished his friend well and as Adam rode off, John hoped he would see him return.

John began building the house on his own, on the bottomland, where the soil would be good for a garden. It was a rough structure compared to the house on the Sheep River, but it would at least keep them warm in winter and would do until he could build something more permanent.

Mildred was nearing her due date, and since there were no doctors or midwives in the immediate vicinity, John took her and the children into Brooks, about twenty miles south, where her parents were living. He had to get back to the homestead and told Mildred that he would return in a couple of weeks to collect her and their four children. But bad news awaited him when he did: the baby, a boy, had died shortly after it was born. The doctor could only say that it had arrived in a weak condition and never strengthened, that it was sometimes the way of the world. Mildred was saddened but not completely surprised. Something had not felt right during the last few months of her pregnancy; however, she had kept it to herself, sure that John had many other things to fret about.

She fell into a depression, made worse by surroundings she was not happy with. But Nettie, Bobby, and Billy, and endless chores, kept her busy and in time she was able to leave the sadness behind. The remainder of the year flew by and the new century began with Mildred announcing that she was pregnant once again. A baby girl was born in the fall and they named her Mildred. It had been a good year for the Wares, and with another healthy child in the household, they were content. A New Year was in the offing, and they looked forward to it, but it would not bring the good tidings they hoped for.

One April morning, John rose as usual at dawn to milk the cow. He sat up, swung his legs around, and lowered his feet to the floor; they settled in two inches of water. He had only been half-awake until that moment, but he knew instantly what was happening. He leaped up, grabbing his clothes from the chair beside the bed. "Mildred!" he said loudly to awaken her, but she was already stirring. "The river's floodin'! Get the children up and ready to leave. I'll hitch up the wagon."

He donned his clothes, pulled on his boots, and splashed outside. In the grey light he could see that the entire valley bottom was under water and the level was rising. He rushed to the corral, got Molly and the other horse he kept there, and hitched them to the wagon, then led them to the front of the house. Both animals were edgy and restless. Mildred had the children dressed and assisted them into the wagon, instructing Nettie to hold the baby. She and John saved whatever household goods and tools they could. The first thing John got was the axe, Mildred the pictures of their wedding and family, some pots and pans and food. Meanwhile, the water continued to rise and was soon swirling around John's boot tops.

"We gotta get outta here," he urged Mildred. "We can make do with what we got." He steered the team through the water to a nearby coulee that led out of the valley to the prairie above.

As the sun rose over the horizon, they sat at the rim of the valley and watched in awe as the river rose high enough around their house to dislodge it, break it into individual logs, and carry it away. The corral and privy went too. Mildred wept and so did the children, as much because their mother was crying as anything else. John felt like weeping too. He had overcome so many obstacles in his life, particularly those associated with his colour, and now here were two major setbacks—having to leave his beautiful home on the Sheep River and losing this one. He wondered when it would end, wondered if God was trying to discover his breaking point.

Mildred leaned against him and he put his arm around her. She collected herself and dried her tears on her dress sleeve. Sniffing, she said without a hint of rancour, "Well it looks as if we're sitting on what's going to be the roof over our heads for the next while."

John hugged her tighter for a moment, then got busy gathering wood. They needed a fire to cook breakfast and to dry their clothes. And its warmth would probably go a long way toward improving their outlook on life.

He had to go even further afield for suitable logs to build a new home, which did little to improve his disposition. Nevertheless, his mood brightened considerably two days later, when he heard from another rancher that a large boom of spruce logs had broken away from a sawmill at Red Deer, a hundred and fifty miles or so upstream. They now belonged to anyone with the skill and fortitude to retrieve them from the river.

He had Mildred and Nettie keep an eye on the river and watch for the logs. They had not been looking long before Nettie called excitedly, "I think one's coming, Poppa!"

John got a rope from the wagon and rode Molly to where the river narrowed slightly. Dismounting as the log approached, he cast the rope and managed to snag the stub of a sawed-off limb. He pulled it to shore where he could get a better hold on it, hoping the rope would not slip off. It held. Wading into the water, he placed the loop around the whole log, pulling it tight, and wrapped the other end of the rope around his waist. He climbed on Molly and heeled her forward. The big log came sliding up onto land as slick as a newborn baby enters the world. It improved his mood markedly.

He retrieved a dozen more logs in the same fashion and, using a team of horses, dragged them all up the coulee to high ground, where he would build the new house, near a small stream that posed no threat if it flooded. T-shaped, the house would be permanent, with three good-sized rooms. The kitchen would be at the bottom of the T, separated from the main part of the house by a storage room and entrance. That way, if a fire started where they usually start—in the kitchen—he might be able to save the living area of the house. He did not need another major disaster in his life.

He had begun to level the land to lay the first logs when he saw a mounted figure coming from the south. It was Adam Newby, home from the war in South Africa. He had got off the train at Brooks and rented a horse at the local livery, curious to know how the Wares were doing. They welcomed their friend and John thought that Adam had changed considerably. He looked older by more than the two years that he had been gone. He did not mention his involvement in the war, and John sensed that he should ask about it only if Adam broached the subject. Mildred made tea and afterwards Adam said, "We'd better get your house built so this family of yours has a real roof over its head."

Adam stayed to help dig a well and when he did go, seemed to do so only because John was heading off for the spring roundup. During his entire stay, Adam never spoke a single word about his experience in South Africa, but John understood it had affected him profoundly. He was not the same man John had known at the Sheep River, and he wondered if Adam had stayed with them as long as he had because he did not want to face the loneliness of his own ranch. John vowed that the next time he was in Calgary, he would rent a horse and ride down for a visit.

June and July passed uninterrupted by trouble, and John was pleased with the improvement in their lives. With the logs and Adam's help, he thought that perhaps God was not out to test him after all. That is, until the day he rode out to check on his stock and noticed lesions on the rump of one of the animals. At first he dismissed them, thinking that they were self-inflicted, caused by some casual rubbing against something. But then he noticed lesions on a few of the other animals, on different parts of their bodies—shoulders, legs, and necks—and knew he had a huge problem on his hands.

He galloped back to the house and Mildred saw the look of concern on his face.

"There's something troubling you, John. I could feel it before you even rode up. You never thunder in here like that."

"The mange," he said, disgusted. "It's come. Our herd's got it."

"Oh, Lord!"

"I'm headin' into Brooks. Better make a late supper for me."

He took no time to add anything, simply pointed Molly toward Brooks and spurred her into an easy lope.

Mange had ravaged herds south of the border some time ago and more recently along the Little Bow River. A mite burrowing beneath an animal's skin, which became itchy, caused it. In serious cases, rubbed areas turned into scabs and looked like elephant skin. The disease was ugly, but worse, the affected cattle usually didn't feed properly and did not gain weight, which was bad news for a cattleman. The Stock Growers Association had expressed concern that the mite would spread even farther north, and it looked as if their concern had become a reality.

In Brooks, John went straight to an association rep and reported his findings. Within a few days, a handful of men with a wagonload of materials arrived on the ranch to build a dipping vat. They dug a trench thirty feet long and lined it with concrete and boards. Once it was completed, they filled it with a soupy sulphur solution that would kill the parasites.

John wasted no time running his cattle through, and ranchers from miles around brought their herds for treatment. Knowing of John's reputation for breaking horses, they also brought wild ones for him to tame. For a month or more, the ranch seemed to play host to a giant rodeo and he cherished every minute of it. Mildred loved to watch him ride in spite of the fact that it still scared her nearly half to death. The horses jerked him around so much, she wondered how he managed to stay in the saddle, yet she could have sworn he looked ten years younger every time he got on one of those whirling devils. His contentment, though, did nothing to alleviate her fears. She said to him, after a ride on a particularly nasty horse, words she had uttered before, "If you break your darned fool neck, where does that leave us?"

John considered that an impossibility. "That ain't gonna happen, Mildred. And that's a God-given fact."

"I'll pray that it is so. But it seems to me God deals more in 'perhaps' and 'maybe' than He does in facts."

EIGHTEEN

Ain't never considered myself a fool.

Near the end of April the following year, John went by train to Calgary to get some medicine for Mildred, who was pregnant again and not feeling well. This would be their fifth child and that would have to be enough. Mildred wanted a dozen, but she was thirty-one now, an advanced age for having babies, and this was the second time she had not been well during a pregnancy. The doctor offered no guarantees that the child would survive, and it was getting equally dangerous for her.

John hated leaving her and the children alone, especially when she was ailing, but he could not get what she needed in Brooks. He enjoyed coming to Calgary now. The days when he was no better than a pariah dog were long gone. Calgary was a cow town and the people there admired his skills as a cowboy. They smiled and said hello. Merchants called him Mr. Ware and said it with respect.

However, he was unprepared for the grim mood that gripped the town when he arrived this time. There had been a huge rockslide in southwestern Alberta, in the Crowsnest Pass. An entire mountainside had broken away and buried the town of Frank and the seventy-five people living there. Several volunteers were heading to the area to see if anyone had survived. Few held out much hope.

John would have gone himself, but getting Mildred's medicine was his first priority. He also wanted to see Adam Newby, and since the train back to Brooks did not leave until the next morning, he rented a horse and rode down to the Sheep River. The weather was cold, the sky dark, and John thought it might snow, even though May was only a day away. He hoped Adam had not gone off to the Frank slide—it would be like him to do that—and that his friend was faring better. The last time John had been down this way, Adam had still not escaped from the doldrums that he had grappled with since his return from the war.

Badger, Adam's hound, heard John coming, his throaty bark sounding a warning. But he soon recognized John, wagging his tail and whimpering. At the house, John dismounted and scratched the dog behind the ear, wondering where his master was. Badger might have been wondering too, because he was fidgety, and John was concerned. He was certain that if Adam were around, he would have acknowledged his visitor's presence by now, and if he had gone to Frank, he definitely would not have left the dog on its own. John knocked on the door. Maybe his friend was ill or sleeping. When there was no answer, he opened the door and called, "Hello, Adam! It's John." The house remained quiet. There were only two rooms, the main living and kitchen area, and a bedroom. John checked the bedroom. It was empty, the bed made. That was also like Adam, everything in its place and everything in the place tidy.

He went outside and walked over to the stable to see if Adam's horse was gone. He opened the door and nearly choked. Adam was hanging by the neck from one of the roof beams. John was stunned, his brain not comprehending what his eyes were seeing. He ran to Adam, pulling out his pocketknife. He righted the box that Adam had used to stand on, climbed up, and cut the body down. His friend's bowels had evacuated and the odour was foul.

John laid him on the floor. "Ah, Adam," he said aloud, "what have you done?" He folded Adam's arms across his chest and uttered a short prayer, then covered him with a horse blanket. He could do little else. He barred the barn door to keep out scavenging animals and led Badger into High River to let the authorities know of the tragedy; they would deal with the body and he could get back to Mildred.

When he left Calgary, the weather had turned; snow was falling heavily, and it got worse during the train ride. The wind had picked up and he could see it swirling in eddies across the prairie. He arrived in Brooks during the worst snowstorm of the year. Walking from the train station to the livery where he had stabled Molly, he could see barely ten yards in front of him.

The livery owner looked grim. "I hope you're not planning to ride home in this, John."

"Not plannin', Walter," John replied. "Doin'. And to be doin' it I need my tack. I'd be obliged if you fetched it for me."

"But you can't see the buildings across the street, and the snow's piled so deep now the trail will be covered!"

"The wife needs somethin' I got and she's waited long enough for it."

"I've never called a customer a fool before, but if you go out there, John, you're as good as lost, maybe dead. You won't be found until the thaw, and how will that help Mildred?"

Reluctantly, he retrieved John's tack and John paid him. He saddled Molly, Walter opened the door, and John rode out. "Good luck!" the owner cried.

John pointed Molly north, into the teeth of the wind that bit at him like a sandstorm. Molly had her head down and was reluctant to face into the storm. Her instincts told her to turn around and put her rump to the wind. John used the end of the reins against her and talked to her, "Come on, girl! Come on! We got people that need us." Despite his urgings, she stopped after a quarter of a mile and would go no further. No amount of coaxing would change her mind. John did not have the heart to force her forward, so he turned her around. Already the trail she had left was disappearing in the snow.

"We'll go back to the barn, old girl," he said, patting her neck.

He gave Molly her head and she did not need any more incentive. Before long, they were back in Brooks at the livery stable.

"I knew you wouldn't make it!" Walter said self-righteously. "You can sleep in the loft if you like. Maybe the storm will have blown itself out by morning."

"I ain't stayin' nowhere but at home. I'll thank you to look after Molly until I can get back to fetch her."

"You're going on foot?" The stableman was incredulous. "Surely you're not *that* big a fool."

"Ain't never considered myself a fool, Walter. I see somethin' that needs doin' and do it."

He borrowed some binder twine from Walter to tie around his pant legs to keep the snow out of his boots, pulled the collar of his sheepskin coat up around his face, and left the liveryman shaking his head. He had twenty miles in front of him to the ranch, which lay directly north of the town. If he stayed heading into the wind, he had no doubt that he would reach his destination. If the wind shifted and he did not detect it, well, that was a different story.

The wind and snow beat at him and felt like where it probably came from—the Arctic. He sank his chin even further into his collar so that only his eyes showed. Luckily, the land was flat and there were no hills to scale. He kicked his way through the snow, mile after mile after mile, until he eventually had to stop and rest. He managed to get his watch out of its pocket and saw that he had been walking for four hours. In good weather, four hours would have been almost enough to see him at home, but right now he had no idea where he was along the imaginary string that he felt connecting himself to Mildred. He found his mind drifting off and that he was enjoying sitting down a little too much. He could easily have stretched out in the snow and gone to sleep, but he forced himself to his feet and trudged on. He thought he heard on the wind cattle bellowing but could not be sure. He knew that his herd, as well as others in the area, would be in distress, but he could do nothing until the storm blew itself out.

Yet instead of abating, the wind seemed to grow fiercer and required most of John's strength to lean into it and advance. On a wrong step, it sometimes knocked him off-balance and he would stumble. He was breathing heavily and sweating, and from time to time had to brush away the ice that formed on his eyebrows. He must have been walking with his eyes shut, or maybe he was sleepwalking or daydreaming, because he ran into a barbed-wire fence without seeing it. It jolted him back to reality. A sense of relief shot through him. The fence belonged to a homesteader, and he knew that the man's cabin was somewhere in the vicinity. But that was not where he wanted to go. Home was his destination and he was now within four miles of it.

It was full dark when he saw the kerosene lantern in the window of his cabin, a beacon, as if Mildred knew he would come and she wanted to guide him home. When he swung the door open and stepped into the warmth of his sanctuary, encrusted in snow and exhausted, Mildred and the children froze in what they were doing. They stared at him, slack-jawed; Nettie began to cry.

"My God, John," said Mildred. "You look like a ghost!"

<hr />

The medicine helped her, or at least she said it did, after what John had gone through to bring it to her. But she had few words to offer him as comfort after the storm subsided four days later and he rode out to discover dead cattle in the coulees. He was in for an even greater disappointment when he left with fellow cattlemen on the spring roundup, which for him now began in Medicine Hat, because the Red Deer, South Saskatchewan, and Bow Rivers boxed in most of the area's cattle.

It was his first time in the town that sat in the South Saskatchewan River valley. It was a divisional point for the Canadian Pacific Railway, which accounted for its existence and rapid growth. With a handful of other cattlemen, he liveried his horse and went to check in at the Cosmopolitan Hotel. After a sixty-mile ride, he was tired and looking forward to a bath and a good night's sleep before the roundup began in earnest the next morning. At the desk, he said, "John Ware. I have a reservation."

The clerk, a thin-faced young man who reminded John of Harold Wootton, gave him a withering look. "I'm sorry. Coloureds aren't allowed here."

John was flabbergasted. The thought that someone would deny him service because of his skin colour had never crossed his mind during the entire journey to Medicine Hat. In fact, he thought he was done with that sort of nonsense in Alberta forever, at least on the southern range where everybody seemed to know him. Everybody, apparently, except the bigot on the other side of the desk. He felt the old anger rising in his chest; he wanted to haul the pompous ass across the desk and poke his eyes out so that colour would never concern him again. But he held himself back and said through clenched teeth, "You're gonna be a whole lot sorrier, young fella, if you don't find a way to give me a room."

"If that's a threat, I can send for the police and have them deal with it."

Before John could reply, another cattleman stepped around him. "Either you let Mr. Ware have a room or you're going to lose a lot of business. Now that might not bother you, but I expect your boss wouldn't like it a bit. So if you still have objections, you'd best run and fetch him, or you're gonna have trouble like you've never seen trouble before."

Damn you! John thought. I don't need you buttin' in. I can fight my own battles! But on the heels of that thought was another, that this was only a single battle in what was bound to be a long war before it was over, if it ever was. And since no one ever wins a war alone, he let it go and enjoyed the spectacle of the clerk, red-faced now, looking nervously at the stolid-faced men behind John. Clearing his throat, the young man turned the ledger. "That won't be necessary, sir. Sign here, Mr. Ware."

That was how the roundup started; it ended with John having lost more than a hundred head to that vicious storm. He was devastated. The odds seemed to be stacking up against him again, and he was depressed when he arrived home. Thank goodness for Mildred and the children. They were his lifeline to all that was right with the world.

When he told Mildred how he had been greeted in Medicine Hat and how much it had bothered him, she said, "You've come too far and earned too much respect to let something like that eat at you, John. A man who tries to hold you down is really only holding himself down. I shouldn't have to tell you that."

That summer he made a trip to Calgary, and set aside time to visit Duffy's and Adam Newby's graves in High River. Like the town, the cemetery had grown bigger with each passing year, and he knew more people buried there than he cared to. It made him ponder his own mortality, and he balked at the idea of his lifeless body mouldering beneath the ground, although it wasn't so much the fact of death as the loss of life that bothered him. It had taken him a long time to build a good one and he was in no hurry to lose it.

In town, he learned why Adam had taken his life. John had missed the note in Adam's cabin that told of how he had been part of a patrol that, in a fit of anger, had murdered two Boer families: two men, two women, and three children. They had then burned their houses down. He was ashamed of the depth of his immorality and depravity. He had gone to war to fight for a righteous cause, only to discover that he was not the man he thought he was, that he was capable of committing horrific deeds he once believed only lesser people committed. He apologized and said he could no longer live with that knowledge. He had looked for self-forgiveness but could not find it.

Mildred gave birth to another boy and they named him Arthur. She was frail afterwards and to John never seemed to regain her strength. Even so, she didn't complain, because she had a husband who would never think of complaining himself. She carried on fulfilling her duties as she saw them, through another long winter and stiflingly hot summer. It was during the spring of 1905 that she really began to feel unwell, and it took all of her will to tell John, knowing how much he needed her on the ranch.

"Maybe we ought to get you into Calgary to see a doctor," he suggested.

Mildred did not say anything for a moment, unwilling to leave her home. Reluctantly, she agreed. "I think maybe you're right."

While John took Mildred to Calgary, Esther Lewis came up from Brooks to look after the children, who preferred to be at home rather than in town. At the hospital, the doctor told him not to worry, that Mildred would be well looked after. He hated to leave her but had to return to the ranch, because it would not run without either him or Mildred there.

But it seemed an odd place without her around, and despite Esther's presence, he mostly felt lost. She had the gift of the gab, Esther, and it was pretty much non-stop from the moment

John walked in the door. She recounted every small detail of what the children had done, and when that ran out, there were her dreams, which she felt a need to reveal and analyze. He loved her dearly, but listening to her tired him out more than the ranch work did.

On a windy prairie evening a few days later, she was telling John about a vivid dream she'd had of the Royal Hotel in Calgary catching on fire and burning to the ground. She was trying to figure out what it meant when she glanced out the window and saw a horse and rider approaching.

"Looks as if we have company," she said.

People stopped by on regular basis, so John thought nothing of it. It might even prove to be a welcome break from Esther. He went out to greet their visitor and did not recognize him.

"Mr. John Ware?"

John nodded. "Yes. And you are?"

"Telegram, sir."

He handed John an envelope and left. John took it inside for Esther to read. He figured it was from the hospital in Calgary, letting him know that it was time to pick Mildred up. Esther took only a moment to read it and looked as if she might faint.

"God save us," she breathed.

"What is it?" John asked, alarmed.

"Our Mildred is gone."

According to the doctor, pneumonia and typhoid were the thieves that had conspired to steal her life. That John would outlive her was such an impossible notion that he had never entertained it. He was, after all, nearly thirty years her senior. But his love, his life was gone, taken by a god he was coming to understand less and less with each passing year. He felt as if someone had placed a stick of dynamite beneath his heart and blown it clear out of his chest, leaving nothing but a monstrous, gaping hole.

Funeral services were held in Calgary, and John wept to see her lying in her casket. She had not even celebrated her thirty-third birthday. He stood next to her coffin for a long time, willing it to be someone else in there. Her face was so gaunt that she bore only a faint resemblance to the woman he had known and loved. He wanted someone to tell him that a grievous error had been committed and that Mildred was waiting for him at the hospital. But no one came with that good news.

John could not tend to the ranch and to the children, so the Lewises took the little ones in. Esther said that with Nettie's help, she could look after them, but Nettie wanted to be with her father. At twelve years of age she was, in her own mind, quite capable of performing the chores that had been her mother's; after all, she had been helping for more than a year. She insisted on going with him to the ranch. John bent in front of her and cupped her face gently. "I know you can do the chores, Nettie, but Grandma needs you here. Your momma'll rest a whole lot easier knowin' that you're helpin' out with your brothers and sisters. We wouldn't ask you if it wasn't real important." He gathered her into his arms, nearly overwhelmed with the memory of another twelve-year-old child who had offered more than any child should ever have to. "Your Aunt Nettie would've been awful proud if she'd lived to know you."

John returned to the ranch, but without Mildred and the children, it had lost much of its meaning. He occupied the space that had once been a bedroom, dining room, and living room for the entire family, and it felt as empty as the prairie outside. He was not sleeping well either, and that did not help. It now baffled him how bachelor men survived being alone, without the love of a wife, without the sound of children. How had he survived? He did not know, only that he was lucky to have found Mildred, to have gone to the I.G. Baker store on the same day as Dan Lewis.

As the summer passed, he grew tired of being alone. With fall lurking around the corner, he rode into Brooks to visit the children and to ask Bobby if he wanted to return to the ranch with him for a while. "You want to learn the cowboy trade from your poppa?"

Bobby didn't need to answer. John could tell by the light in his eyes before he said yes that he meant it.

Bobby was only eleven and had more of his mother's qualities than John's; he would never be as big and sturdy, but he was a quick study and determined, and in that was very much like his father. He already knew how to take care of a horse and to ride, but not how to work with cattle.

John began the lessons there. He cut Bobby a shorter rope and showed him how to use it, just as Emmett Cole had taught him so many years ago. Bobby was smoother with it than John had ever been, and unlike John, who had practised because he felt a need to be better than everyone else, Bobby practised because he loved throwing the rope. John was showing him how to use a branding iron on a fence board when an order came from a meat packer in Calgary for twelve of John's prime beeves. It was the perfect opportunity for another lesson.

The pair rode out to the herd the next day, father and son, to gather the animals and drive them to the stockyard in Brooks. "This'll be your first cattle drive, boy. You'll find that them beeves'll wanna go in every direction but the one you want 'em to go. So it'll be your job to keep 'em in line."

"That should be easy, Pa, if there's only twelve. You said that you used to drive thousands."

"Yep and that's the truth of it. But the first herd I ever drove that I *owned* was only nine little mavericks. It don't matter much how big a herd is, though. It's full of cattle and there ain't one that's been born that don't have a contrary streak somewhere in it. Nine, twelve, or a thousand, it don't mean a thing. They'll keep you on your toes. Besides, you gotta start somewhere, and startin' small don't hurt none."

Not in a hurry, they ambled along in the warm September sun, one of those perfect fall days that the prairies rise to every so often. John loved this country, despite its ability to deal a cruel hand occasionally. He had always been able to play the cards and come away with something, and a man could be proud of that. He was proud, too, that he had come so far from a rice plantation in South Carolina—and in more ways than one. By the sheer power of his character, he had forced people to see John Ware the man, not John Ware the coloured man, although he knew that his experience in Medicine Hat told a story that was a long way from a happy conclusion. But this was as good as he'd felt in a long time, out here on his ranch, riding side by side with his oldest boy, the son he was first proud of, teaching him as a lad the things that John had not learned until he was a man. There would be good money in the sale of the beeves, and he would make sure some of it went into the boy's pocket. No one should work for nothing unless he works for himself.

Suddenly, Molly stumbled and lurched as she stepped in a badger hole, lost her balance, and went down, with John underneath her. He heard more than felt a tremendous *crack* in his neck. Molly scrambled to her feet, unhurt, but John could not move, yet he could have sworn he was trying. He saw Bobby looking down on him, terrified and confused.

Ah, Bobby, I believe I've gone and broke my damned fool neck.

The words formed in his mind but not in his mouth. There was much more that he wanted to say but a kaleidoscope of images, so vivid and clear, replaced his thoughts. The last one sent him tumbling into the dark abyss from which he had risen at birth.

EPILOGUE

News of John's death reverberated across the southern range. Ranchers were in shock. John Ware dead? Impossible! He had been one of those rare human beings who seemed invincible. And even more impossible was the way he died. After he had broken hundreds of wild horses, a tame one did him in. The irony was stunning.

His funeral service was held at the Baptist Church, Mildred's church, where her own service had been held. Few of those attending could believe that the flower-bedecked coffin contained the body of John Ware. Speaker after speaker—anyone who cared to—arose and told stories of mythological proportions that would become part of John's legend, and if they were not quite the truth, then, as Mark Twain said, they ought to have been. Others told stories about how John had touched their lives, about his generosity, how he always gave and asked for nothing in return. Perhaps the most heartfelt tribute came from a young horse rancher from British Columbia who had once worked with John at the Quorn. He said, "Everything I know about how to make my ranch work, and everything I know about horses, I learned from John. But the most important lesson he taught me was that the highest honour you can pay another human being is not love but respect. He showed me that through his actions as much as he did through his words. That's how the best teachers teach, and John was one of the best."

Calgarians had never before witnessed a procession as long as the one that followed John's coffin to Union Cemetery, where his family and friends laid him to rest beside Mildred. Modest to a fault, he would have been surprised had he been able to see it.

His estate included a thousand head of cattle and many horses, and was settled by a lawyer named R.B. Bennett, who would become prime minister of Canada many years later. Nearby ranchers bought the stock. In 1958, the house near the Red Deer River was dismantled and relocated in Alberta's Dinosaur Provincial Park to a spot not far from its original site. It is on display for visitors to the park. The last surviving members of the Ware family were Nettie, who died in March 1989 in Vulcan, Alberta, and Arthur, who died two months later in Burnaby, British Columbia.

With John's passing, the old ways of the west had begun their own slide into oblivion. There was little left of the southern range that was not in use and cut into smaller parcels. It had become difficult to tell the difference between a farmer and a rancher, because in most cases they were the same. But thirty-five years after John's unexpected departure from the home he had worked so hard to find, when the old ways had all but disappeared completely, a group of men gathered to found the John Ware Society, because they thought that both deserved to be remembered.

AUTHOR'S NOTE

The "factual" parts of *High Rider* are based on Grant MacEwan's *John Ware's Cattle Country*. First published in 1960, it is the "definitive" work on John Ware; however, MacEwan does not provide his sources of information. Some of it may have come from older ranchers who remembered Ware, and some, possibly, from Nettie and Arthur, who were still alive when he wrote the book. That said, they were so young when their father died, it's hard to know how much they actually knew of him and how much was hearsay. But if we can accept that MacEwan's words are facts, then the following elements in this story are true: Ware was a slave on a plantation in South Carolina; he did confront his master over the maltreatment of his little sister and was whipped for it; he did meet up with his ex-master on the way out of town after the war, but did not seek revenge; and he did walk to Texas. (Surely he must have had adventures along the way, so the single chapter of his trek is fiction.) He learned his ranching skills from a family named Murphy, whose name I changed to Cole because there wasn't enough information available to present them fairly. But Ware did have a wild ride toward the Brazos River. He was invited to stay in the Murphys' house because they liked him so much, and he stayed for a decade. He rode in the horse race as described and was given the horse for his efforts. He trailed cattle north with the Murphys' son, and while MacEwan says that Ware assumed responsibility for the herd while the rest of the crew enjoyed Dodge City, there's room for speculation. With the limited information available to him at the time, MacEwan might have assumed that Dodge wouldn't be a welcoming place to a black man, when, in fact, it was just the opposite. So the Dodge City chapter is pure fiction, but Holliday and the Earps were there at the time, as were Eddie Foy and the man who tried to kill him.

The trail drive out of Texas probably terminated in Montana rather than Ogallala, and though the adventures experienced along the way may not apply to Ware's journey, they are all based on historical fact. Ware did go to Virginia City to mine silver with his friend, although his friend's name was Bill Moodie. They did separate and eventually meet up in Pocatello, where they joined Tom Lynch on the drive to Alberta. Since I couldn't find out what happened to Moodie, he became Duffy, whose life and death are fictional.

In Alberta, all the characters are real (including Molly and Bismarck), except Duffy, of course; Adam Newby, who is a composite character; Jack Strong; and the magistrate—but he is based on a real magistrate who dropped drunk and disorderly charges against Ware and paid him to break a wild horse. Ware may or may not have played a part in the Jumbo Fisk affair, but he was working in Calgary for the I.G. Baker Company at the time. The British noblemen are based on real characters who visited the Quorn Ranch. They did go on a "fox" hunt, and Ware did scoop up one of them, who later rewarded him with a Prince Albert coat. All of the other events in Alberta are real too, from Ware riding Mustard over the cutbank to his death from Molly's stumble.

ACKNOWLEDGMENTS

My thanks to: Diamond Joe White, whose great song "High Rider" first brought the story of John Ware to my attention; Jean Gallup, Interpretation Officer at the Bar U Ranch National Historical Site of Canada for her warm welcome there; and Ross Fritz, cowboy, also of the Bar U, for taking some time away from his beautiful Percherons to chat about John Ware over a cup of coffee. Thanks also to all the talented folks at TouchWood Editions who helped put this book together, especially Marlyn Horsdal and Cailey Cavallin for their expert guidance. And, as always, thanks to Jaye for her unfailing encouragement.

BILL GALLAHER is a well-known singer and songwriter. He is the author of The Wild Jack Strong trilogy, which includes *The Frog Lake Massacre*, *The Luck of the Horseman*, and *The Horseman's Last Call*. Please visit